THE WIND FROM

DRAWINGS BY DENNIS NEAL SMITH

A BURNING WOMAN

Greg Bear

ARKHAM HOUSE PUBLISHERS, INC.

ACKNOWLEDGMENTS

"Hardfought," copyright © 1982 by Davis Publications, Inc. for *Isaac Asimov's Science Fiction Magazine,* February 1983.

"Mandala," copyright © 1978 by Robert Silverberg for *New Dimensions 8.*

"Petra," copyright © 1981 by Omni Publications International, Ltd. for *Omni,* February 1982.

"Scattershot," copyright © 1978 by Terry Carr for *Universe 8.*

"The White Horse Child," copyright © 1979 by Terry Carr for *Universe 9.*

"The Wind from a Burning Woman," copyright © 1978 by The Condé Nast Publications, Inc. for *Analog Science Fiction/Science Fact,* October 1978; title used by permission of Michael Bishop, from his poem "Postcards to Athena."

Library of Congress Cataloging in Publication Data

Bear, Greg, 1951–
    The wind from a burning woman.

    Contents: The wind from a burning woman—The white horse child—Petra—[etc.]
    1. Science fiction, American. I. Title.
PS3552.E157W5   1983   813'.54   82-16395
ISBN 0-87054-094-7

Printed in the United States of America
Second Printing

For David Clark

CONTENTS

PREFACE
ix

THE WIND FROM A BURNING WOMAN
1

THE WHITE HORSE CHILD
39

PETRA
65

SCATTERSHOT
91

MANDALA
133

HARDFOUGHT
191

PREFACE

I have had a passion for science fiction and fantasy ever since I can remember. Science fiction has been a wonderful mother for my mind, showing me that the world is far bigger and stranger than it seems within my province. And in the past few years—after many more years of apprenticeship—it has become a fine, broad landscape on which to test my imagination.

Occasionally I've felt the pressure of limited editors and markets, but I have yet to run up against an artistic boundary. If a thought is expressible in human language, a science fiction story can be written about it. The same cannot be said of any other genre.

Through reading science fiction, I became interested in other forms of literature, in astronomy and the sciences, in history and philosophy. Specifically, discovering James Blish's *Case of Conscience* when I was sixteen led me to read James Joyce; L. Sprague de Camp, Fletcher Pratt, Poul Anderson, and others have given me solid reasons to explore history. Arthur C. Clarke—and through Clarke, Olaf Stapledon—sent me on a wild search through philosophy, looking for similar insights and experiences. (I've usually been disappointed; Stapledon is unique.) In short, my intellect has been nurtured and guided by science fiction.

Some people, reading the above, will sneer the ineradicable sneer. The hell with them. C. P. Snow pinned their little grey moth in *The Two Cultures and the Scientific Revolution;* they are ignorant or afraid of science. They reject the universe in favor of a small human circle, limited in time and place to their own lifetimes. You are not one of them if you have read this far. You are one of the brave ones.

So I will open my heart to you a little bit and talk about the stories that follow.

I have friends who believe the world will come to an end in twenty or thirty years. They foresee complete collapse, perhaps nuclear war. They look on the prospect with either stunned indifference or some relish. Serve everybody right, they seem to say.

What they are actually saying is that within the next few decades—certainly within the next sixty or seventy years—*they* will come to an end. *Their* world will darken. And, solipsists that many of us are, it seems perfectly logical to take everybody and everything with us. The future does not really exist, certainly not the far and unknowable future. Why talk about it?

They are still my friends, but they are as wrong as wrong can be. The future will come, and it will be different, unimaginably so. Then why do I bother to try imagining it?

I could sing you a long number on how science fiction is seldom intended to be prophetic. But I'm willing to bet, in our deepest hearts, that we all hope one of our more optimistic imagined futures, or some aspect of a literary time to come, will closely parallel reality. Then we will be admired for our perspicacity. People in the future, if they still read, might come across an even more fantastic concept and say, "Hey, that crazy Greg Bear stuff!"

Perhaps. But it will be accident, not prophecy.

Like my pessimistic friends, I'm not going to live forever. I may see the first starships; I may not.

But when I write, I not only live to see one future, I experience dozens. I chart their courses, lay out histories, try to create new cultures and extend the range of discovery. When I write—

When I write, I'm immortal.

Sometimes I enter into a kind of trance state and engage so many thoughts and ideas and abilities that I seem to rise onto another plane. And though I seldom think about it while I'm on that plane, I seem to become everyone who has ever thought about the future. I join the greats, past and present, at least for a moment.

I've been writing since I was eight or nine years old. In 1966, when I was fifteen, through something of a fluke I sold my first professional short story. Five years passed before I sold another. The apprenticeship is still not over, and may never be. None of those earlier efforts are represented in this collection; the earliest piece here, "Mandala," was written in 1975 and first appeared in 1978. It also comprises the first third of my novel, *Strength of Stones,* published in 1981.

There isn't much remarkable to record about the writing of these stories. Writing is usually quite dull to an outside observer. It consists of long periods of apparent loafing around, punctuated by hours at a typewriter, highlighted by moments of desk-pounding and finger-chewing puzzlement. (All this, to contrast with the above-mentioned trance state.)

"Mandala" and "Hardfought" were about equally difficult to write, for different reasons. "The White Horse Child" was one of the easiest; like "Scattershot," it emerged while I sat at the typewriter, consciously unaware of what was going to pour out. "Petra" went through several stages, becoming progressively stranger and stranger. (One of the great difficulties with creativity is trying to impose order on the results.)

"The Wind from a Burning Woman" also began as an exercise in sitting blankly at the typewriter. As in most instances where such stories turn out well, there was a strong emotion lurking behind the apparent blankness—that of repugnance to terrorism. Do the weak have the right to force the strong to do their bidding by terrorist action? To handle the issue honestly, I had to make the "Burning Woman" fight for a cause that I, myself, would cherish. One editor, reading the story for an anthology on space colonies, rejected it because it didn't overtly support the cause. It would have been dishonest to force the story into such a mold; however pleasant or unpleasant the result, my stories must work themselves out within their own framework, not according to some market principle or philosophical bias.

It may be remarkable that, with such views, I've come as far as I have in publishing, where large conglomerates seem to dictate overall marketing of science fiction as if it were some piecework commodity. ("Take dragon/unicorn/spaceship, add vaguely medieval/ magical setting, mix well with wise old wizard/cute sidekick . . .") Don't get me wrong, I've enjoyed stories with all those elements, but enough is enough. Science fiction is much too restless to accept the same kind of genre regimentation displayed by, for example, Westerns or hard-boiled detective novels, where one Western Town or corrupt Big City can serve as stage settings for an infinity of retold tales.

But enough authorial interference. I will tell you no more about these stories until we meet in person; perhaps not even then, for I'm not certain my interpretations are always correct. "Mandala," for example, has defied my analysis for seven years, and yet I knew what I wanted to say when I wrote it.

That's when I'm happiest with my own work—when the stories say so many things that they become playgrounds for the mind. I hope you feel the same way.

GREG BEAR

Spring Valley, California

THE WIND FROM A BURNING WOMAN

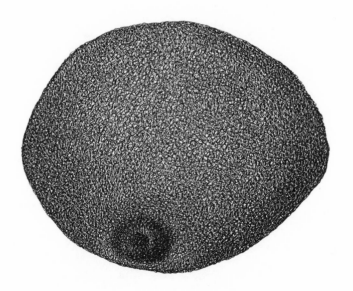

FIVE YEARS LATER THE GLASS BUBBLES WERE INTACT, THE WIRES AND PIPES WERE taut, and the city—strung across Psyche's surface like a dewy spider's web wrapped around a thrown rock—was still breathtaking. It was also empty. Hexamon investigators had swept out the final dried husks and bones. The asteroid was clean again. The plague was over.

Giani Turco turned her eyes away from the port and looked at the displays. Satisfied by the approach, she ordered a meal and put her work schedule through the processor for tightening and trimming. She had six tanks of air, enough to last her three days. There was no time to spare. The robot guards in orbit around Psyche hadn't been operating for at least a year and wouldn't offer any resistance, but four small pursuit bugs had been planted in the bubbles. They turned themselves off whenever possible, but her presence would activate them. Time spent in avoiding and finally destroying them: one hour forty minutes, the processor said. The final schedule was projected in front of her by a pen hooked around her ear. She happened to be staring at Psyche when the readout began; the effect—red numerals and letters over grey rock and black space—was pleasingly graphic, like a film in training.

Turco had dropped out of training six weeks early. She had no need for a final certificate, approval from the Hexamon, or any other nicety. Her craft was stolen from Earth orbit, her papers and cards forged, and her intentions entirely opposed to those of the sixteen corporeal desks. On Earth, some hours hence, she would be hated and reviled.

The impulse to sneer was strong—pure theatrics, since she was alone—but she didn't allow it to break her concentration. (Worse than sheep, the seekers-after-security, the cowardly citizens who tacitly supported the forces that had driven her father to suicide and murdered her grandfather; the seekers-after-security who lived by technology but believed in the just influences: Star, Logos, Fate, and Pneuma . . .)

To calm her nerves, she sang a short song while she selected her landing site.

The ship, a small orbital tug, touched the asteroid like a mote settling on a boulder and made itself fast. She stuck her arms and legs into the suit receptacles, and the limb covers automatically hooked themselves to the thorax. The cabin was too cramped to get into a suit any other way. She reached up and brought down the helmet, pushed until all the semifluid seals seized and beeped, and began the evacuation of the cabin's atmosphere. Then the cabin parted down the middle, and she floated slowly, fell more slowly still, to Psyche's surface.

She turned once to watch the cabin clamp together and to see if the propulsion rods behind the tanks had been damaged by the unusually long journey. They'd held up well.

She took hold of a guide wire after a flight of twenty or twenty-five meters and pulled for the nearest glass bubble. Five years before, the milky spheres had been filled with the families of workers setting the charges that would form Psyche's seven internal chambers. Holes had been bored from the Vlasseg and Janacki poles, on the narrow ends of the huge rock, through the center. After the formation of the chambers, materials necessary for atmosphere would have been pumped into Psyche through the bore-holes while motors increased her natural spin to create artificial gravity inside.

In twenty years, Psyche's seven chambers would have been green and beautiful, filled with hope—and passengers. But now the control-bubble hatches had been sealed by the last of the investigators. Since Psyche was not easily accessible, even in its lunar orbit, the seals hadn't been applied carefully. Nevertheless it took her an hour to break in. The glass ball towered above her, a hundred feet in diameter, translucent walls mottled by the shadows of rooms and equipment. Psyche rotated once every three hours, and light from the sun was beginning to flush the top of the bubbles in the local cluster. Moonlight illuminated the shadows. She pushed the rubbery cement seals away, watching them float lazily to the pocked ground. Then she examined the airlock to see if it was still functioning. She wanted to keep the atmosphere inside the bubble, to check it for psychotropic chemicals; she would not leave her suit at any rate.

The locked door opened with a few jerks and closed behind her. She brushed crystals of frost off her faceplate and the inner lock door's port. Then she pushed the button for the inner door, but nothing happened. The external doors were on a different power supply, which was no longer functioning—or, she hoped, had only been turned off.

From her backpack she removed a half-meter pry bar. The break-in took another fifteen minutes. She was now five minutes ahead of schedule.

Across the valley, the fusion power plants that supplied power to the Geshel populations of Tijuana and Chula Vista sat like squat mountains of concrete. By Naderite law, all nuclear facilities were enclosed by multiple domes and pyramids, whether they posed any danger or not. The symbolism was two-fold—it showed the distaste of the ruling Naderites for energy sources that were not nature-kinetic, and it carried on the separation of Naderites-Geshels. Farmer Kollert, advisor to the North American Hexamon and ecumentalist to the California corporeal desk, watched the sun set behind the false peak and wondered vaguely if there was any symbolism in the act. Was not fusion the source of power for the sun? He smiled. Such things seldom occurred to him; perhaps it would amuse a Geshel technician.

His team of five Geshel scientists would tour the plants two days from now and make their report to him. He would then pass on *his* report to the desk, acting as interface for the invariably clumsy, elitist language the Geshel scientists used. In this way, through the medium of advisors across the globe, the Naderites oversaw the production of Geshel power. By their grants and control of capital, his people had once plucked the world from technological overkill, and the battle was ongoing still—a war against some of mankind's darker tendencies.

He finished his evening juice and took a package of writing utensils from the drawer in the veranda desk. The reports from last month's energy consumption balancing needed to be edited and revised, based on new estimates—and he enjoyed doing the work himself, rather than giving it to the library computer personna. It relaxed him to do things by hand. He wrote on a positive feedback slate, his scrawly letters adjusting automatically into script, with his tongue between his lips and a pleased frown creasing his brow.

"Excuse me, Farmer." His ur-wife, Gestina, stood in the French doors leading to the veranda. She was as slender as when he had married her, despite fifteen years and two children.

"Yes, *cara*, what is it?" He withdrew his tongue and told the slate to store what he'd written.

"Josef Krupkin."

Kollert stood up quickly, knocking the metal chair over. He hurried past his wife into the dining room, dropped his bulk into a chair, and drew up the crystalline cube on the alabaster tabletop. The cube adjusted its picture to meet the angle of his eyes, and Krupkin appeared.

"Josef! This is unexpected."

"Very," Krupkin said. He was a small man with narrow eyes and curly black hair. Compared to Kollert's bulk, he was dapper—but thirty years behind a desk had given him the usual physique of a Hexamon backroomer. "Have you ever heard of Giani Turco?"

Kollert thought for a moment. "No, I haven't. Wait—Turco. Related to Kimon Turco?"

"Daughter. California should keep better track of its radical Geshels, shouldn't it?"

"Kimon Turco lived on the Moon."

"His daughter lived in your district."

"Yes, fine. What about her?" Kollert was beginning to be perturbed. Krupkin enjoyed roundabouts even in important situations—and to call him at this address, at such a time, something important had happened.

"She's calling for you. She'll only talk to you, none of the rest. She won't even accept President Praetori."

"Yes. Who is she? What has she done?"

"She's managed to start up Psyche. There was enough reaction mass left in the Beckmann motors to alter it into an Earth-intersect orbit." The left side of the cube was flashing bright red, indicating the call was being scrambled.

Kollert sat very still for a few seconds. There was no need acting incredulous. Krupkin was in no position to joke. But the enormity of what he said—and the impulse to disbelieve, despite the bearer of the news—froze Kollert for an unusually long time. He ran his hand through lank blond hair.

"Kollert," Krupkin said. "You look like you've been—"

"Is she telling the truth?"

Krupkin shook his head. "No, Kollert, you don't understand. She hasn't *claimed* these accomplishments. She hasn't said anything about them yet. She just wants to speak to you. But our tracking stations say there's no doubt. I've spoken with the officer who commanded the last inspection. He says there was enough mass left in the Beckmann drive positioning motors to push—"

"This is incredible! No precautions were taken? The mass wasn't drained, or something?"

"I'm no Geshel, Farmer. My technicians tell me the mass was left on Psyche because it would have cost several hundred million—"

"That's behind us now. Let the journalists worry about that, if they ever hear of it." He looked up and saw Gestina still standing in the French doors. He held up his hand to tell her to stay where she was. She was going to have to keep to the house, incommunicado, for as long as it took to straighten this out.

"You're coming?"

"Which center?"

"Does it matter? She's not being discreet. Her message is hitting an entire hemisphere, and there are hundreds of listening stations to pick it up. Several aren't under our control. Once anyone pinpoints the source, the story is going to be clear. For your convenience, go to Baja Station. Mexico is signatory to all the necessary pacts."

"I'm leaving now," Kollert said. Krupkin nodded, and the cube went blank.

"What was he talking about?" Gestina asked. "What's *Psyche*?"

"A chunk of rock, dear," he said. Her talents lay in other directions —she wasn't stupid. Even for a Naderite, however, she was unknowledgeable about things beyond the Earth.

He started to plan the rules for her movements, then thought better of it and said nothing. If Krupkin was correct—and he would be —there was no need. The political considerations, if everything turned out right, would be enormous. He could run as Governor of the Desk, even President of the Hexamon . . .

And if everything didn't turn out right, it wouldn't matter where anybody was.

Turco sat in the middle of her grandfather's control center and cried. She was tired and sick at heart. Things were moving rapidly now, and she wondered just how sane she was. In a few hours she would be the worst menace the Earth had ever known, and for what cause? Truth, justice? They had murdered her grandfather, discredited her father and driven him to suicide—but all seven billion of them, Geshels and Naderites alike?

She didn't know whether she was bluffing or not. Psyche's fall was still controllable, and she was bargaining it would never hit the Earth. Even if she lost and everything was hopeless, she might divert it, causing a few tidal disruptions, minor earthquakes perhaps, but still passing over four thousand kilometers from the Earth's surface. There was enough reaction mass in the positioning motors to allow a broad margin of safety.

Resting lightly on the table in front of her was a chart that showed the basic plan of the asteroid. The positioning motors surrounded a crater at one end of the egg-shaped chunk of nickel-iron and rock. Catapults loaded with huge barrels of reaction mass had just a few hours earlier launched a salvo to rendezvous above the crater's center. Beckmann drive beams had then surrounded the mass with a halo of energy, releasing its atoms from the bonds of nature's weak force. The blast had bounced off the crater floor, directed by the geometric patterns of heat-resistant slag. At the opposite end, a smaller guidance engine was in position, but it was no longer functional and didn't figure in her plans. The two tunnels that reached from the poles to the center of Psyche opened into seven blast chambers, each containing a fusion charge. She hadn't checked to see if the charges were still armed. There were so many things to do.

She sat with her head bowed, still suited up. Though the bubbles contained enough atmosphere to support her, she had no intention

of unsuiting. In one gloved hand she clutched a small ampoule with a nozzle for attachment to air and water systems piping. The Hexamon Nexus's trumped-up excuse of madness caused by near-weightless conditions was now a shattered, horrible lie. Turco didn't know why, but the Psyche project had been deliberately sabotaged, and the psychotropic drugs still lingered.

Her grandfather hadn't gone mad contemplating the stars. The asteroid crew hadn't mutinied out of misguided Geshel zeal and space sickness.

Her anger rose again, and the tears stopped. "You deserve whoever governs you," she said quietly. "Everyone is responsible for the actions of their leaders."

The computer display cross-haired the point of impact. It was ironic—the buildings of the Hexamon Nexus were only sixty kilometers from the zero point. She had no control over such niceties, but nature and fate seemed to be as angry as she was.

"Moving an asteroid is like carving a diamond," the Geshel advisor said. Kollert nodded his head, not very interested. "The charges for initial orbit change—moving it out of the asteroid belt—have to be placed very carefully or the mass will break up and be useless. When the asteroid is close enough to the Earth-Moon system to meet the major crew vessels, the work has only begun. Positioning motors have to be built—"

"Madness," Kollert's secretary said, not pausing from his monitoring of communications between associate committees.

"And charge tunnels drilled. All of this was completed on the asteroid ten years ago."

"Are the charges still in place?" Kollert asked.

"So far as I know," the Geshel said.

"Can they be set off now?"

"I don't know. Whoever oversaw dismantling should have disarmed to protect his crew—but then, the reaction mass should have been jettisoned, too. So who can say? The report hasn't cleared top secrecy yet."

And not likely to, either, Kollert thought. "If they haven't been disarmed, can they be set off now? What would happen if they were?"

"Each charge has a complex communications system. They were designed to be set off by coded signals and could probably be set off now, yes, if we had the codes. Of course, those are top secret, too."

"What would happen?" Kollert was becoming impatient with the Geshel.

"I don't think the charges were ever given a final adjustment. It all depends on how well the initial alignment was performed. If they're out of true, or the final geological studies weren't taken into account, they could blow Psyche to pieces. If they are true, they'll do what they were intended to do—form chambers inside the rock. Each chamber would be about fifteen kilometers long, ten kilometers in diameter—"

"If the asteroid were blown apart, how would that affect our situation?"

"Instead of having one mass hit, we'd have a cloud, with debris twenty to thirty kilometers across and smaller."

"Would that be any better?" Kollert asked.

"Sir?"

"Would it be better to be hit by such a cloud than one chunk?"

"I don't think so. The difference is pretty moot—either way, the surface of the Earth would be radically altered, and few life forms would survive."

Kollert turned to his secretary. "Tell them to put a transmission through to Giani Turco."

The communications were arranged. In the meantime Kollert tried to make some sense out of the Geshel advisor's figures. He was very good at mathematics, but in the past sixty years many physics and chemistry symbols had diverged from those used in biology and psychology. To Kollert, the Geshel mathematics was irritatingly dense and obtuse.

He put the paper aside when Turco appeared on the cube in front of him. A few background beeps and noise were eliminated, and her image cleared. "Ser Turco," he said.

"Ser Farmer Kollert," she replied several seconds later. A beep signaled the end of one side's transmission. She sounded tired.

"You're doing a very foolish thing."

"I have a list of demands," she said.

Kollert laughed. "You sound like the Good Man himself, Ser Turco.

The tactic of direct confrontation. Well, it didn't work all the time, even for him."

"I want the public—Geshels and Naderites both—to know why the Psyche project was sabotaged."

"It was not sabotaged," Kollert said calmly. "It was unfortunate proof that humans cannot live in conditions so far removed from the Earth."

"Ask those on the Moon!" Turco said bitterly.

"The Moon has a much stronger gravitational pull than Psyche. But I'm not briefed to discuss all the reasons why the Psyche project failed."

"I have found psychotropic drugs—traces of drugs and containers—in the air and water the crew breathed and drank. That's why I'm maintaining my suit integrity."

"No such traces were found by our investigating teams. But, Ser Turco, neither of us is here to discuss something long past. Speak your demands—your price—and we'll begin negotiations." Kollert knew he was walking a loose rope. Several Hexamon terrorist team officers were listening to everything he said, waiting to splice in a timely splash of static. Conversely, there was no way to stop Turco's words from reaching open stations on the Earth. He was sweating heavily under his arms. Stations on the Moon—the bastards there would probably be sympathetic to her—could pick up his messages and relay them back to the Earth. A drop of perspiration trickled from armpit to sleeve, and he shivered involuntarily.

"That's my only demand," Turco said. "No money, not even amnesty. I want nothing for myself. I simply want the people to know the truth."

"Ser Turco, you have an ideal platform to tell them all you want them to hear."

"The Hexamons control most major reception centers. Everything else—except for a few ham and radio-astronomy amateurs—is cabled and controlled. To reach the most people, the Hexamon Nexus will have to reveal its part in the matter."

Before speaking to her again, Kollert asked if there was any way she could be fooled into believing her requests were being carried out. The answer was ambiguous—a few hundred people were thinking it over.

"I've conferred with my staff, Ser Turco, and I can assure you, so far as the most privy of us can tell, nothing so villainous was ever done to the Psyche project." At a later time, his script suggested, he might indicate that some tests had been overlooked, and that a junior officer had suggested lunar sabotage on Psyche. That might shift the heat. But for the moment, any admission that drugs existed in the asteroid's human environments could backfire.

"I'm not arguing," she said. "There's no question that the Hexamon Nexus had somebody sabotage Psyche."

Kollert held his tongue between his lips and punched key words into his script processor. The desired statements formed over Turco's image. He looked at the camera earnestly. "If we had done anything so heinous, surely we would have protected ourselves against an eventuality like this—drained the reaction mass in the positioning motors—" One of the terrorist team officers was waving at him frantically and scowling. The screen's words showed red where they were being covered by static. There was to be no mention of how Turco had gained control of Psyche. The issue was too sensitive, and blame hadn't been placed yet. Besides, there was still the option of informing the public that Turco had never gained control of Psyche at all. If everything worked out, the issue would have been solved without costly admissions.

"Excuse me," Turco said a few seconds later. The time lag between communications was wearing on her nerves, if Kollert was any judge. "Something was lost there."

"Ser Turco, your grandfather's death on Psyche was accidental, and your actions now are ridiculous. Destroying the Hexamon Nexus"—much better than saying *Earth*—"won't mean a thing." He leaned back in the seat, chewing on the edge of his index finger. The gesture had been approved an hour before the talks began, but it was nearly genuine. His usual elegance of speech seemed to be wearing thin in this encounter. He'd already made several embarrassing misjudgments.

"I'm not doing this for logical reasons," Turco finally said. "I'm doing it out of hatred for you and all the people who support you. What happened on Psyche was purely evil—useless, motivated by the worst intentions, resulting in the death of a beautiful dream, not to mention people I loved. No talk can change my mind about those things."

"Then why talk to me at all? I'm hardly the highest official in the Nexus."

"No, but you're in an ideal position to know who the higher officials involved were. You're a respected politician. And I suspect you had a great deal to do with suggesting the plot. I just want the truth. I'm tired. I'm going to rest for a few hours now."

"Wait a moment," Kollert said sharply. "We haven't discussed the most important things yet."

"I'm signing off. Until later."

The team leader made a cutting motion across his throat that almost made Kollert choke. The young bastard's indiscreet symbol was positively obscene in the current situation. Kollert shook his head and held his fingertips to his temples. "We didn't even have time to begin," he said.

The team leader stood and stretched his arms.

"You're doing quite well so far, Ser Kollert," he said. "It's best to ease into these things."

"I'm Advisor Kollert to you, and I don't see how we have much time to take it easy."

"Yes, sir. Sorry."

She needed the rest, but there was far too much to do. She pushed off from the seat and floated gently for a few moments before drifting down. The relaxation of weightlessness would have been welcome, and Psyche's pull was very weak, but just enough to remind her there was no time for rest.

One of the things she had hoped she could do—checking the charges deep inside the asteroid to see if they were armed—was impossible. The main computer and the systems board indicated the transport system through the boreholes was no longer operative. It would take her days to crawl or float the distance down the shafts, and she wasn't about to take the small tug through a tunnel barely fifty meters wide. She wasn't that well-trained a pilot.

So she had a weak spot. The bombs couldn't be disarmed from where she was. They could be set off by a ship positioned along the axis of the tunnels, but so far none had shown up. That would take another twelve hours or so, and by then time would be running out. She hoped that all negotiations would be completed.

The woman desperately wanted out of the suit. The catheters and cups were itching fiercely; she felt like a ball of tacky glue wrapped in wool. Her eyes were stinging from strain and sweat buildup on the lids. If she had a moment of irritation when something crucial was happening, she could be in trouble. One way or another, she had to clean up a bit—and there was no way to do that unless she risked exposure to the residue of drugs. She stood unsteadily for several minutes, vacillating, and finally groaned, slapping her thigh with a gloved palm. "I'm *tired*," she said. "Not thinking straight."

She looked at the computer. There was a solution, but she couldn't see it clearly. "Come on, girl. So simple. But what?"

The drug would probably have a limited life, in case the Nexus wanted to do something with Psyche later. But how limited? Ten years? She chuckled grimly. She had the ampoule and its cryptic chemical label. Would a Physician's Desk Reference be programmed into the computers?

She hooked herself into the console again. "PDR," she said. The screen was blank for a few seconds. Then it said, "Ready."

"Iropentaphonate," she said. "Two-seven diboltene."

The screen printed out the relevant data. She searched through the technical maze for a full minute before finding what she wanted. "Effective shelf life, four months two days from date of manufacture."

She tested the air again—it was stale but breathable—and unhooked her helmet. It was worth any risk. A bare knuckle against her eye felt so good.

The small lounge in the Baja Station was well-furnished and comfortable, but suited more for Geshels than Naderites—bright rather than natural colors, abstract paintings of a mechanistic tendency, modernist furniture. To Kollert it was faintly oppressive. The man sitting across from him had been silent for the past five minutes, reading through a sheaf of papers.

"Who authorized this?" the man asked.

"Hexamon Nexus, Mr. President."

"But who proposed it?"

Kollert hesitated. "The advisory committee."

"Who proposed it to the committee?"

"I did."

"Under what authority?"

"It was strictly legal," Kollert said defensively. "Such activities have been covered under the emergency code, classified section fourteen."

The president nodded. "She came to the right man when she asked for you, then. I wonder where she got her information. None of this can be broadcast—why was it done?"

"There were a number of reasons, among them financial—"

"The project was mostly financed by lunar agencies. Earth had perhaps a five percent share, so no controlling interest—and there was no connection with radical Geshel groups, therefore no need to invoke section fourteen on revolutionary deterrence. I read the codes, too, Farmer."

"Yes, sir."

"What were you afraid of? Some irrational desire to pin the butterflies down? Jesus God, Farmer, the Naderite beliefs don't allow anything like this. But you and your committee took it upon yourselves to covertly destroy the biggest project in the history of mankind. You think this follows in the tracks of the Good Man?"

"You're aware of lunar plans to build particle guidance guns. They're canceled now because Psyche is dead. They were to be used to push asteroids like Psyche into deep space, so advanced Beckmann drives could be used."

"I'm not technically minded, Farmer."

"Nor am I. But such particle guns could have been used as weapons—considering lunar sympathies, probably would have been used. They could cook whole cities on Earth. The development of potential weapons *is* a matter of concern for Naderites, sir. And there are many studies showing that human behavior changes in space. It becomes less Earth-centered, less communal. Man can't live in space and remain human. We were trying to preserve humanity's right to a secure future. Even now the Moon is a potent political force, and war has been suggested by our strategists . . . it's a dire possibility. All this because of the separation of a group of humans from the parent body, from wise government and safe creed."

The president shook his head and looked away. "I am ashamed such a thing could happen in my government. Very well, Kollert, this remains your ball game until she asks to speak to someone else. But my advisors are going to go over everything you say. I doubt you'll have the chance to botch anything. We're already acting with the Moon to stop this before it gets any worse. And you can thank God—for your life, not your career, which is already dead—that our Geshels have come up with a way out."

Kollert was outwardly submissive, but inside he was fuming. Not even the President of the Hexamon had the right to treat him like a child or, worse, a criminal. He was an independent advisor, of a separate desk, elected by Naderites of high standing. The ecumentalist creed was apparently much tighter than the president's. "I acted in the best interests of my constituency," he said.

"You no longer have a constituency, you no longer have a career. Nor do any of the people who planned this operation with you, or those who carried it out. Up and down the line. A purge."

Turco woke up before the blinking light and moved her lips in a silent curse. How long had she been asleep? She panicked briefly—a dozen hours would be crucial—but then saw the digital clock. Two hours. The light was demanding her attention to an incoming radio signal.

There was no video image. Kollert's voice returned, less certain, almost cowed. "I'm here," she said, switching off her camera as well. The delay was a fraction shorter than when they'd first started talking.

"Have you made any decisions?" Kollert asked.

"I should be asking that question. My course is fixed. When are you and your people going to admit to sabotage?"

"We'd—I'd almost be willing to admit, just to—" He stopped. She was about to speak when he continued. "We could do that, you know. Broadcast a worldwide admission of guilt. A cheap price to pay for saving all life on Earth. Do you really understand what you're up to? What satisfaction, what revenge, could you possibly get out of this? My God, Turco, you—" There was a burst of static. It sounded suspiciously like the burst she had heard some time ago.

"You're editing him," she said. Her voice was level and calm. "I don't want anyone editing anything between us, whoever you are. Is that understood? One more burst of static like that, and I'll . . ." She had already threatened the ultimate. "I'll be less tractable. Remember —I'm already a fanatic. Want me to be a hardened fanatic? Repeat what you were saying, Ser Kollert."

The digital readout indicated one-way delay time of 1.496 seconds. She would soon be closer to the Earth than the Moon was.

"I was saying," Kollert repeated, something like triumph in his tone, "that you are a very young woman, with very young ideas—like a child leveling a loaded pistol at her parents. You may not be a fanatic. But you aren't seeing things clearly. We have no evidence here on Earth that you've found anything, and we won't have evidence—nothing will be solved—if the asteroid collides with us. That's obvious. But if it veers aside, goes into an Earth orbit perhaps, then an—"

"That's not one of my options," Turco said.

"—investigating team could reexamine the crew quarters," Kollert continued, not to be interrupted for a few seconds, "do a more detailed search. Your charges could be verified."

"I can't go into Earth orbit without turning around, and this is a one-way rock, remember that. My only other option is to swing around the Earth, be deflected a couple of degrees, and go into a solar orbit. By the time any investigating team reached me, I'd be on the other side of the sun, and dead. I'm the daughter of a Geshel, Ser Kollert—don't forget that. I have a good technical education, and my training under Hexamon auspices makes me a competent pilot and spacefarer. Too bad there's so little long-range work for my type— just Earth-Moon runs. But don't try to fool me or kid me. I'm far more expert than you are. Though I'm sure you have Geshel people on your staff." She paused. "Geshels! I can't call you traitors—you in the background—because you might be thinking I'm crazy, out to destroy all of you. But do you understand what these men have done to our hopes and dreams? I've never seen a finished asteroid starship, of course—Psyche was to have been the first. But I've seen good simulations. It would have been like seven Shangri-las inside, hollowed out of solid rock and metal, seven valleys separated by walls four kilometers high, each self-contained, connected with the others by tube trains. The valley floors reach up to the sky, like magic, everything wonderfully topsy-turvy. And quiet—so much insulation none of the engine sounds reach inside." She was crying again.

"Psyche would consume herself on the way to the stars. By the time she arrived, there'd be little left besides a cylinder thirty kilometers wide, and two hundred ninety long. Like the core of an apple, and the passengers would be luxurious worms—star travelers. Now ask why, *why* did these men sabotage such a marvelous thing? Because they are blind unto pure evil—blind, ugly-minded, weak men who hate big ideas . . ." She paused. "I don't know what you think of all this, but remember, they took something away from you. I know. I've seen the evidence here. Sabotage and murder." She pressed the button and waited wearily for a reply.

"Ser Turco," Kollert said, "you have ten hours to make an effective course correction. We estimate you have enough reaction mass left to extend your orbit and miss the Earth by about four thousand kilometers. There is nothing we can do here but try to convince you—"

She stopped listening, trying to figure out what was happening behind the scenes. Earth wouldn't take such a threat without exploring a large number of alternatives. Kollert's voice droned on as she tried to think of the most likely action, and the most effective.

She picked up her helmet and placed a short message, paying no attention to the transmission from Earth. "I'm going outside for a few minutes."

The acceleration had been steady for two hours, but now the weightlessness was just as oppressive. The large cargo handler was fully loaded with extra fuel and a bulk William Porter was reluctant to think about. With the ship turned around for course correction, he could see the Moon glowing with Earthshine, and a bright crescent so thin it was almost a hair.

He had about half an hour to relax before the real work began, and he was using it to read an excerpt from a novel by Anthony Burgess. He'd been a heavy reader all his memorable life, and now he allowed himself a possible last taste of pleasure.

Like most inhabitants of the Moon, Porter was a Geshel, with a physicist father and a geneticist mother. He'd chosen a career as a pilot rather than a researcher out of romantic predilections established long before he was ten years old. There was something immediately effective and satisfying about piloting, and he'd turned out to be well suited to the work. He'd never expected to take on a mission like this. But then, he'd never paid much attention to politics, either. Even if he had, the disputes between Geshels and Naderites would have been hard to spot—they'd been settled, most experts believed, fifty years before, with the Naderites emerging as a ruling class. Outside of grumbling at restrictions, few Geshels complained. Responsibility had been lifted from their shoulders. Most of the population of both Earth and Moon was now involved in technical and scientific work, yet the mistakes they made would be blamed on Naderite policies—and the disasters would likewise be absorbed by the leadership. It wasn't a hard situation to get used to.

William Porter wasn't so sure, now, that it was the ideal. He had two options to save Earth, and one of them meant he would die.

He'd listened to the Psyche-Earth transmissions during acceleration, trying to make sense out of Turco's position, to form an opinion of her character and sanity, but he was more confused than ever. If she was right—and not a raving lunatic, which didn't seem to fit the facts—then the Hexamon Nexus had a lot of explaining to do and probably wouldn't do it under the gun. The size of Turco's gun was far too imposing to be rational—the destruction of the human race, the wiping of a planet's surface.

He played back the computer diagram of what would happen if Psyche hit the Earth. At the angle it would strike, it would speed the rotation of the Earth's crust and mantle by an appreciable fraction. The asteroid would cut a gouge from Maine to England, several thousand kilometers long and at least a hundred kilometers deep. The impact would vault hundreds of millions of tons of surface material into space, and that would partially counteract the speedup of rotation. The effect would be a monumental jerk, with the energy finally being released as heat. The continents would fracture in several directions, forming new faults, even new plate orientations, which would generate earthquakes on a scale never before seen. The impact basin would be a hell of molten crust and mantle, with water on the perimeter bursting violently into steam, altering weather patterns around the world. It would take decades to cool and achieve some sort of stability.

Turco may not have been raving, but she was coldly suggesting a cataclysm to swat what amounted to a historical fly. That made her a lunatic in anyone's book, Geshel or Naderite. And his life was well worth the effort to thwart her.

That didn't stop him from being angry, though.

Kollert impatiently let the physician check him over and administer a few injections. He talked to his wife briefly, which left him more nervous than before, then listened to the team leader's theories on how Turco's behavior would change in the next few hours. He nodded at only one statement: "She's going to see she'll be dead, too, and that's a major shock for even the most die-hard terrorist."

Then Turco was back on the air, and he was on stage again.

"I've seen your ship," she said. "I went outside and looked around in the direction where I thought it would be. There it was—treachery all around. Goddamned hypocrites! Talk friendly to the little girl, but shiv her in the back! Public face cool, private face snarl! Well, just remember, before he can kill me, I can destroy all controls to the positioning engines. It would take a week to rewire them. You don't have the time!" The beep followed.

"Giani, we have only one option left, and that's to do as you say. We'll admit we played a part in the sabotage of Psyche. It's confession under pressure, but we'll do it." Kollert pressed his button and waited, holding his full chin with one hand.

"No way it's so simple, Kollert. No public admission and then public denial after the danger is over—you'd all come across as heroes. No. There has to be some record-keeping, payrolls if nothing else. I want full disclosure of all records, and I want them transmitted around the world—facsimile, authenticated. I want uninvolved government officials to see them and sign that they've seen them. And I want the actual documents put on display where anyone can look at them—memos, plans, letters, whatever. All of it that's still available."

"That would take weeks," Kollert said, "if they existed."

"Not in this age of electronic wizardry. I want you to take a lie-detector test, authenticated by half a dozen experts with their careers on the line—and while you're at it, have the other officials take tests, too."

"That's not only impractical, it won't hold up in a court of law."

"I'm not interested in formal courts. I'm not a vengeful person, no matter what I may seem now. I just want the truth. And if I still see that goddamn ship up there in an hour, I'm going to stop negotiations right now and blow myself to pieces."

Kollert looked at the team leader, but the man's face was blank.

"Let me talk to her, then," Porter suggested. "Direct person-to-person. Let me explain the plans. She really can't change them any, can she? She has no way of making them worse. If she fires her engines or does any positive action, she simply stops the threat. So I'm the one who holds the key to the situation."

"We're not sure that's advisable, Bill," Lunar Guidance said.

"I can transmit to her without permission, you know," he said testily.

"Against direct orders, that's not like you."

"Like me, hell," he said, chuckling. "Listen, just get me permission. Nobody else seems to be doing anything effective." There was a few minutes' silence, then Lunar Guidance returned.

"Okay, Bill. You have permission. But be very careful what you say. Terrorist team officers on Earth think she's close to the pit."

With that obstacle cleared away, he wondered how wise the idea was in the first place. Still, they were both Geshels—they had something in common compared to the elite Naderites running things on Earth.

Far away, Earth concurred and transmissions were cleared. They couldn't censor his direct signal, so Baja Station was unwillingly cut from the circuit.

"Who's talking to me now?" Turco asked when the link was made.

"This is Lieutenant William Porter, from the Moon. I'm a pilot—not a defense pilot usually, either. I understand you've had pilot's training."

"Just enough to get by." The lag was less than a hundredth of a second, not noticeable.

"You know I'm up here to stop you, one way or another. I've got two options. The one I think more highly of is to get in line-of-sight of your boreholes and relay the proper coded signals to the charges in your interior."

"Killing me won't do you any good."

'That's not the plan. The fore end of your rock is bored with a smaller hole by thirty meters. It'll release the blast wastes more slowly than the aft end. The total explosive force should give the rock enough added velocity to get it clear of the Earth by at least sixty kilometers. The damage would be negligible. Spectacular view from Greenland, too, I understand. But if we've miscalculated, or if one or more charges doesn't go, then I'll have to impact with your aft crater and release the charge in my cargo hold. I'm one floating megaboom now, enough to boost the rock up and out by a few additional kilometers. But that means I'll be dead, and not enough left of me to memorialize or pin a medal on. Not too good, hm?"

"None of my sweat."

"No, I suppose not. But listen, sister—"

"No sister to a lackey."

Porter started to snap a retort, but stopped himself. "Listen, they tell me to be soft on you, but I'm under pressure, too, so please reciprocate. I don't see the sense in all of it. If you get your way, you've set back your cause by God knows how many decades—because once you're out of range and blown your trump, they'll deny it all, say it was manufactured evidence and testimony under pressure—all that sort of thing. And if they decide to hard-line it, force me to do my dirty work, or God forbid let you do yours—we've lost our homeworld. You've lost Psyche, which can still be salvaged and finished. Everything will be lost, just because a few men may or may not have done a very wicked thing. Come on, honey. That isn't the Geshel creed, and you know it."

"What is our creed? To let men rule our lives who aren't competent to read a thermometer? Under the Naderites, most of the leaders on Earth haven't got the technical expertise to . . . to . . . I don't know what. To tie their goddamn shoes! They're blind, dedicated to some half-wit belief that progress is the most dangerous thing conceived by man. But they can't live without technology, so we provide it for them. And when they won't touch our filthy nuclear energy, we get stuck with it—because otherwise we all have to go back four hundred years, and sacrifice half the population. Is that good planning, sound policy? And if they do what I say, Psyche won't be damaged. All they'll have to do is fetch it back from orbit around the sun."

"I'm not going to argue on their behalf, sister. I'm a Geshel, too, and a Moonman besides. I never have paid attention to Earth politics because it never made much sense to me. But now I'm talking to you one-to-one, and you're telling me that revenging someone's irrational system is worth wiping away a planet?"

"I'm willing to take that risk."

"I don't think you are. I hope you aren't. I hope it's all bluff, and I won't have to smear myself against your backside."

"I hope you won't, either. I hope they've got enough sense down there to do what I want."

"I don't think they have, sister. I don't put much faith in them, myself. They probably don't even know what would happen if you hit the Earth with your rock. Think about that. You're talking about scientific innocents—flat-Earthers almost, naive. Words fail me. But think on it. They may not even know what's going on."

"They know. And remind them that if they set off the charges, it'll probably break up Psyche and give them a thousand rocks to contend with instead of one. That plan may backfire on them."

"What if they—we—don't have any choice?"

"I don't give a damn what choice you have," Turco said. "I'm not talking for a while. I've got more work to do."

Porter listened to the final click with a sinking feeling. She was a tough one. How would he outwit her? He smiled grimly at his chutzpah for even thinking he could. She'd committed herself all the way—and now, perhaps, she was feeling the power of her position. One lonely woman, holding the key to a world's existence. He wondered how it felt.

Then he shivered, and the sweat in his suit felt very, very cold. If he would have a grave for someone to walk over . . .

For the first time, she realized they wouldn't accede to her demands. They were more traitorous than even she could have imagined. Or—the thought was too horrible to accept—she'd misinterpreted the evidence, and they weren't at fault. Perhaps a madman in the Psyche crew had sought revenge and caused the whole mess. But that didn't fit the facts. It would have taken at least a dozen people to set all the psychotropic vials and release them at once—a concerted preplanned effort. She shook her head. Besides, she had the confidential reports a friend had accidentally plugged into while troubleshooting a Hexamon computer plex. There was no doubt about who was responsible, just uncertainty about the exact procedure. Her evidence for Farmer Kollert's guilt was circumstantial but not baseless.

She sealed her suit and helmet and went outside the bubble again, just to watch the stars for a few minutes. The lead-grey rock under her feet was pitted by eons of micrometeoroids. Rills several kilometers across attested to the rolling impacts of other asteroids, any one of which would have caused a major disaster on Earth. Earth had been hit before, not often by pieces as big as Psyche, but several times at least, and had survived. Earth would survive Psyche's impact, and life would start anew. Those plants and animals—even humans— that survived would eventually build back to the present level, and perhaps it would be a better world, more daunted by the power of past evil. She might be a force for positive regeneration.

The string of bubbles across Psyche's surface was serenely lovely in the starlight. The illumination brightened slowly as Earth rose above the Vlasseg pole, larger now than the Moon. She had a few more hours to make the optimum correction. Just above the Earth was a tiny moving point of light—Porter in his cargo vessel. He was lining up with the smaller borehole to send signals, if he had to.

Again she wanted to cry. She felt like a little child, full of hatred and frustration, but caught now in something so immense and inexorable that all passion was dwarfed. She couldn't believe she was the controlling factor, that she held so much power. Surely something was behind her, some impersonal, objective force. Alone she was nothing, and her crime would be unbelievable—just as Porter had said. But with a cosmic justification, the agreeing nod of some vast all-seeing God, she was just a tool, bereft of responsibility.

She grasped the guide wires strung between the bubbles and pulled herself back to the airlock hatch. With one gloved hand she pressed the button. Under her palm she felt the metal vibrate for a second, then stop. The hatch was still closed. She pressed again and nothing happened.

Porter listened carefully for a full minute, trying to pick up the weak signal. It had cut off abruptly a few minutes before, during his final lineup with the borehole through the Vlasseg pole. He called his director and asked if any signals had been received from Turco. Since he was out of line-of-sight now, the Moon had to act as a relay.

"Nothing," Lunar Guidance said. "She's been silent for an hour."

"That's not right. We've only got an hour and a half left. She should be playing the situation for all it's worth. Listen, LG, I received a weak signal from Psyche several minutes ago. It could have been a freak, but I don't think so. I'm going to move back to where I picked it up."

"Negative, Porter. You'll need all your reaction mass in case Plan A doesn't go off properly."

"I've got plenty to spare, LG. I have a bad feeling about this. Something's gone wrong on Psyche." It was clear to him the instant he said it. "Jesus Christ, LG, the signal must have come from Turco's area on Psyche! I lost it just when I passed out of line-of-sight from her bubble."

Lunar Guidance was silent for a long moment. "Okay, Porter, we've got clearance for you to regain that signal."

"Thank you, LG." He pushed the ship out of its rough alignment and coasted slowly away from Psyche until he could see the equatorial ring of domes and bubbles. Abruptly his receiver again picked up the weak signal. He locked his tracking antenna to it, boosted it, and cut in the communications processor to interpolate through the hash.

"This is Turco. William Porter, listen to me! This is Turco. I'm locked out. Something has malfunctioned in the control bubble. I'm locked out . . ."

"I'm getting you, Turco," he said. "Look at my spot above the Vlasseg pole. I'm in line-of-sight again." If her suit was a standard model, her transmissions would strengthen in the direction she was facing.

"God bless you, Porter. I see you. Everything's gone wrong down here. I can't get back in."

"Try again, Turco. Do you have any tools with you?"

"That's what started all this, breaking in with a chisel and a pry bar. It must have weakened something, and now the whole mechanism is frozen. No, I left the bar inside. No tools. Jesus, this is awful."

"Calm down. Keep trying to get in. I'm relaying your signal to Lunar

Guidance and Earth." That settled it. There was no time to waste now. If she didn't turn on the positioning motors soon, any miss would be too close for comfort. He had to set off the internal charges within an hour and a half for the best effect.

"She's outside?" Lunar Guidance asked when the transmissions were relayed. "Can't get back in?"

"That's it," Porter said.

"That cocks it, Porter. Ignore her and get back into position. Don't bother lining up with the Vlasseg pole, however. Circle around to the Janacki pole borehole and line up for code broadcast there. You'll have a better chance of getting the code through, and you can prepare for any further action."

"I'll be cooked, LG."

"Negative—you're to relay code from an additional thousand kilometers and boost yourself out of the path just before detonation. That will occur—let's see—about four point three seconds after the charges receive the code. Program your computer for sequencing; you'll be too busy."

"I'm moving, LG." He returned to Turco's wavelength. "It's out of your hands now," he said. "We're blowing the charges. They may not be enough, so I'm preparing to detonate myself against the Janacki pole crater. Congratulations, Turco."

"I still can't get back in, Porter."

"I said, congratulations. You've killed both of us and ruined Psyche for any future projects. You know that she'll go to pieces when she drops below Roche's limit? Even if she misses, she'll be too close to survive. You know, they might have gotten it all straightened out in a few administrations. Politicos die, or get booted out of office—even Naderites. I say you've cocked it good. Be happy, Turco." He flipped the switch viciously and concentrated on his approach program display.

Farmer Kollert was slumped in his chair, eyes closed but still awake, half-listening to the murmurs in the control room. Someone tapped him on the shoulder, and he jerked up in his seat.

"I had to be with you, Farmer." Gestina stood over him, a nervous smile making her dimples obvious. "They brought me here to be with you."

"Why?" he asked.

Her voice shook. "Because our house was destroyed. I got out just in time. What's happening, Farmer? Why do they want to kill me? What did I do?"

The team officer standing beside her held out a piece of paper, and Kollert took it. Violence had broken out in half a dozen Hexamon centers, and numerous officials had had to be evacuated. Geshels weren't the only ones involved—Naderites of all classes seemed to share indignation and rage at what was happening. The outbreaks weren't organized—and that was even more disturbing. Wherever transmissions had reached the unofficial grapevines, people were reacting.

Gestina's large eyes regarded him without comprehension, much less sympathy. "I had to be with you, Farmer," she repeated. "They wouldn't let me stay."

"Quiet, please," another officer said. "More transmissions coming in."

"Yes," Kollert said softly. "Quiet. That's what we wanted. Quiet and peace and sanity. Safety for our children to come."

"I think something big is happening," Gestina said. "What is it?"

Porter checked the alignment again, put up his visual shields, and instructed the processor to broadcast the coded signal. With no distinguishable pause, the ship's engines started to move him out of the path of the particle blast.

Meanwhile Giani Turco worked at the hatch with a bit of metal bracing she had broken off her suitpack. The sharp edge just barely fit into the crevice, and by gouging and prying she had managed to force the door up half a centimeter. The evacuation mechanism hadn't been activated, so frosted air hissed from the crack, making the work doubly difficult. The Moon was rising above the Janacki pole.

Deep below her, seven prebalanced but unchecked charges, mounted on massive fittings in their chambers, began to whir. Four processors checked the timings, concurred, and released safety shields.

Six of the charges went off at once. The seventh was late by ten thousandths of a second, its blast muted as the casing melted prematurely. The particle shock waves streamed out through the bore-holes, now pressure release valves, and formed a long neck and tail of flame and ionized particles that grew steadily for a thousand kilometers, then faded. The tail from the Vlasseg pole was thinner and shorter, but no less spectacular. The asteroid shuddered, vibrations rising from deep inside to pull the ground away from Turco's boots, then swing it back to kick her away from the bubble and hatch. She floated in space, disoriented, ripped free of the guide wires, her back to the asteroid, faceplate aimed at peaceful stars, turning slowly as she reached the top of her arc.

Her leisurely descent gave her plenty of time to see the secondary plume of purple and white and red forming around the Janacki pole. The stars were blanked out by its brilliance. She closed her eyes. When she opened them again, she was nearer the ground, and her faceplate had polarized against the sudden brightness. She saw the bubble still intact, and the hatch wide open now. It had been jarred free. Everything was vibrating . . . and with shock she realized the asteroid was slowly moving out from beneath her. Her fall became a drawn-out curve, taking her away from the bubble toward a ridge of lead-grey rock, without guide wires, where she would bounce and continue on unchecked. To her left, one dome ruptured and sent a feathery wipe of debris into space. Pieces of rock and dust floated past her, shaken from Psyche's weak surface grip. Then her hand was only a few meters from a guide wire torn free and swinging outward. It came closer like a dancing snake, hesitated, rippled again, and came within reach. She grabbed it and pulled herself down.

"Porter, this is Lunar Guidance. Earth says the charges weren't enough. Something went wrong."

"She held together, LG," Porter said in disbelief. "She didn't break up. I've got a fireworks show like you've never seen before."

"Porter, listen. She isn't moving fast enough. She'll still impact."

"I *heard* you, LG," Porter shouted. "I heard! Leave me alone to get things done." Nothing more was said between them.

Turco reached the hatch and crawled into the airlock, exhausted. She closed the outer door and waited for equalization before opening the inner. Her helmet was off and floating behind as she walked and bounced and guided herself into the control room. If the motors were still functional, she'd fire them. She had no second thoughts now. Something had gone wrong, and the situation was completely different.

In the middle of the kilometers-wide crater at the Janacki pole, the borehole was still spewing debris and ionized particles. But around the perimeter, other forces were at work. Cannisters of reaction mass were flying to a point three kilometers above the crater floor. The Beckmann drive engines rotated on their mountings, aiming their nodes at the cannister's rendezvous point.

Porter's ship was following the tail of debris down to the crater floor. He could make out geometric patterns of insulating material. His computers told him something was approaching a few hundred meters below. There wasn't time for any second guessing. He primed his main cargo and sat back in the seat, lips moving, not in prayer, but repeating some stray, elegant line from the Burgess novel, a final piece of pleasure.

One of the cannisters struck the side of the cargo ship just as the blast began. A brilliant flare spread out above the crater, merging with and twisting the tail of the internal charges. Four cannisters were knocked from their course and sent plummeting into space. The remaining six met at the assigned point and were hit by beams from the Beckmann drive nodes. Their matter was stripped down to pure energy.

All of this, in its lopsided, incomplete way, bounced against the crater floor and drove the asteroid slightly faster.

When the shaking subsided, Turco let go of a grip bar and asked the computers questions. No answers came back. Everything except minimum life support was out of commission. She thought briefly of returning to her tug, if it was still in position, but there was nowhere to go. So she walked and crawled and floated to a broad viewwindow in the bubble's dining room. Earth was rising over the Vlasseg pole again, filling half her view, knots of storm and streaks of brown continent twisting slowly before her. She wondered if it had been enough—it hadn't felt right. There was no way of knowing for sure, but the Earth looked much too close.

"It's too close to judge," the president said, deliberately standing with his back to Kollert. "She'll pass over Greenland, maybe just hit the upper atmosphere."

The terrorist team officers were packing their valises and talking to each other in subdued whispers. Three of the president's security men looked at the screen with dazed expressions. The screen was blank except for a display of seconds until accession of picture. Gestina was asleep in the chair next to Kollert, her face peaceful, hands wrapped together in her lap.

"We'll have relay pictures from Iceland in a few minutes," the president said. "Should be quite a sight." Kollert frowned. The man was almost cocky, knowing he would come through it untouched. Even with survival uncertain, his government would be preparing explanations. Kollert could predict the story: a band of lunar terrorists, loosely tied with Giani Turco's father and his rabid spacefarers, was responsible for the whole thing. It would mean a few months of ill-feeling on the Moon, but at least the Nexus would have found its scapegoats.

A communicator beeped in the room, and Kollert looked around for its source. One of the security men reached into a pocket and pulled out a small earplug, which he inserted. He listened for a few seconds, frowned, then nodded. The other two gathered close, and they whispered.

Then, quietly, they left the room. The president didn't notice they were gone, but to Kollert their absence spoke volumes.

Six Nexus police entered a minute later. One stood by Kollert's chair, not looking at him. Four waited by the door. Another approached the president and tapped him on the shoulder. The president turned.

"Sir, fourteen desks have requested your impeachment. We're instructed to put you under custody, for your own safety."

Kollert started to rise, but the officer beside him put a hand on his shoulder.

"May we stay to watch?" the president asked. No one objected.

Before the screen was switched on, Kollert asked, "Is anyone going to get Turco, if it misses?"

The terrorist team leader shrugged when no one else answered. "She may not even be alive."

Then, like a crowd of children looking at a horror movie, the men and women in the communications center grouped around the large screen and watched the dark shadow of Psyche blotting out stars.

From the bubble window, Turco saw the sudden aurorae, the spray of ionized gases from the Earth's atmosphere, the awesomely rapid passage of the ocean below, and the blur of white as Greenland flashed past. The structure rocked and jerked as the Earth exerted enormous tidal strains on Psyche.

Sitting in the plastic chair, numb, tightly gripping the arms, Giani looked up—down—at the bright stars, feeling Psyche die beneath her.

Inside, the still-molten hollows formed by the charges began to collapse. Cracks shot outward to the surface, where they became gaping chasms. Sparks and rays of smoke jumped from the chasms. In minutes the passage was over. Looking closely, she saw roiling storms forming over Earth's seas and the spreading shock wave of the asteroid's sudden atmospheric compression. Big winds were blowing, but they'd survive.

It shouldn't have gone this far. They should have listened reasonably, admitted their guilt—

Absolved, girl, she wanted her father to say. She felt him very near. *You've destroyed everything we worked for—a fine architect of Pyrrhic victories.* And now he was at a great distance, receding.

The room was cold, and her skin tingled.

One huge chunk rose to block out the sun. The cabin screamed, and the bubble was filled with sudden flakes of air.

THE
WHITE HORSE
CHILD

WHEN I WAS SEVEN YEARS OLD, I MET AN OLD MAN BY THE SIDE OF THE DUSTY road between school and farm. The late afternoon sun had cooled, and he was sitting on a rock, hat off, hands held out to the gentle warmth, whistling a pretty song. He nodded at me as I walked past. I nodded back. I was curious, but I knew better than to get involved with strangers. Nameless evils seemed to attach themselves to strangers, as if they might turn into lions when no one but a little kid was around.

"Hello, boy," he said.

I stopped and shuffled my feet. He looked more like a hawk than a lion. His clothes were brown and grey and russet, and his hands were pink like the flesh of some rabbit a hawk had just plucked up. His face was brown except around the eyes, where he might have worn glasses; around the eyes he was white, and this intensified his gaze.

"Hello," I said.

"Was a hot day. Must have been hot in school," he said.

"They got air conditioning."

"So they do, now. How old are you?"

"Seven," I said. "Well, almost eight."

"Mother told you never to talk to strangers?"

"And Dad, too."

"Good advice. But haven't you seen me around here before?"

I looked him over. "No."

"Closely. Look at my clothes. What color are they?"

His shirt was grey, like the rock he was sitting on. The cuffs, where they peeped from under a russet jacket, were white. He didn't smell bad, but he didn't look particularly clean. He was smooth-shaven, though. His hair was white, and his pants were the color of the dirt below the rock. "All kinds of colors," I said.

"But mostly I partake of the landscape, no?"

"I guess so," I said.

"That's because I'm not here. You're imagining me, at least part of me. Don't I look like somebody you might have heard of?"

"Who are you supposed to look like?" I asked.

"Well, I'm full of stories," he said. "Have lots of stories to tell little boys, little girls, even big folk, if they'll listen."

I started to walk away.

"But only if they'll listen," he said. I ran. When I got home, I told my older sister about the man on the road, but she only got a worried look and told me to stay away from strangers. I took her advice. For some time afterward, into my eighth year, I avoided that road and did not speak with strangers more than I had to.

The house that I lived in, with the five other members of my family and two dogs and one beleaguered cat, was white and square and comfortable. The stairs were rich dark wood overlaid with worn carpet. The walls were dark oak paneling up to a foot above my head, then white plaster, with a white plaster ceiling. The air was full of smells—bacon when I woke up, bread and soup and dinner when I came home from school, dust on weekends when we helped clean.

Sometimes my parents argued, and not just about money, and those were bad times; but usually we were happy. There was talk about selling the farm and the house and going to Mitchell where Dad could work in a computerized feed-mixing plant, but it was only talk.

It was early summer when I took to the dirt road again. I'd forgotten about the old man. But in almost the same way, when the sun was cooling and the air was haunted by lazy bees, I saw an old woman. Women strangers are less malevolent than men, and rarer. She was sitting on the grey rock, in a long green skirt summer-dusty, with a daisy-colored shawl and a blouse the precise hue of cottonwoods seen in a late hazy day's muted light. "Hello, boy," she said.

"I don't recognize you, either," I blurted, and she smiled.

"Of course not. If you didn't recognize him, you'd hardly know me."

"Do you know him?" I asked. She nodded. "Who was he? Who are you?"

"We're both full of stories. Just tell them from different angles. You aren't afraid of us, are you?"

I was, but having a woman ask the question made all the difference. "No," I said. "But what are you doing here? And how do you know—?"

"Ask for a story," she said. "One you've never heard of before." Her eyes were the color of baked chestnuts, and she squinted into the sun so that I couldn't see her whites. When she opened them wider to look at me, she didn't have any whites.

"I don't want to hear stories," I said softly.

"Sure you do. Just ask."

"It's late. I got to be home."

"I knew a man who became a house," she said. "He didn't like it. He stayed quiet for thirty years, and watched all the people inside grow up, and be just like their folks, all nasty and dirty and leaving his walls to flake, and the bathrooms were unbearable. So he spit them out one morning, furniture and all, and shut his doors and locked them."

"What?"

"You heard me. Upchucked. The poor house was so disgusted he changed back into a man, but he was older and he had a cancer and his heart was bad because of all the abuse he had lived with. He died soon after."

I laughed, not because the man had died, but because I knew such things were lies. "That's silly," I said.

"Then here's another. There was a cat who wanted to eat butterflies. Nothing finer in the world for a cat than to stalk the grass, waiting for black-and-pumpkin butterflies. It crouches down and wriggles its rump to dig in the hind paws, then it jumps. But a butterfly is no sustenance for a cat. It's practice. There was a little girl about your age—might have been your sister, but she won't admit it—who saw the cat and decided to teach it a lesson. She hid in the taller grass with two old kites under each arm and waited for the cat to come by stalking. When it got real close, she put on her mother's dark glasses, to look all bug-eyed, and she jumped up flapping the kites. Well, it was just a little too real, because in a trice she found herself flying, and she was much smaller than she had been, and the cat jumped at her. Almost got her, too. Ask your sister about that sometime. See if she doesn't deny it."

"How'd she get back to be my sister again?"

"She became too scared to fly. She lit on a flower and found herself crushing it. The glasses broke, too."

"My sister did break a pair of Mom's glasses once."

The woman smiled.

"I got to be going home."

"Tomorrow you bring me a story, okay?"

I ran off without answering. But in my head, monsters were already rising. If she thought I was scared, wait until she heard the story I had to tell! When I got home my oldest sister, Barbara, was fixing lemonade in the kitchen. She was a year older than I but acted as if she were grown-up. She was a good six inches taller, and I could beat her if I got in a lucky punch, but no other way—so her power over me was awesome. But we were usually friendly.

"Where you been?" she asked, like a mother.

"Somebody tattled on you, " I said.

Her eyes went doe-scared, then wizened down to slits. "What're you talking about?"

"Somebody tattled about what you did to Mom's sunglasses."

"I already been whipped for that," she said nonchalantly. "Not much more to tell."

"Oh, but *I* know more."

"Was *not* playing doctor," she said. The youngest, Sue-Ann, weakest and most full of guile, had a habit of telling the folks somebody or other was playing doctor. She didn't know what it meant—I just barely did—but it had been true once, and she held it over everybody as her only vestige of power.

"No," I said, "but I know what you were doing. And I won't tell anybody."

"You don't know nothing," she said. Then she accidentally poured half a pitcher of lemonade across the side of my head and down my front. When Mom came in I was screaming and swearing like Dad did when he fixed the cars, and I was put away for life plus ninety years in the bedroom I shared with younger brother Michael. Dinner smelled better than usual that evening, but I had none of it. Somehow I wasn't brokenhearted. It gave me time to think of a scary story for the country-colored woman on the rock.

School was the usual mix of hell and purgatory the next day. Then the hot, dry winds cooled and the bells rang and I was on the dirt road again, across the southern hundred acres, walking in the lees and shadows of the big cottonwoods. I carried my Road-Runner lunch pail and my pencil box and one book—a handwriting manual I hated so much I tore pieces out of it at night, to shorten its lifetime—and I walked slowly, to give my story time to gel.

She was leaning up against a tree, not far from the rock. Looking back, I can see she was not so old as a boy of eight years thought. Now I see her lissome beauty and grace, despite the dominance of grey in her reddish hair, despite the crow's-feet around her eyes and the smile-haunts around her lips. But to the eight-year-old she was simply a peculiar crone. And he had a story to tell her, he thought, that would age her unto graveside.

"Hello, boy," she said.

"Hi." I sat on the rock.

"I can see you've been thinking," she said.

I squinted into the tree shadow to make her out better. "How'd you know?"

"You have the look of a boy that's been thinking. Are you here to listen to another story?"

"Got one to tell, this time," I said.

"Who goes first?"

It was always polite to let the woman go first, so I quelled my haste and told her she could. She motioned me to come by the tree and sit on a smaller rock, half-hidden by grass. And while the crickets in the shadow tuned up for the evening, she said, "Once there was a dog. This dog was a pretty usual dog, like the ones that would chase you around home if they thought they could get away with it—if they didn't know you or thought you were up to something the big people might disapprove of. But this dog lived in a graveyard. That is, he belonged to the caretaker. You've seen a graveyard before, haven't you?"

"Like where they took Grandpa."

"Exactly," she said. "With pretty lawns, and big white-and-grey stones, and for those who've died recently, smaller grey stones with names and flowers and years cut into them. And trees in some places, with a mortuary nearby made of brick, and a garage full of black cars, and a place behind the garage where you wonder what goes on." She knew the place, all right. "This dog had a pretty good life. It was his job to keep the grounds clear of animals at night. After the gates were locked, he'd be set loose, and he wandered all night long. He was almost white, you see. Anybody human who wasn't supposed to be there would think he was a ghost, and they'd run away.

"But this dog had a problem. His problem was, there were rats that didn't pay much attention to him. A whole gang of rats. The leader was a big one, a good yard from nose to tail. These rats made their living by burrowing under the ground in the old section of the cemetery."

That did it. I didn't want to hear any more. The air was a lot colder than it should have been, and I wanted to get home in time for dinner and still be able to eat it. But I couldn't go just then.

"Now the dog didn't know what the rats did, and just like you and I, probably, he didn't much care to know. But it was his job to keep them under control. So one day he made a truce with a couple of cats that he normally tormented and told them about the rats. These cats were scrappy old toms, and they'd long since cleared out the competition of other cats, but they were friends themselves. So the dog made them a proposition. He said he'd let them use the cemetery anytime they wanted, to prowl or hunt in or whatever, if they would put the fear of God into a few of the rats. The cats took him up on it. 'We get to do whatever we want,' they said, 'whenever we want, and you won't bother us.' The dog agreed.

"That night the dog waited for the sounds of battle. But they never came. Nary a yowl." She glared at me for emphasis. "Not a claw scratch. Not even a twitch of tail in the wind." She took a deep breath, and so did I. "Round about midnight the dog went out into

the graveyard. It was very dark, and there wasn't wind or bird or speck of star to relieve the quiet and the dismal inside-of-a-box-camera blackness. He sniffed his way to the old part of the graveyard and met with the head rat, who was sitting on a slanty, cracked wooden grave marker. Only his eyes and a tip of tail showed in the dark, but the dog could smell him. 'What happened to the cats?' he asked. The rat shrugged his haunches. 'Ain't seen any cats,' he said. 'What did you think—that you could scare us out with a couple of cats? Ha. Listen—if there had been any cats here tonight, they'd have been strung and hung like meat in a shed, and my youn'uns would have grown fat on—'"

"No-o-o!" I screamed, and I ran away from the woman and the tree until I couldn't hear the story anymore.

"What's the matter?" she called after me. "Aren't you going to tell me your story?" Her voice followed me as I ran.

It was funny. That night, I wanted to know what happened to the cats. Maybe nothing had happened to them. Not knowing made my visions even worse—and I didn't sleep well. But my brain worked like it had never worked before.

The next day, a Saturday, I had an ending—not a very good one in retrospect—but it served to frighten Michael so badly he threatened to tell Mom on me.

"What would you want to do that for?" I asked. "Cripes, I won't ever tell you a story again if you tell Mom!"

Michael was a year younger and didn't worry about the future. "You never told me stories before," he said, "and everything was fine. I won't miss them."

He ran down the stairs to the living room. Dad was smoking a pipe and reading the paper, relaxing before checking the irrigation on the north thirty. Michael stood at the foot of the stairs, thinking. I was almost down to grab him and haul him upstairs when he made his decision and headed for the kitchen. I knew exactly what he was considering—that Dad would probably laugh and call him a little scaredy-cat. But Mom would get upset and do me in proper.

She was putting a paper form over the kitchen table to mark it for fitting a tablecloth. Michael ran up to her and hung on to a pants leg while I halted at the kitchen door, breathing hard, eyes threatening eternal torture if he so much as peeped. But Michael didn't worry about the future much.

"Mom," he said.

"Cripes!" I shouted, high-pitching on the *i*. Refuge awaited me in the tractor shed. It was an agreed-upon hiding place. Mom didn't know I'd be there, but Dad did, and he could mediate.

It took him a half hour to get to me. I sat in the dark behind a workbench, practicing my pouts. He stood in the shaft of light falling from the unpatched chink in the roof. Dust motes maypoled around his legs. "Son," he said. "Mom wants to know where you got that story."

Now, this was a peculiar thing to be asked. The question I'd expected had been, "Why did you scare Michael?" or maybe, "What made you think of such a thing?" But no. Somehow she had plumbed the problem, planted the words in Dad's mouth, and impressed upon him that father-son relationships were temporarily suspended.

"I made it up," I said.

"You've never made up that kind of story before."

"I just started."

He took a deep breath. "Son, we get along real good, except when you lie to me. We know better. Who told you that story?"

This was uncanny. There was more going on than I could understand—there was a mysterious adult thing happening. I had no way around the truth. "An old woman," I said.

Dad sighed even deeper. "What was she wearing?"

"Green dress," I said.

"Was there an old man?"

I nodded.

"Christ," he said softly. He turned and walked out of the shed. From outside he called me to come into the house. I dusted off my overalls and followed him. Michael sneered at me.

"'Locked them in coffins with old dead bodies,'" he mimicked. "Phhht! You're going to get it."

The folks closed the folding door to the kitchen with both of us outside. This disturbed Michael, who'd expected instant vengeance. I was too curious and worried to take my revenge on him, so he skulked out the screen door and chased the cat around the house. "Lock you in a coffin!" he screamed.

Mom's voice drifted from behind the louvered doors. "Do you hear that? The poor child's going to have nightmares. It'll warp him."

"Don't exaggerate," Dad said.

"Exaggerate what? That those filthy people are back? Ben, they must be a hundred years old now! They're trying to do the same thing to your son that they did to your brother . . . and just look at *him!* Living in sin, writing for those hell-spawned girlie magazines."

"He ain't living in sin, he's living alone in an apartment in New York City. And he writes for all kinds of places."

"They tried to do it to you, too! Just thank God your aunt saved you."

"Margie, I hope you don't intend—"

"Certainly do. She knows all about them kind of people. She chased them off once, she can sure do it again!"

All hell had broken loose. I didn't understand half of it, but I could feel the presence of Great Aunt Sybil Danser. I could almost hear her crackling voice and the shustle of her satchel of Billy Grahams and Zondervans and little tiny pamphlets with shining light in blue offset on their covers.

I knew there was no way to get the full story from the folks short of listening in, but they'd stopped talking and were sitting in that stony kind of silence that indicated Dad's disgust and Mom's determination. I was mad that nobody was blaming me, as if I were some idiot child not capable of being bad on my own. I was mad at Michael for precipitating the whole mess.

And I was curious. Were the man and woman more than a hundred years old? Why hadn't I seen them before, in town, or heard about them from other kids? Surely I wasn't the only one they'd seen on the road and told stories to. I decided to get to the source. I walked up to the louvered doors and leaned my cheek against them. "Can I go play at George's?"

"Yes," Mom said. "Be back for evening chores."

George lived on the next farm, a mile and a half east. I took my bike and rode down the old dirt road going south.

They were both under the tree, eating a picnic lunch from a wicker basket. I pulled my bike over and leaned it against the grey rock, shading my eyes to see them more clearly.

"Hello, boy," the old man said. "Ain't seen you in a while."

I couldn't think of anything to say. The woman offered me a cookie, and I refused with a muttered, "No, thank you, ma'am."

"Well then, perhaps you'd like to tell us your story."

"No, ma'am."

"No story to tell us? That's odd. Meg was sure you had a story in you someplace. Peeking out from behind your ears maybe, thumbing its nose at us."

The woman smiled ingratiatingly. "Tea?"

"There's going to be trouble," I said.

"Already?" The woman smoothed the skirt in her lap and set a plate of nut bread into it. "Well, it comes sooner or later, this time sooner. What do you think of it, boy?"

"I think I got into a lot of trouble for not much being bad," I said. "I don't know why."

"Sit down, then," the old man said. "Listen to a tale, then tell us what's going on."

I sat down, not too keen about hearing another story but out of politeness. I took a piece of nut bread and nibbled on it as the woman sipped her tea and cleared her throat. "Once there was a city on the shore of a broad blue sea. In the city lived five hundred children and nobody else, because the wind from the sea wouldn't let anyone grow old. Well, children don't have kids of their own, of course, so when the wind came up in the first year the city never grew any larger."

"Where'd all the grown-ups go?" I asked. The old man held his fingers to his lips and shook his head.

"The children tried to play all day, but it wasn't enough. They became frightened at night and had bad dreams. There was nobody to comfort them because only grown-ups are really good at making nightmares go away. Now, sometimes nightmares are white horses that come out of the sea, so they set up guards along the beaches and fought them back with wands made of blackthorn. But there was another kind of nightmare, one that was black and rose out of the ground, and those were impossible to guard against. So the children got together one day and decided to tell all the scary stories there were to tell, to prepare themselves for all the nightmares. They found it was pretty easy to think up scary stories, and every one of them had a story or two to tell. They stayed up all night spinning yarns about ghosts and dead things, and live things that shouldn't have been, and things that were neither. They talked about death and about monsters that suck blood, about things that live way deep in the earth and long, thin things that sneak through cracks in doors to lean over the beds at night and speak in tongues no one could understand. They talked about eyes without heads, and vice versa, and little blue shoes that walk across a cold empty white room, with no one in them, and a bunk bed that creaks when it's empty, and a printing press that produces newspapers from a city that never was. Pretty soon, by morning, they'd told all the scary stories. When the black horses came out of the ground the next night, and the white horses from the sea, the children greeted them with cakes and ginger ale, and they held a big party. They also invited the pale sheet-things from the clouds, and everyone ate hearty and had a good time. One white horse let a little boy ride on it and took him wherever he wanted to go. So there were no more bad dreams in the city of children by the sea."

I finished the piece of bread and wiped my hands on my crossed legs. "So that's why you tried to scare me," I said.

She shook her head. "No. I never have a reason for telling a story, and neither should you."

"I don't think I'm going to tell stories anymore," I said. "The folks get too upset."

"Philistines," the old man said, looking off across the fields.

"Listen, young man. There is nothing finer in the world than the telling of tales. Split atoms if you wish, but splitting an infinitive—and getting away with it—is far nobler. Lance boils if you wish, but pricking pretensions is often cleaner and always more fun."

"Then why are Mom and Dad so mad?"

The old man shook his head. "An eternal mystery."

"Well, I'm not so sure," I said. "I scared my little brother pretty bad, and that's not nice."

"Being scared is nothing," the old woman said. "Being bored, or ignorant—now that's a crime."

"I still don't know. My folks say you have to be a hundred years old. You did something to my uncle they didn't like, and that was a long time ago. What kind of people are you, anyway?"

The old man smiled. "Old, yes. But not a hundred."

"I just came out here to warn you. Mom and Dad are bringing out my great aunt, and she's no fun for anyone. You better go away." With that said, I ran back to my bike and rode off, pumping for all I was worth. I was between a rock and a hard place. I loved my folks, but I itched to hear more stories. Why wasn't it easier to make decisions?

That night I slept restlessly. I didn't have any dreams, but I kept waking up with something pounding at the back of my head, like it wanted to be let in. I scrunched my face up and pressed it back.

At Sunday breakfast, Mom looked across the table at me and put on a kind face. "We're going to pick up Auntie Danser this afternoon, at the airport," she said.

My face went like warm butter.

"You'll come with us, won't you?" she asked. "You always did like the airport."

"All the way from where she lives?" I asked.

"From Omaha," Dad said.

I didn't want to go, but it was more a command than a request. I nodded, and Dad smiled at me around his pipe.

"Don't eat too many biscuits," Mom warned him. "You're putting on weight again."

"I'll wear it off come harvest. You cook as if the whole crew was here, anyway."

"Auntie Danser will straighten it all out," Mom said, her mind elsewhere. I caught the suggestion of a grimace on Dad's face, and the pipe wriggled as he bit down on it harder.

The airport was something out of a TV space movie. It went on forever, with stairways going up to restaurants and big smoky windows that looked out on the screaming jets, and crowds of people, all leaving, except for one pear-shaped figure in a cotton print dress with fat ankles and glasses thick as headlamps. I knew her from a hundred yards.

When we met, she shook hands with Mom, hugged Dad as if she didn't want to, then bent down and gave me a smile. Her teeth were yellow and even, sound as a horse's. She was the ugliest woman I'd ever seen. She smelled of lilacs. To this day lilacs take my appetite away.

She carried a bag. Part of it was filled with knitting, part with books and pamphlets. I always wondered why she never carried a Bible—just Billy Grahams and Zondervans. One pamphlet fell out, and Dad bent to pick it up.

"Keep it, read it," Auntie Danser instructed him. "Do you good." She turned to Mom and scrutinized her from the bottom of a swimming pool. "You're looking good. He must be treating you right."

Dad ushered us out the automatic doors into the dry heat. Her one suitcase was light as a mummy and probably just as empty. I carried it, and it didn't even bring sweat to my brow. Her life was not in clothes and toiletry but in the plastic knitting bag.

We drove back to the farm in the big white station wagon. I leaned my head against the cool glass of the rear seat window and considered puking. Auntie Danser, I told myself, was like a mental dose of castor oil. Or like a visit to the dentist. Even if nothing was going to happen her smell presaged disaster, and like a horse sniffing a storm, my entrails worried.

Mom looked across the seat at me—Auntie Danser was riding up front with Dad—and asked, "You feeling okay? Did they give you anything to eat? Anything funny?"

I said they'd given me a piece of nut bread. Mom went, "Oh, Lord."

"Margie, they don't work like that. They got other ways." Auntie Danser leaned over the backseat and goggled at me. "Boy's just worried. I know all about it. These people and I have had it out before."

Through those murky glasses, her flat eyes knew me to my young pithy core. I didn't like being known so well. I could see that Auntie Danser's life was firm and predictable, and I made a sudden commitment. I liked the man and woman. They caused trouble, but they were the exact opposite of my great aunt. I felt better, and I gave her a reassuring grin. "Boy will be okay," she said. "Just a colic of the upset mind."

Michael and Barbara sat on the front porch as the car drove up. Somehow a visit by Auntie Danser didn't bother them as much as it did me. They didn't fawn over her, but they accepted her without complaining—even out of adult earshot. That made me think more carefully about them. I decided I didn't love them any the less, but I couldn't trust them, either. The world was taking sides, and so far on my side I was very lonely. I didn't count the two old people on my side, because I wasn't sure they were—but they came a lot closer than anybody in my family.

Auntie Danser wanted to read Billy Graham books to us after dinner, but Dad snuck us out before Mom could gather us together— all but Barbara, who stayed to listen. We watched the sunset from the loft of the old wood barn, then tried to catch the little birds that lived in the rafters. By dark and bedtime I was hungry, but not for food. I asked Dad if he'd tell me a story before bed.

"You know your mom doesn't approve of all that fairy-tale stuff," he said.

"Then no fairy tales. Just a story."

"I'm out of practice, son," he confided. He looked very sad. "Your mom says we should concentrate on things that are real and not waste our time with make-believe. Life's hard. I may have to sell the farm, you know, and work for that feed-mixer in Mitchell."

I went to bed and felt like crying. A whole lot of my family had died that night, I didn't know exactly how, or why. But I was mad.

I didn't go to school the next day. During the night I'd had a dream, which came so true and whole to me that I had to rush to the stand of cottonwoods and tell the old people. I took my lunch box and walked rapidly down the road.

They weren't there. On a piece of wire bradded to the biggest tree they'd left a note on faded brown paper. It was in a strong feminine hand, sepia-inked, delicately scribed with what could have been a goose-quill pen. It said: "We're at the old Hauskopf farm. Come if you must."

Not "Come if you can." I felt a twinge. The Hauskopf farm, abandoned fifteen years ago and never sold, was three miles farther down the road and left on a deep-rutted fork. It took me an hour to get there.

The house still looked deserted. All the white paint was flaking, leaving dead grey wood. The windows stared. I walked up the porch steps and knocked on the heavy oak door. For a moment I thought no one was going to answer. Then I heard what sounded like a gust of wind, but inside the house, and the old woman opened the door. "Hello, boy," she said. "Come for more stories?"

She invited me in. Wildflowers were growing along the baseboards, and tiny roses peered from the brambles that covered the walls. A quail led her train of inch-and-a-half fluffball chicks from under the stairs, into the living room. The floor was carpeted, but the flowers in the weave seemed more than patterns. I could stare down and keep picking out detail for minutes. "This way, boy," the woman said. She took my hand. Hers was smooth and warm, but I had the impression it was also hard as wood.

A tree stood in the living room, growing out of the floor and sending its branches up to support the ceiling. Rabbits and quail and a lazy-looking brindle cat stared at me from tangles of roots. A wooden bench surrounded the base of the tree. On the side away from us, I heard someone breathing. The old man poked his head around and smiled at me, lifting his long pipe in greeting. "Hello, boy," he said.

"The boy looks like he's ready to tell us a story, this time," the woman said.

"Of course, Meg. Have a seat, boy. Cup of cider for you? Tea? Herb biscuit?"

"Cider, please," I said.

The old man stood and went down the hall to the kitchen. He came back with a wooden tray and three steaming cups of mulled cider. The cinnamon tickled my nose as I sipped.

"Now. What's your story?"

"It's about two hawks," I said, and then hesitated.

"Go on."

"Brother hawks. Never did like each other. Fought for a strip of land where they could hunt."

"Yes?"

"Finally, one hawk met an old crippled bobcat that had set up a place for itself in a rockpile. The bobcat was learning itself magic so it wouldn't have to go out and catch dinner, which was awful hard for it now. The hawk landed near the bobcat and told it about his brother, and how cruel he was. So the bobcat said, 'Why not give him the land for the day? Here's what you can do.' The bobcat told him how he could turn into a rabbit, but a very strong rabbit no hawk could hurt."

"Wily bobcat," the old man said, smiling.

" 'You mean, my brother wouldn't be able to catch me?' the hawk asked. 'Course not,' the bobcat said. 'And you can teach him a lesson. You'll tussle with him, scare him real bad—show him what tough animals there are on the land he wants. Then he'll go away and hunt somewheres else.' The hawk thought that sounded like a fine idea. So he let the bobcat turn him into a rabbit, and he hopped back to the land and waited in a patch of grass. Sure enough, his brother's shadow passed by soon, and then he heard a swoop and saw the claws held out. So he filled himself with being mad and jumped up and practically bit all the tail feathers off his brother. The hawk just flapped up and rolled over on the ground, blinking and gawking with his beak wide. 'Rabbit,' he said, 'that's not natural. Rabbits don't act that way.'

" 'Round here they do,' the hawk-rabbit said. 'This is a tough old land, and all the animals here know the tricks of escaping from bad birds like you.' This scared the brother hawk, and he flew away as best he could and never came back again. The hawk-rabbit hopped to the rockpile and stood up before the bobcat, saying, 'It worked real fine. I thank you. Now turn me back, and I'll go hunt my land.' But the bobcat only grinned and reached out with a paw and broke the rabbit's neck. Then he ate him, and said, 'Now the land's mine, and no hawks can take away the easy game.' And that's how the greed of two hawks turned their land over to a bobcat."

The old woman looked at me with wide baked-chestnut eyes and smiled. "You've got it," she said. "Just like your uncle. Hasn't he got it, Jack?" The old man nodded and took his pipe from his mouth. "He's got it fine. He'll make a good one."

"Now, boy, why did you make up that story?"

I thought for a moment, then shook my head. "I don't know," I said. "It just came up."

"What are you going to do with the story?"

I didn't have an answer for that question, either.

"Got any other stories in you?"

I considered, then said, "Think so."

A car drove up outside, and Mom called my name. The old

woman stood and straightened her dress. "Follow me," she said. "Go out the back door, walk around the house. Return home with them. Tomorrow, go to school like you're supposed to do. Next Saturday, come back, and we'll talk some more."

"Son? You in there?"

I walked out the back and came around to the front of the house. Mom and Auntie Danser waited in the station wagon. "You aren't allowed out here. Were you in that house?" Mom asked. I shook my head.

My great aunt looked at me with her glassed-in flat eyes and lifted the corners of her lips a little. "Margie," she said, "go have a look in the windows."

Mom got out of the car and walked up the porch to peer through the dusty panes. "It's empty, Sybil."

"Empty, boy, right?"

"I don't know," I said. "I wasn't inside."

"I could hear you, boy," she said. "Last night. Talking in your sleep. Rabbits and hawks don't behave that way. You know it, and I know it. So it ain't no good thinking about them that way, is it?"

"I don't remember talking in my sleep," I said.

"Margie, let's go home. This boy needs some pamphlets read into him."

Mom got into the car and looked back at me before starting the engine. "You ever skip school again, I'll strap you black and blue. It's real embarrassing having the school call, and not knowing where you are. Hear me?"

I nodded.

Everything was quiet that week. I went to school and tried not to dream at night and did everything boys are supposed to do. But I didn't feel like a boy. I felt something big inside, and no amount of Billy Grahams and Zondervans read at me could change that feeling.

I made one mistake, though. I asked Auntie Danser why she never read the Bible. This was in the parlor one evening after dinner and cleaning up the dishes. "Why do you want to know, boy?" she asked.

"Well, the Bible seems to be full of fine stories, but you don't carry it around with you. I just wondered why."

"Bible is a good book," she said. "The only good book. But it's difficult. It has lots of camouflage. Sometimes—" She stopped. "Who put you up to asking that question?"

"Nobody," I said.

"I heard that question before, you know," she said. "Ain't the first time I been asked. Somebody else asked me, once."

I sat in my chair, stiff as a ham.

"Your father's brother asked me that once. But we won't talk about him, will we?"

I shook my head.

Next Saturday I waited until it was dark and everyone was in bed. The night air was warm, but I was sweating more than the warm could cause as I rode my bike down the dirt road, lamp beam swinging back and forth. The sky was crawling with stars, all of them looking at me. The Milky Way seemed to touch down just beyond the road, like I might ride straight up it if I went far enough.

I knocked on the heavy door. There were no lights in the windows and it was late for old folks to be up, but I knew these two didn't behave like normal people. And I knew that just because the house looked empty from the outside didn't mean it was empty within. The wind rose up and beat against the door, making me shiver. Then it opened. It was dark for a moment, and the breath went out of me. Two pairs of eyes stared from the black. They seemed a lot taller this time. "Come in, boy," Jack whispered.

Fireflies lit up the tree in the living room. The brambles and wild-flowers glowed like weeds on a sea floor. The carpet crawled, but not to my feet. I was shivering in earnest now, and my teeth chattered.

I only saw their shadows as they sat on the bench in front of me. "Sit," Meg said. "Listen close. You've taken the fire, and it glows bright. You're only a boy, but you're just like a pregnant woman now. For the rest of your life you'll be cursed with the worst affliction known to humans. Your skin will twitch at night. Your eyes will see things in the dark. Beasts will come to you and beg to be ridden. You'll never know one truth from another. You might starve, because few will want to encourage you. And if you do make good in this world, you might lose the gift and search forever after, in vain.

Some will say the gift isn't special. Beware them. Some will say it is special, and beware them, too. And some—"

There was a scratching at the door. I thought it was an animal for a moment. Then it cleared its throat. It was my great aunt.

"Some will say you're damned. Perhaps they're right. But you're also enthused. Carry it lightly and responsibly."

"Listen in there. This is Sybil Danser. You know me. Open up."

"Now stand by the stairs, in the dark where she can't see," Jack said. I did as I was told. One of them—I couldn't tell which—opened the door, and the lights went out in the tree, the carpet stilled, and the brambles were snuffed. Auntie Danser stood in the doorway, outlined by star glow, carrying her knitting bag. "Boy?" she asked. I held my breath.

"And you others, too."

The wind in the house seemed to answer. "I'm not too late," she said. "Damn you, in truth, damn you to hell! You come to our towns, and you plague us with thoughts no decent person wants to think. Not just fairy stories, but telling the way people live and why they shouldn't live that way! Your very breath is tainted! Hear me?" She walked slowly into the empty living room, feet clonking on the wooden floor. "You make them write about us and make others laugh at us. Question the way we think. Condemn our deepest prides. Pull out our mistakes and amplify them beyond all truth. What right do you have to take young children and twist their minds?"

The wind sang through the cracks in the walls. I tried to see if Jack or Meg was there, but only shadows remained.

"I know where you come from, don't forget that! Out of the ground! Out of the bones of old wicked Indians! Shamans and pagan dances and worshiping dirt and filth! I heard about you from the old squaws on the reservation. Frost and Spring, they called you, signs of the turning year. Well, now you got a different name! Death and demons, I call you, hear me?"

She seemed to jump at a sound, but I couldn't hear it. "Don't you argue with me!" she shrieked. She took her glasses off and held out both hands. "Think I'm a weak old woman, do you? You don't know how deep I run in these communities! I'm the one who had them books taken off the shelves. Remember me? Oh, you hated it—not being able to fill young minds with your pestilence. Took them off high school shelves and out of lists—burned them for junk! Remember? That was me. I'm not dead yet! Boy, where are you?"

"Enchant her," I whispered to the air. "Magic her. Make her go away. Let me live here with you."

"Is that you, boy? Come with your aunt, now. Come with, come away!"

"Go with her," the wind told me. "Send your children this way, years from now. But go with her."

I felt a kind of tingly warmth and knew it was time to get home. I snuck out the back way and came around to the front of the house. There was no car. She'd followed me on foot all the way from the farm. I wanted to leave her there in the old house, shouting at the dead rafters, but instead I called her name and waited.

She came out crying. She knew.

"You poor sinning boy," she said, pulling me to her lilac bosom.

PETRA

> "God is dead, God is dead" . . . Perdition! When God dies,
> you'll know it.   —CONFESSIONS OF ST. ARGENTINE

I'M AN UGLY SON OF STONE AND FLESH, THERE'S NO DENYING IT. I DON'T REMEM-
ber my mother. It's possible she abandoned me shortly after my
birth. More than likely she is dead. My father—ugly beaked half-
winged thing, if he resembles his son—I have never seen.

Why should such an unfortunate aspire to be a historian? I think I
can trace the moment my choice was made. It's among my earliest
memories, and it must have happened about thirty years ago, though
I'm sure I lived many years before that—years now lost to me. I was
squatting behind thick, dusty curtains in a vestibule, listening to a
priest instructing other novitiates, all of pure flesh, about Mortdieu.
His words are still vivid.

"As near as I can discover," he said, "Mortdieu occurred about
seventy-seven years ago. Learned ones deny that magic was set
loose on the world, but few deny that God, as such, had died."

Indeed. That's putting it mildly. All the hinges of our once-great
universe fell apart, the axis tilted, cosmic doors swung shut, and the
rules of existence lost their foundations. The priest continued in
measured, awed tones to describe that time.

"I have heard wise men speak of the slow decline. Where human
thought was strong, reality's sudden quaking was reduced to a
tremor. Where thought was weak, reality disappeared completely,
swallowed by chaos. Every delusion became as real as solid matter."
His voice trembled with emotion. "Blinding pain, blood catching fire

in our veins, bones snapping and flesh powdering. Steel flowing like liquid. Amber raining from the sky. Crowds gathering in streets that no longer followed any maps, if the maps themselves had not altered. They knew not what to do. Their weak minds could not grab hold . . ."

Most humans, I take it, were entirely too irrational to begin with. Whole nations vanished or were turned into incomprehensible whirlpools of misery and depravity. It is said that certain universities, libraries, and museums survived, but to this day we have little contact with them.

I think often of those poor victims of the early days of Mortdieu. They had known a world of some stability; we have adapted since. They were shocked by cities turning into forests, by their nightmares taking shape before their eyes. Prodigal crows perched atop trees that had once been buildings, pigs ran through the streets on their hind legs . . . and so on. (The priest did not encourage contemplation of the oddities. "Excitement," he said, "breeds even more monsters.")

Our Cathedral survived. Rationality in this neighborhood, however, had weakened some centuries before Mortdieu, replaced only by a kind of rote. The Cathedral suffered. Survivors—clergy and staff, worshipers seeking sanctuary—had wretched visions, dreamed wretched dreams. They saw the stone ornaments of the Cathedral come alive. With someone to see and believe, in a universe lacking any other foundation, my ancestors shook off stone and became flesh. Centuries of rock celibacy weighed upon them. Forty-nine nuns who had sought shelter in the Cathedral were discovered and were not entirely loath, so the coarser versions of the tale go. Mortdieu had had a surprising aphrodisiacal effect on the faithful, and conjugation took place.

No definite gestation period has been established, for at that time the great stone wheel had not been set twisting back and forth to count the hours. Nor had anyone been given the chair of Kronos to watch over the wheel and provide a baseline for everyday activities.

But flesh did not reject stone, and there came into being the sons and daughters of flesh and stone, including me. Those who had fornicated with the inhuman figures were cast out to raise—or reject—their monstrous young in the highest hidden recesses. Those who had accepted the embraces of the stone saints and other human

figures were less abused but still banished to the upper reaches. A wooden scaffolding was erected, dividing the great nave into two levels. A canvas drop cloth was fastened over the scaffold to prevent offal raining down, and on the second level of the Cathedral the more human offspring of stone and flesh set about creating a new life.

I have long tried to find out how some semblance of order came to the world. Legend has it that it was the archexistentialist Jansard—crucifier of the beloved St. Argentine—who, realizing and repenting his error, discovered that mind and thought could calm the foaming sea of reality.

The priest finished his all-too-sketchy lecture by touching on this point briefly: "With the passing of God's watchful gaze, humanity had to reach out and grab hold the unraveling fabric of the world. Those left alive—those who had the wits to keep their bodies from falling apart—became the only cohesive force in the chaos."

I had picked up enough language to understand what he said; my memory was good—still is—and I was curious enough to want to know more.

Creeping along stone walls behind the curtains, I listened to other priests and nuns intoning scripture to gaggles of flesh children. That was on the ground floor, and I was in great danger; the people of pure flesh looking on my kind as abominations. But it was worth it.

I was able to steal a psalter and learned to read. I stole other books; they defined my world by allowing me to compare it with others. At first I couldn't believe the others had ever existed; only the Cathedral was real. I still have my doubts. I can look out a tiny round window on one side of my room and see the great forest and river that surround the Cathedral, but I can see nothing else. So my experience with other worlds is far from direct.

No matter. I read a great deal, but I'm no scholar. What concerns me is recent history—the final focus of that germinal hour listening to the priest. From the metaphysical to the acutely personal.

I am small—barely three English feet in height—but I can run quickly through most of the hidden passageways. This lets me observe without attracting attention. I may be the only historian in this whole structure. Others who claim the role disregard what's before their eyes, in search of ultimate truths, or at least Big Pictures. So if you prefer history where the historian is not involved, look to the others. Objective as I try to be, I do have my favorite subjects. . . .

In the time when my history begins, the children of stone and flesh were still searching for the Stone Christ. Those of us born of the union of the stone saints and gargoyles with the bereaved nuns thought our salvation lay in the great stone celibate, who came to life as all the other statues had.

Of smaller import were the secret assignations between the bishop's daughter and a young man of stone and flesh. Such assignations were forbidden even between those of pure flesh; and as these two lovers were unmarried, their compound sin intrigued me.

Her name was Constantia, and she was fourteen, slender of limb, brown of hair, mature of bosom. Her eyes carried the stupid sort of divine life common in girls that age. His name was Corvus, and he was fifteen. I don't recall his precise features, but he was handsome enough and dextrous: he could climb through the scaffolding almost as quickly as I. I first spied them talking when I made one of my frequent raids on the repository to steal another book. They were in shadow, but my eyes are keen. They spoke softly, hesitantly. My heart ached to see them and to think of their tragedy, for I knew right away that Corvus was not pure flesh and that Constantia was the daughter of the bishop himself. I envisioned the old tyrant meting out the usual punishment to Corvus for such breaches of level and morality—castration. But in their talk was a sweetness that almost masked the closed-in stench of the lower nave.

"Have you ever kissed a man before?"

"Yes."

"Who?"

"My brother." She laughed.

"And?" His voice was sharper; he might kill her brother, he seemed to say.

"A friend named Jules."

"Where is he?"

"Oh, he vanished on a wood-gathering expedition."

"Oh." And he kissed her again. I'm a historian, not a voyeur, so I discreetly hide the flowering of their passion. If Corvus had had any sense, he would have reveled in his conquest and never returned.

But he was snared and continued to see her despite the risk. This was loyalty, love, faithfulness, and it was rare. It fascinated me.

I have just been taking in sun, a nice day, and looking out over the buttresses. The Cathedral is like a low-bellied lizard, and the buttresses are its legs. There are little houses at the base of each buttress, where rainspouters with dragon faces used to lean out over the trees (or city or whatever was down below once). Now people live there. It wasn't always that way—the sun was once forbidden. Corvus and Constantia from childhood were denied its light, and so even in their youthful prime they were pale and dirty with the smoke of candles and tallow lamps. The most sun anyone received in those days was obtained on wood-gathering expeditions.

After spying on one of the clandestine meetings of the young lovers, I mused in a dark corner for an hour, then went to see the copper giant Apostle Thomas. He was the only human form to live so high in the Cathedral. He carried a ruler on which was engraved his real name—he had been modeled after the Cathedral's restorer in times past, the architect Viollet-le-Duc. He knew the Cathedral better than anyone, and I admired him greatly. Most of the monsters left him alone—out of fear, if nothing else. He was huge, black as night, but flaked with pale green, his face creased in eternal thought. He was sitting in his usual wooden compartment near the base of the spire, not twenty feet from where I write now, thinking about times none of the rest of us ever knew: of joy and past love, some say; others say of the burden that rested on him now that the Cathedral was the center of this chaotic world.

It was the giant who selected me from the ugly hordes when he saw me with a psalter. He encouraged me in my efforts to read. "Your eyes are bright," he told me. "You move as if your brain were quick, and you keep yourself dry and clean. You aren't hollow like the rainspouters—you have substance. For all our sakes, put it to use and learn the ways of the Cathedral."

And so I did.

He looked up as I came in. I sat on a box near his feet and said, "A daughter of flesh is seeing a son of stone and flesh."

He shrugged his massive shoulders. "So it shall be, in time."

"Is it not a sin?"

"It is something so monstrous it is past sin and become necessity," he said. "It will happen more as time passes."

"They're in love, I think, or will be."

He nodded. "I—and One Other—were the only ones to abstain from fornication on the night of Mortdieu," he said. "I am—except for the Other—alone fit to judge."

I waited for him to judge, but he sighed and patted me on the shoulder. "And I never judge, do I, ugly friend?"

"Never," I said.

"So leave me alone to be sad." He winked. "And more power to them."

The bishop of the Cathedral was an old, old man. It was said he hadn't been bishop before the Mortdieu, but a wanderer who came in during the chaos, before the forest had replaced the city. He had set himself up as titular head of this section of God's former domain by saying it had been willed to him.

He was short, stout, with huge hairy arms like the clamps of a vise. He had once killed a spouter with a single squeeze of his fist, and spouters are tough things, since they have no guts like you (I suppose) and I. The hair surrounding his bald pate was white, thick, and unruly, and his eyebrows leaned over his nose with marvelous flexibility. He rutted like a pig, ate hugely, and shat liquidly (I know all). A man for this time, if ever there was one.

It was his decree that all those not pure of flesh be banned and that those not of human form be killed on sight.

When I returned from the giant's chamber, I saw that the lower nave was in an uproar. They had seen someone clambering about in the scaffold, and troops had been sent to shoot him down. Of course it was Corvus. I was a quicker climber than he and knew the beams better, so when he found himself trapped in an apparent cul-de-sac, it was I who gestured from the shadows and pointed to a hole large enough for him to escape through. He took it without a breath of thanks, but etiquette has never been important to me. I entered the stone wall through a nook a spare hand's width across and wormed my way to the bottom to see what else was happening. Excitement was rare.

A rumor was passing that the figure had been seen with a young girl, but the crowds didn't know who the girl was. The men and women who mingled in the smoky light, between the rows of open-roofed hovels, chattered gaily. Castrations and executions were among the few joys for us then; I relished them too, but I had a stake in the potential victims now and I worried.

My worry and my interest got the better of me. I slid through an unrepaired gap and fell to one side of the alley between the outer wall and the hovels. A group of dirty adolescents spotted me. "There he is!" they screeched. "He didn't get away!"

The bishop's masked troops can travel freely on all levels. I was almost cornered by them, and when I tried one escape route, they waited at a crucial spot in the stairs—which I had to cross to complete the next leg—and I was forced back. I prided myself in knowing the Cathedral top to bottom, but as I scrambled madly, I came upon a tunnel I had never noticed before. It led deep into a broad stone foundation wall. I was safe for the moment but afraid that they might find my caches of food and poison my casks of rainwater. Still, there was nothing I could do until they had gone, so I decided to spend the anxious hours exploring the tunnel.

The Cathedral is a constant surprise; I realize now I didn't know half of what it offered. There are always new ways to get from here to there (some, I suspect, created while no one is looking), and sometimes even new theres to be discovered. While troops snuffled about the hole above, near the stairs—where only a child of two or three could have entered—I followed a flight of crude steps deep into the stone. Water and slime made the passage slippery and difficult. For a moment I was in darkness deeper than any I had experienced before—a gloom more profound than mere lack of light could explain. Then below I saw a faint yellow gleam. More cautious, I slowed and progressed silently. Behind a rusting, scabrous metal gate, I set foot into the lighted room. There was the smell of crumbling stone, a tang of mineral water, slime—and the stench of a dead spouter. The beast lay on the floor of the narrow chamber, several months gone but still fragrant. I have mentioned that spouters are very hard to kill—and this one had been murdered. Three candles stood freshly placed in nooks around the chamber, flickering in a faint draft from above. Despite my fears, I walked across the stone floor, took a candle, and peered into the next section of tunnel.

It sloped down for several dozen feet, ending at another metal gate. It was here that I detected an odor I had never before encountered—the smell of the purest of stones, as of rare jade or virgin marble. Such a feeling of light-headedness passed over me that I almost laughed, but I was too cautious for that. I pushed aside the gate and was greeted by a rush of the coldest, sweetest air, like a draft from the tomb of a saint whose body does not corrupt but, rather, draws corruption away and expels it miraculously into the nether pits. My beak dropped open. The candlelight fell across the darkness onto a figure I at first thought to be an infant. But I quickly disagreed with myself. The figure was several ages at once. As I blinked, it became a man of about thirty, well formed, with a high forehead and elegant hands, pale as ice. His eyes stared at the wall behind me. I bowed down on scaled knee and touched my forehead as best I could to the cold stone, shivering to my vestigial wing tips. "Forgive me, Joy of Man's Desiring," I said. "Forgive me." I had stumbled upon the hiding place of the Stone Christ.

"You are forgiven," He said wearily. "You had to come sooner or later. Better now than later, when . . ." His voice trailed away and He shook His head. He was very thin, wrapped in a grey robe that still bore the scars of centuries of weathering. "Why did you come?"

"To escape the bishop's troops," I said.

He nodded. "Yes. The bishop. How long have I been here?"

"Since before I was born, Lord. Sixty or seventy years." He was thin, almost ethereal, this figure I had imagined as a husky carpenter. I lowered my voice and beseeched, "What may I do for you, Lord?"

"Go away," He said.

"I could not live with such a secret," I said. "You are salvation. You can overthrow the bishop and bring all the levels together."

"I am not a general or a soldier. Please go away and tell no—"

I felt a breath behind me, then the whisper of a weapon. I leaped aside, and my hackles rose as a stone sword came down and shattered on the floor beside me. The Christ raised His hand. Still in shock, I stared at a beast much like myself. It stared back, face black with rage, stayed by the power of His hand. I should have been more wary—something had to have killed the spouter and kept the candles fresh.

"But, Lord," the beast rumbled, "he will tell all."

"No," the Christ said. "He'll tell nobody." He looked half at me, half through me, and said, "Go, go."

Up the tunnels, into the orange dark of the Cathedral, crying, I crawled and slithered. I could not even go to the giant. I had been silenced as effectively as if my throat had been cut.

The next morning I watched from a shadowy corner of the scaffold as a crowd gathered around a lone man in a dirty sackcloth robe. I had seen him before—his name was Psalo, and he was left alone as an example of the bishop's largesse. It was a token gesture; most of the people regarded him as barely half-sane.

Yet this time I listened and, in my confusion, found his words striking responsive chords in me. He was exhorting the bishop and his forces to allow light into the Cathedral again by dropping the canvas tarps that covered the windows. He had talked about this before, and the bishop had responded with his usual statement—that with the light would come more chaos, for the human mind was now a pesthole of delusions. Any stimulus would drive away whatever security the inhabitants of the Cathedral had.

At this time it gave me no pleasure to watch the love of Constantia and Corvus grow. They were becoming more careless. Their talk was bolder:

"We shall announce a marriage," Corvus said.

"They will never allow it. They'll . . . cut you."

"I'm nimble. They'll never catch me. The church needs leaders, brave revolutionaries. If no one breaks with tradition, everyone will suffer."

"I fear for your life—and mine. My father would push me from the flock like a diseased lamb."

"Your father is no shepherd."

"He is my father," Constantia said, eyes wide, mouth drawn tight.

I sat with beak in paws, eyes half-lidded, able to mimic each statement before it was uttered. Undying love . . . hope for a bleak future . . . shite and onions! I had read it all before, in a cache of romance novels in the trash of a dead nun. As soon as I made the connection and realized the timeless banality—and the futility—of what I was seeing, and when I compared their prattle with the infinite sadness of the Stone Christ, I went from innocent to cynic. The transition dizzied me, leaving little backwaters of noble emotion, but the future seemed clear. Corvus would be caught and executed; if it hadn't been for me, he would already have been gelded, if not killed. Constantia would weep, poison herself; the singers would sing of it (those selfsame warble-throats who cheered the death of her lover), perhaps I would write of it (I was planning this chronicle even then), and afterward, perhaps, I would follow them both, having succumbed to the sin of boredom.

With night, things become less certain. It was easy to stare at a dark wall and let dreams become manifest. At one time, I've deduced from books, dreams could not take shape beyond sleep or brief fantasy. All too often I've had to fight things generated in my dreams, flowing from the walls, suddenly independent and hungry. People often die in the night, devoured by their own nightmares.

That evening, falling to sleep with visions of the Stone Christ in my head, I dreamed of holy men, angels, and saints. I came awake abruptly, by training, and one had stayed behind. The others I saw vaguely, flitting outside the round window, where they whispered and made plans for flying off to heaven. The wraith who remained was a dark shape in one corner. His breathing was harsh. "I am Peter," he said, "also called Simon. I am the Rock of the Church, and popes are told that they are heir to my task."

"I'm rock, too," I said. "At least in part."

"So be it, then. You are heir to my task. Go forth and be pope. Do not revere the Stone Christ, for a Christ is only as good as He does, and if He does nothing, there is no salvation in Him."

The shadow reached out to pat my head, and I saw his eyes grow wide as he made out my form. He muttered some formula for banishing devils and oozed out the window to join his fellows.

I imagined that if such a thing were actually brought before the council, it would be decided under the law that the benison of a dream person is not binding. I did not care. This was better advice than any I'd had since the giant told me to read and learn.

But to be pope, one must have a hierarchy of servants to carry out one's orders. The biggest of rocks does not move by itself. So, swelled with power, I decided to appear in the upper nave and announce myself to the people.

It took a great deal of courage to appear in daylight, without cloak, and to walk across the scaffold's surface, on the second level, through crowds of vendors setting up the market for the day. Some reacted with typical bigotry and sought to kick or deride me. My beak discouraged them. I clambered to the top of a prominent stall and stood in a murky lamp's circle, clearing my throat to announce myself. Under a hail of rotten pomegranates and limp vegetables, I told the throng who I was, and I told them about my vision. Jeweled with beads of offal, I jumped down in a few minutes and fled to a tunnel entrance too small for most men. Some boys followed me, and one lost a finger while trying to slice me with a fragment of colored glass.

I recognized that the tactic of open revelation was worthless. There are levels of bigotry, and I was at the very bottom of any list.

My next strategy was to find some way to disrupt the Cathedral from top to bottom. Even bigots, when reduced to a mob, could be swayed by the presence of one obviously ordained and capable. I spent two days skulking through the walls. There had to be a basic flaw in so fragile a structure as the church, and, while I wasn't contemplating total destruction, I wanted something spectacular, unavoidable.

While I thought, hanging from the bottom of the second scaffold, above the community of pure flesh, the bishop's deep gravelly voice roared over the noise of the crowd. I opened my eyes and looked down. The masked troops were holding a bowed figure, and the bishop was intoning over its head, "Know all who hear me now, this young bastard of flesh and stone—"

Corvus, I told myself. Finally caught. I shut one eye, but the other refused to close out the scene.

"—has violated all we hold sacred and shall atone for his crimes on this spot, tomorrow at this time. Kronos! Mark the wheel's progress." The elected Kronos, a spindly old man with dirty grey hair down to his buttocks, took a piece of charcoal and marked an X on the huge bulkhead chart, behind which the wheel groaned and sighed in its circuit.

The crowd was enthusiastic. I saw Psalo pushing through the people.

"What crime?" he called out. "Name the crime!"

"Violation of the lower level!" the head of the masked troops declared.

"That merits a whipping and an escort upstairs," Psalo said. "I detect a more sinister crime here. What is it?"

The bishop looked Psalo down coldly. "He tried to rape my daughter, Constantia."

Psalo could say nothing to that. The penalty was castration and death. All the pure humans accepted such laws. There was no other recourse.

I mused, watching Corvus being led to the dungeons. The future that I desired at that moment startled me with its clarity. I wanted that part of my heritage that had been denied to me—to be at peace with myself, to be surrounded by those who accepted me, by those no better than I. In time that would happen, as the giant had said. But would I ever see it? What Corvus, in his own lusty way, was trying to do was equalize the levels, to bring stone into flesh until no one could define the divisions.

Well, my plans beyond that point were very hazy. They were less plans than glowing feelings, imaginings of happiness and children playing in the forest and fields beyond the island as the world knit itself under the gaze of God's heir. My children, playing in the forest. A touch of truth came to me at this moment. I had wished to be Corvus when he tupped Constantia.

So I had two tasks, then, that could be merged if I was clever. I had to distract the bishop and his troops, and I had to rescue Corvus, fellow revolutionary.

I spent that night in feverish misery in my room. At dawn I went to the giant and asked his advice. He looked me over coldly and said, "We waste our time if we try to knock sense into their heads. But we have no better calling than to waste our time, do we?"

"What shall I do?"

"Enlighten them."

I stomped my claw on the floor. "They are bricks! Try enlightening bricks!"

He smiled his sad, narrow smile. "Enlighten them," he said.

I left the giant's chamber in a rage. I did not have access to the great wheel's board of time, so I couldn't know exactly when the execution would take place. But I guessed—from memories of a

grumbling stomach—that it would be in the early afternoon. I traveled from one end of the nave to the other and, likewise, the transept. I nearly exhausted myself. Then, traversing an empty aisle, I picked up a piece of colored glass and examined it, puzzled. Many of the boys on all levels carried these shards with them, and the girls used them as jewelry—against the wishes of their elders, who held that bright objects bred more beasts in the mind. Where did they get them?

In one of the books I had perused years before, I had seen brightly colored pictures of the Cathedral windows. "Enlighten them," the giant had said.

Psalo's request to let light into the Cathedral came to mind.

Along the peak of the nave, in a tunnel running its length, I found the ties that held the pulleys of the canvases over the windows. The best windows, I decided, would be the huge ones of the north and south transepts. I made a diagram in the dust, trying to decide what season it was and from which direction the sunlight would come—pure theory to me, but at this moment I was in a fever of brilliance. All the windows had to be clear. I could not decide which was best.

I was ready by early afternoon, just after sext prayers in the upper nave. I had cut the major ropes and weakened the clamps by prying them from the walls with a pick stolen from the bishop's armory. I walked along a high ledge, took an almost vertical shaft through the wall to the lower floor, and waited.

Constantia was watching from a wooden balcony, the bishop's special box for executions. She had a terrified, fascinated look on her face. Corvus was on the dais across the nave, right in the center of the cross of the transept. Torches illumined him and his executioners, three men and an old woman.

I knew the procedure. The old woman would castrate him first, then the men would remove his head. He was dressed in the condemned's red robe to hide any blood. Blood excitement among the impressionable was the last thing the bishop wanted. Troops waited around the dais to purify the area with scented water.

I didn't have much time. It would take minutes for the system of ropes and pulleys to clear and the canvases to fall. I went to my station and severed the remaining ties. Then, as the Cathedral filled with a hollow creaking sound, I followed the shaft back to my viewing post.

In three minutes the canvases were drooping. I saw Corvus look up, his eyes glazed. The bishop was with his daughter in the box. He pulled her back into the shadows. In another two minutes the canvases fell onto the upper scaffold with a hideous crash. Their weight was too great for the ends of the structure, and it collapsed, allowing the canvas to cascade to the floor many yards below. At first the illumination was dim and bluish, filtered perhaps by a passing cloud. Then, from one end of the Cathedral to the other, a burst of light threw my smoky world into clarity. The glory of thousands of pieces of colored glass, hidden for decades and hardly touched by childish vandals, fell upon upper and lower levels at once. A cry from the crowds nearly wrenched me from my post. I slid quickly to the lower level and hid, afraid of what I had done. This was more than simple sunlight. Like the blossoming of two flowers, one brighter than the other, the transept windows astounded all who beheld them.

Eyes accustomed to orangey dark, to smoke and haze and shadow, cannot stare into such glory without drastic effect. I shielded my own face and tried to find a convenient exit.

But the population was increasing. As the light brightened and more faces rose to be locked, phototropic, the splendor unhinged some people. From their minds poured contents too wondrous to be accurately cataloged. The monsters thus released were not violent, however, and most of the visions were not monstrous.

The upper and lower nave shimmered with reflected glories, with dream figures and children clothed in baubles of light. Saints and prodigies dominated. A thousand newly created youngsters squatted on the bright floor and began to tell of marvels, of cities in the East, and times as they had once been. Clowns dressed in fire entertained from the tops of the market stalls. Animals unknown to the Cathedral cavorted between the dwellings, giving friendly advice. Abstract things, glowing balls in nets of gold and ribbons of silk, sang and floated around the upper reaches. The Cathedral became a great vessel of all the bright dreams known to its citizens.

Slowly, from the lower nave, people of pure flesh climbed to the scaffold and walked the upper nave to see what they couldn't from below. From my hideaway I watched the masked troops of the bishop carrying his litter up narrow stairs. Constantia walked behind, stumbling, her eyes shut in the new brightness.

All tried to cover their eyes, but none for long succeeded.

I wept. Almost blind with tears, I made my way still higher and looked down on the roiling crowds. I saw Corvus, his hands still wrapped in restraining ropes, being led by the old woman. Constantia saw him, too, and they regarded each other like strangers, then joined hands as best they could. She borrowed a knife from one of her father's soldiers and cut his ropes away. Around them the brightest dreams of all began to swirl, pure white and blood-red and sea-green, coalescing into visions of all the children they would innocently have.

I gave them a few hours to regain their senses—and to regain my own. Then I stood on the bishop's abandoned podium and shouted over the heads of those on the lowest level.

"The time has come!" I cried. "We must all unite now; we must unite—"

At first they ignored me. I was quite eloquent, but their excitement was still too great. So I waited some more, began to speak again, and was shouted down. Bits of fruit and vegetables arced up. "Freak!" they screamed, and drove me away.

I crept along the stone stairs, found the narrow crack, and hid in it, burying my beak in my paws, wondering what had gone wrong. It took a surprisingly long time for me to realize that, in my case, it was less the stigma of stone than the ugliness of my shape that doomed my quest for leadership.

I had, however, paved the way for the Stone Christ. He will surely be able to take His place now, I told myself. So I maneuvered along the crevice until I came to the hidden chamber and the yellow glow. All was quiet within. I met first the stone monster, who looked me over suspiciously with glazed grey eyes. "You're back," he said. Overcome by his wit, I leered, nodded, and asked that I be presented to the Christ.

"He's sleeping."

"Important tidings," I said.

"What?"

"I bring glad tidings."

"Then let me hear them."

"His ears only."

Out of the gloomy corner came the Christ, looking much older now. "What is it?" He asked.

"I have prepared the way for you," I said. "Simon called Peter told me I was the heir to his legacy, that I should go before you—"

The Stone Christ shook His head. "You believe I am the fount from which all blessings flow?"

I nodded, uncertain.

"What have you done out there?"

"Let in the light," I said.

He shook His head slowly. "You seem a wise enough creature. You know about Mortdieu."

"Yes."

"Then you should know that I barely have enough power to keep myself together, to heal myself, much less to minister to those out there." He gestured beyond the walls. "My own source has gone away," He said mournfully. "I'm operating on reserves, and those none too vast."

"He wants you to go away and stop bothering us," the monster explained.

"They have their light out there," the Christ said. "They'll play with that for a while, get tired of it, go back to what they had before. Is there any place for you in that?"

I thought for a moment, then shook my head. "No place," I said. "I'm too ugly."

"You are too ugly, and I am too famous," He said. "I'd have to come from their midst, anonymous, and that is clearly impossible. No, leave them alone for a while. They'll make me over again, perhaps, or better still, forget about me. About us. We don't have any place there."

I was stunned. I sat down hard on the stone floor, and the Christ patted me on my head as He walked by. "Go back to your hiding place; live as well as you can," He said. "Our time is over."

I turned to go. When I reached the crevice, I heard His voice behind, saying, "Do you play bridge? If you do, find another. We need four to a table."

I clambered up the crack, through the walls, and along the arches over the revelry. Not only was I not going to be pope—after an appointment by Saint Peter himself!—but I couldn't convince someone much more qualified than I to assume the leadership.

It is the sign of the eternal student, I suppose, that when his wits fail him, he returns to the teacher.

I returned to the copper giant. He was lost in meditation. About his feet were scattered scraps of paper with detailed drawings of parts of the Cathedral. I waited patiently until he saw me. He turned, chin in hand, and looked me over.

"Why so sad?"

I shook my head. Only he could read my features and recognize my moods.

"Did you take my advice below? I heard a commotion."

"Mea maxima culpa," I said.

"And . . . ?"

I slowly, hesitantly, made my report, concluding with the refusal of the Stone Christ. The giant listened closely without interrupting. When I was done, he stood, towering over me, and pointed with his ruler through an open portal.

"Do you see that out there?" he asked. The ruler swept over the forests beyond the island, to the far green horizon. I replied that I did and waited for him to continue. He seemed to be lost in thought again.

"Once there was a city where trees now grow," he said. "Artists came by the thousands, and whores, and philosophers, and academics. And when God died, all the academics and whores and artists couldn't hold the fabric of the world together. How do you expect us to succeed now?"

Us? "Expectations should not determine whether one acts or not," I said. "Should they?"

The giant laughed and tapped my head with the ruler. "Maybe we've been given a sign, and we just have to learn how to interpret it correctly."

I leered to show I was puzzled.

"Maybe Mortdieu is really a sign that we have been weaned. We must forage for ourselves, remake the world without help. What do you think of that?"

I was too tired to judge the merits of what he was saying, but I had never known the giant to be wrong before. "Okay. I grant that. So?"

"The Stone Christ indicates his charge is running down. If God weans us from the old ways, we can't expect His Son to replace the nipple, can we?"

"No . . ."

He hunkered next to me, his face bright. "I wondered who would really stand forth. It's obvious He won't. So, little one, who's the next choice?"

"Me?" I asked, meekly. The giant looked me over almost pityingly.

"No," he said after a time. "I am the next. We're *weaned!*" He did a little dance, startling my beak up out of my paws. I blinked. He grabbed my vestigial wing tips and pulled me upright. "Stand straight. Tell me more."

"About what?"

"Tell me all that's going on below, and whatever else you know."

"I'm trying to figure out what you're saying," I protested, trembling a bit.

"Dense as stone!" Grinning, he bent over me. Then the grin went away, and he tried to look stern. "It's a grave responsibility. We must remake the world ourselves now. We must coordinate our thoughts, our dreams. Chaos won't do. What an opportunity, to be the architect of an entire universe!" He waved the ruler at the ceiling. "To build the very skies! The last world was a training ground, full of harsh rules and strictures. Now we've been told we're ready to leave that behind, move on to something more mature. Did I teach you any of the rules of architecture? I mean, the aesthetics. The need for harmony, interaction, utility, beauty?"

"Some," I said.

"Good. I don't think making the universe anew will require any better rules. No doubt we'll need to experiment, and perhaps one or more of our great spires will topple. But now we work for ourselves, to our own glory, and to the greater glory of the God who made us! No, ugly friend?"

Like many histories, mine must begin with the small, the tightly focused, and expand into the large. But unlike most historians, I don't have the luxury of time. Indeed, my story isn't even concluded yet.

Soon the legions of Viollet-le-Duc will begin their campaigns. Most have been schooled pretty thoroughly. Kidnapped from below, brought up in the heights, taught as I was. We'll begin returning them, one by one.

I teach off and on, write off and on, observe all the time.

The next step will be the biggest. I haven't any idea how we're going to do it.

But, as the giant puts it, "Long ago the roof fell in. Now we must push it up again, strengthen it, repair the beams." At this point he smiles to the pupils. "Not just repair them. Replace them! Now *we* are the beams. Flesh and stone become something much stronger."

Ah, but then some dolt will raise a hand and inquire, "What if our arms get tired holding up the sky?"

Our task, you see, will not soon be over.

SCATTERSHOT

THE TEDDY BEAR SPOKE EXCELLENT MANDARIN. IT WAS ABOUT FIFTY CENTIMETERS tall, plump, with close-set eyes above a nose unusually long for the generally pug breed. It paced around me, muttering to itself.

I rolled over and felt barbs down my back and sides. My arms were reluctant to move. There was something about my will to get up and the way my muscles reacted that was out-of-kilter; the nerves weren't conveying properly. So it was, I thought, with my eyes and the small black-and-white beast they claimed to see: a derangement of phosphene patterns, cross-tied with childhood memories and snatches of linguistics courses ten years past.

It began speaking Russian. I ignored it and focused on other things. The rear wall of my cabin was unrecognizable, covered with geometric patterns that shifted in and out of bas-relief and glowed faintly in the shadow cast by a skewed panel light. My fold-out desk had been torn from its hinges and now lay on the floor, not far from my head. The ceiling was cream-colored. Last I remembered it had been a pleasant shade of burnt orange. Thus totaled, half my cabin was still present. The other half had been ferried away in the—

Disruption. I groaned, and the bear stepped back nervously. My body was gradually coordinating. Bits and pieces of disassembled vision integrated and stopped their random flights, and still the creature walked, and still it spoke, though getting deep into German.

It was not a minor vision. It was either real or a full-fledged hallucination.

"What's going on?" I asked.

It bent over me, sighed, and said, "Of all the fated arrangements. A

speaking I know not the best of—Anglo." It held out its arms and shivered. "Pardon the distraught. My cords of psyche—nerves?—they
have not decided which continuum to obey this moment."

"Mine, too," I said cautiously. "Who are you?"

"Psyche, we are all psyche. Take this care and be not content with
illusion, this path, this merriment. Excuse. Some writers in English. All
I know is from the read."

"Am I still on my ship?"

"So we are all, and *hors de combat*. We limp for the duration."

I was integrated enough to stand, and I did so, towering above the
bear and rearranging my tunic. My left breast ached with a bruise.
Because we had been riding at one G for five days, I was wearing a
bra, and the bruise lay directly under a strap. Such, to quote, was the
fated arrangement. As my wits gathered and held converse, I considered what might have happened and felt a touch of the "distraughts"
myself. I began to shiver like a recruit in pressure-drop training.

We had survived. That is, at least I had survived, out of a crew of
forty-three. How many others?

"Do you know . . . have you found out—"

"Worst," the bear said. "Some I do not catch, the deciphering of
other things not so hard. Disrupted about seven, eight hours past. It
was a force of many, for I have counted ten separate things not in my
recognition." It grinned. "You are ten, and best yet. We are perhaps
not so far in world-lines."

We'd been told survival after disruption was possible. Practical
statistics indicated one out of a myriad ships, so struck, would remain
integral. For a weapon that didn't actually kill in itself, the probability
disrupter was very effective.

"Are we intact?" I asked.

"Fated," the Teddy bear said. "I cognize we can even move and
seek a base. Depending."

"Depending," I echoed. The creature sounded masculine, despite
size and a childlike voice. "Are you a he? Or—"

"He," the bear said quickly.

I touched the bulkhead above the door and ran my finger along a
familiar, slightly crooked seam. Had the disruption kept me in my
own universe—against incalculable odds—or exchanged me to some
other? Was either of us in a universe we could call our own?

"Is it safe to look around?"

The bear hummed. "Cognize—know not. Last I saw, others had not reached a state of organizing."

It was best to start from the beginning. I looked down at the creature and rubbed a bruise on my forehead. "Wh-where are you from?"

"Same as you, possible," he said. "Earth. Was mascot to captain, for cuddle and advice."

That sounded bizarre enough. I walked to the hatchway and peered down the corridor. It was plain and utilitarian, but neither the right color nor configuration. The hatch at the end was round and had a manual sealing system, six black throw-bolts that no human engineer would ever have put on a spaceship. "What's your name?"

"Have got no official name. Mascot name known only to captain."

I was scared, so my brusque nature surfaced and I asked him sharply if his captain was in sight, or any other aspect of the world he'd known.

"Cognize not," he answered. "Call me Sonok."

"I'm Geneva," I said. "Francis Geneva."

"We are friends?"

"I don't see why not. I hope we're not the only ones who can be friendly. Is English difficult for you?"

"Mind not. I learn fast. Practice make perfection."

"Because I can speak some Russian, if you want."

"Good as I with Anglo?" Sonok asked. I detected a sense of humor —and self-esteem—in the bear.

"No, probably not. English it is. If you need to know anything, don't be embarrassed to ask."

"Sonok hardly embarrassed by anything. Was mascot."

The banter was providing a solid framework for my sanity to grab on to. I had an irrational desire to take the bear and hug him, just for want of something warm. His attraction was undeniable—tailored, I guessed, for that very purpose. But tailored from what? The color suggested panda; the shape did not.

"What do you think we should do?" I asked, sitting on my bunk.

"Sonok not known for quick decisions," he said, squatting on the floor in front of me. He was stubby-limbed but far from clumsy.

"Nor am I," I said. "I'm a software and machinery language expert. I wasn't combat-trained."

"Not cognize 'software,'" Sonok said.

"Programming materials," I explained. The bear nodded and got up to peer around the door. He pulled back and scrabbled to the rear of the cabin.

"They're here!" he said. "Can port shut?"

"I wouldn't begin to know how—" But I retreated just as quickly and clung to my bunk. A stream of serpents flowed by the hatchway, metallic green and yellow, with spatulate heads and red ovals running dorsally.

The stream passed without even a hint of intent to molest, and Sonok climbed down the bas-relief pattern. "What the hell are they doing here?" I asked.

"They are a crew member, I think," Sonok said.

"What—who else is out there?"

The bear straightened and looked at me steadily. "Have none other than to seek," he said solemnly. "Elsewise, we possess no rights to ask. No?" The bear walked to the hatch, stepped over the bottom seal, and stood in the corridor. "Come?"

I got up and followed.

A woman's mind is a strange pool to slip into at birth. It is set within parameters by the first few months of listening and seeing. Her infant mind is a vast blank template that absorbs all and stores it away. In those first few months come role acceptance, a beginning to attitude, and a hint of future achievement. Listening to adults and observing their actions build a storehouse of preconceptions and warnings: *Do not see those ghosts on bedroom walls—they aren't there! None of the rest of us can see your imaginary companions, darling. . . . It's something you have to understand.*

And so, from some dim beginning, not *ex nihilo* but out of totality, the woman begins to pare her infinite self down. She whittles away at this unwanted piece, that undesired trait. She forgets in time that she was once part of all and turns to the simple tune of life, rather than to the endless and symphonic *before.* She forgets those companions who danced on the ceiling above her bed and called to her from the dark. Some of them were friendly; others, even in the dim time, were not pleasant. But they were all *she.* For the rest of her life, the woman seeks some echo of that preternatural menagerie; in the men she chooses to love, in the tasks she chooses to perform, in the way she tries to be. After thirty years of cutting, she becomes Francis Geneva.

When love dies, another piece is pared away, another universe is sheared off, and the split can never join again. With each winter and spring, spent on or off worlds with or without seasons, the woman's life grows more solid, and smaller.

But now the parts are coming together again, the companions out of the dark above the child's bed. Beware of them. They're all the things you once lost or let go, and now they walk on their own, out of your control; reborn, as it were, and indecipherable.

"Do you have understanding?" the bear asked. I shook my head to break my steady stare at the six-bolted hatch.

"Understand what?" I asked.

"Of how we are here."

"Disrupted. By Aighors, I presume."

"Yes, they are the ones for us, too. But how?"

"I don't know," I said. No one did. We could only observe the results. When the remains of disrupted ships could be found, they always resembled floating garbage heaps—plucked from our universe, rearranged in some cosmic grab bag, and returned. What came back was of the same mass, made up of the same basic materials, and recombined with a tendency toward order and viability. But in deep space, even ninety percent viability was tantamount to none at all. If the ship's separate elements didn't integrate perfectly—a one in a hundred thousand chance—there were no survivors. But oh, how interested we were in the corpses! Most were kept behind the Paper Curtain of secrecy, but word leaked out even so—word of ostriches with large heads, blobs with bits of crystalline seawater still adhering to them . . . and now my own additions, a living Teddy bear and a herd of parti-colored snakes. All had been snatched out of terrestrial ships from a maze of different universes.

Word also leaked out that of five thousand such incidents, not once had a human body been returned to our continuum.

"Some things still work," Sonok said. "We are heavy the same."

The gravitation was unchanged—I hadn't paid attention to that. "We can still breathe, for that matter," I said. "We're all from one world. There's no reason to think the basics will change." And that meant there had to be standards for communication, no matter how diverse the forms. Communication was part of my expertise, but thinking about it made me shiver. A ship runs on computers, or their equivalent. How were at least ten different computer systems communicating? Had they integrated with working interfaces? If they hadn't, our time was limited. Soon all hell would join us; darkness, and cold, and vacuum.

I released the six throw-bolts and opened the hatch slowly.

"Say, Geneva," Sonok mused as we looked into the corridor beyond. "How did the snakes get through here?"

I shook my head. There were more important problems. "I want to find something like a ship's bridge, or at least a computer terminal. Did you see something before you found my cabin?"

Sonok nodded. "Other way in corridor. But there were . . . things there. Didn't enjoy the looks, so came this way."

"What were they?" I asked.

"One like trash can," he said. "With breasts."

"We'll keep looking this way," I said by way of agreement.

The next bulkhead was a dead end. A few round displays studded the wall, filled like bull's-eyes with concentric circles of varying thickness. A lot of information could be carried in such patterns, given a precise optical scanner to read them—which suggested a machine more than an organism, though not necessarily. The bear paced back and forth in front of the wall.

I reached out with one hand to touch the displays. Then I got down on my knees to feel the bulkhead, looking for a seam. "Can't see it, but I feel something here—like a ridge in the material."

The bulkhead, displays and all, peeled away like a heart's triplet valve, and a rush of air shoved us into darkness. I instinctively rolled into a fetal curl. The bear bumped against me and grabbed my arm. Some throbbing force flung us this way and that, knocking us against squeaking wet things. I forced my eyes open and unfurled my arms and legs, trying to find a grip. One hand rapped against metal or hard plastic, and the other caught what felt like rope. With some fumbling, I gripped the rope and braced myself against the hard surface. Then I had time to sort out what I was seeing.

The chamber seemed to be open to space, but we were breathing, so obviously a transparent membrane was keeping in the atmosphere. I could see the outer surface of the ship, and it appeared a hell of a lot larger than I'd allowed. Clinging to the membrane in a curve, as though queued on the inside of a bubble, were five or six round nebulosities that glowed dull orange like dying suns. I was hanging on to something resembling a ship's mast, a metal pylon that reached from one side of the valve to the center of the bubble. Ropes were rigged from the pylon to stanchions that seemed suspended in midair, though they had to be secured against the membrane. The ropes and pylon supported clusters of head-sized spheres covered with hairlike plastic tubing. They clucked like brood hens as they slid away from us. *"Góspodi!"* Sonok screeched.

The valve that had given us access was still open, pushing its flaps in and out. I kicked away from the pylon. The bear's grip was fierce. The flaps loomed, slapped against us, and closed with a final sucking throb. We were on the other side, lying on the floor. The bulkhead again was impassively blank.

The bear rolled away from my arm and stood up. "Best to try the other way!" he suggested. "More easily faced, I cognize."

I unshipped the six-bolted hatch, and we crawled through. We doubled back and went past my cabin. The corridor, now that I thought of it, was strangely naked. In any similar region on my ship there would have been pipes, access panels, printed instructions—and at least ten cabin doors.

The corridor curved a few yards past my cabin, and the scenery became more diverse. We found several small cubbyholes, all empty, and Sonok walked cautiously ahead. "Here," he said. "Can was here."

"Gone now," I observed. We stepped through another six-bolt hatch into a chamber that had the vague appearance of a command center. In large details it resembled the bridge of my own ship, and I rejoiced for that small sense of security.

"Can you talk to it?" Sonok asked.

"I can try. But where's a terminal?"

The bear pointed to a curved bench in front of a square, flat surface, devoid of keyboard, speaker, or knobs. It didn't look much like a terminal—though the flat surface resembled a visual display screen—but I wasn't ashamed to try speaking to it. Nor was I abashed when it didn't answer. "No go. Something else."

We looked around the chamber for several minutes but found nothing more promising. "It's like a bridge," I said, "but nothing matches specifically. Maybe we're looking for the wrong thing."

"Machines run themselves, perhaps," Sonok suggested.

I sat on the bench, resting an elbow on the edge of the "screen." Nonhuman technologies frequently use other senses for information exchange than we do. Where we generally limit machine-human interactions to sight, sound, and sometimes touch, the Crocerians use odor, and the Aighors control their machines on occasion with microwave radiation from their nervous systems. I laid my hand across the screen. It was warm to the touch, but I couldn't detect any variation in the warmth. Infrared was an inefficient carrier of information for creatures with visual orientation. Snakes use infrared to seek their prey—

"Snakes," I said. "The screen is warm. Is this part of the snake ship?"

Sonok shrugged. I looked around the cabin to find other smooth surfaces. They were few. Most were crisscrossed with raised grills. Some were warm to the touch. There were any number of possibilities—but I doubted if I would hit on the right one very quickly. The best I could hope for was the survival of some other portion of my ship.

"Sonok, is there another way out of this room?"

"Several. One is around the grey pillar," he said. "Another hatch with six dogs."

"What?"

"Six . . ." He made a grabbing motion with one hand. "Like the others."

"Throw-bolts," I said.

"I thought my Anglo was improving," he muttered sulkily.

"It is. But it's bound to be different from mine, so we both have to adapt." We opened the hatch and looked into the next chamber. The lights flickered feebly, and wrecked equipment gave off acrid smells. A haze of cloying smoke drifted out and immediately set ventilators to work. The bear held his nose and jumped over the seal for a quick walk through the room.

"Is something dead in here," he said when he returned. "Not like human, but not far. It is shot in head." He nodded for me to go with him, and I reluctantly followed. The body was pinned between two bolted seats. The head was a mess, and there was ample evidence that it used red blood. The body was covered by grey overalls and, though twisted into an awkward position, was obviously more canine than human. The bear was correct in one respect: it was closer to me than whiskered balls or rainbow snakes. The smoke was almost clear when I stepped back from the corpse.

"Sonok, any possibility this could be another mascot?"

The bear shook his head and walked away, nose wrinkled. I wondered if I'd insulted him.

"I see nothing like terminal here," he said. "Looks like nothing work now, anyway. Go on?"

We returned to the bridgelike chamber, and Sonok picked out another corridor. By the changing floor curvature, I guessed that all my previous estimates as to ship size were appreciably off. There was no way of telling either the shape or the size of this collage of vessels. What I'd seen from the bubble had appeared endless, but that might have been optical distortion.

The corridor dead-ended again, and we didn't press our luck as to what lay beyond the blank bulkhead. As we turned back, I asked, "What were the things you saw? You said there were ten of them, all different."

The bear held up his paws and counted. His fingers were otterlike and quite supple. "Snakes, number one," he said. "Cans with breasts, two; back wall of your cabin, three; blank bulkhead with circular marks, four; and you, five. Other things not so different, I think now—snakes and six-dog hatches might go together, since snakes know how to use them. Other things—you and your cabin fixtures, so on, all together. But you add dead thing in overalls, fuzzy balls, and who can say where it ends?"

"I hope it ends someplace. I can only face so many variations before I give up. Is there anything left of your ship?"

"Where I was after disruption," the bear said. "On my stomach in bathroom."

Ah, that blessed word! "Where?" I asked. "Is it working?" I'd considered impolitely messing the corridors if there was no alternative.

"Works still, I think. Back through side corridor."

He showed me the way. A lot can be learned from a bathroom—social attitudes, technological levels, even basic psychology, not to mention anatomy. This one was lovely and utilitarian, with fixtures for males and females of at least three sizes. I made do with the largest. The bear gave me privacy, which wasn't strictly necessary—bathrooms on my ship being coed—but appreciated, nonetheless. Exposure to a Teddy bear takes getting used to.

When I was through, I joined Sonok in the hall and realized I'd gotten myself turned around. "Where are we?"

"Is changing," Sonok said. "Where bulkhead was, is now hatch. I'm not sure I cognize how—it's a different hatch."

And it was, in an alarming way. It was battle-armored, automatically controlled, and equipped with heavily shielded detection equipment. It was ugly and khaki-colored and had no business being inside a ship, unless the occupants distrusted each other. "I was in anteroom, outside lavatory," Sonok said, "with door closed. I hear loud sound and something like metal being cut, and I open door to see this."

Vague sounds of machines were still audible, grinding and screaming. We stayed away from the hatch. Sonok motioned for me to follow him. "One more," he said. "Almost forgot." He pointed into a cubbyhole, about a meter deep and two meters square. "Look like fish tank, perhaps?"

It was a large rectangular tank filled with murky fluid. It reached from my knees to the top of my head and fit the cubbyhole perfectly. "Hasn't been cleaned, in any case," I said.

I touched the glass to feel how warm or cold it was. The tank lighted up, and I jumped back, knocking Sonok over. He rolled into a backward flip and came upright, wheezing.

The light in the tank flickered like a strobe, gradually speeding up until the glow was steady. For a few seconds it made me dizzy. The murk was gathering itself together. I bent over cautiously to get a close look. The murk wasn't evenly distributed. It was composed of animals like brine shrimp no more than a centimeter long, with two black eyespots at one end, a pinkish "spine," and a feathery fringe rippling between head and tail. They were forming a dense mass at the center of the tank.

The bottom of the tank was crossed with ordered dots of luminescence, which changed colors across a narrow spectrum: red, blue, amber.

"It's doing something," Sonok said. The mass was defining a shape. Shoulders and head appeared, then torso and arms, sculpted in ghost-colored brine shrimp. When the living sculpture was finished, I recognized myself from the waist up. I held out my arm, and the mass slowly followed suit.

I had an inspiration. In my pants pocket I had a marker for labeling tapas cube blanks. It used soft plastic wrapped in a metal jacket. I took it out and wrote three letters across the transparent front of the tank: WHO. Part of the mass dissolved and re-formed to mimic the letters, the rest filling in behind. WHO they spelled, then they added a question mark.

Sonok chirped, and I came closer to see better. "They understand?" he asked. I shook my head. I had no idea what I was playing with. WHAT ARE YOU? I wrote.

The animals started to break up and return to the general murk. I shook my head in frustration. So near! The closest thing to communication yet.

"Wait," Sonok said. "They're group again."

TENZIONA, the shrimp coalesced. DYSFUNCTIO. GUARDATEO AB PEREGRINO PERAMBULA.

"I don't understand. Sounds like Italian—do you know any Italian?" The bear shook his head.

"'Dysfunctio,'" I read aloud. "That seems plain enough. 'Ab peregrino'? Something about a hawk?"

"Peregrine, it is foreigner," Sonok said.

"Guard against foreigners . . . 'perambula,' as in strolling? Watch for the foreigners who walk? Well, we don't have the grammar, but it seems to tell us something we already know. Christ! I wish I could remember all the languages they filled me with ten years ago."

The marks on the tank darkened and flaked off. The shrimp began to form something different. They grouped into branches and arranged themselves nose-to-tail, upright, to form a trunk, which rooted itself to the floor of the tank.

"Tree," Sonok said.

Again they dissolved, returning in a few seconds to the simulacrum of my body. The clothing seemed different, however—more like a robe. Each shrimp changed its individual color now, making the shape startlingly lifelike. As I watched, the image began to age. The outlines of the face sagged, wrinkles formed in the skin, and the limbs shrank perceptibly. My arms felt cold, and I crossed them over my breasts; but the corridor was reasonably warm.

Of course the universe isn't really held in a little girl's mind. It's one small thread in a vast skein, separated from every other universe by a limitation of constants and qualities, just as death is separated from life by the eternal nonreturn of the dead. Well, now we know the universes are less inviolable than death, for there are ways of crossing from thread to thread. So these other beings, from similar Earths, are not part of my undifferentiated infancy. That's a weak fantasy for a rather unequipped young woman to indulge in. Still, the symbols of childhood lie all around—nightmares and Teddy bears and dreams held in a tank; dreams of old age and death. And a tree, grey and ghostly, without leaves. That's me. Full of winter, wood cracking into splinters. How do *they* know?

A rustling came from the corridor ahead. We turned from the tank and saw the floor covered with rainbow snakes, motionless, all heads aimed at us. Sonok began to tremble.

"Stop it," I said. "They haven't done anything to us."

"You are bigger," he said. "Not meal-sized."

"They'd have a rough time putting you away, too. Let's just sit it out calmly and see what this is all about." I kept my eyes on the snakes and away from the tank. I didn't want to see the shape age any more. For all the sanity of this place, it might have kept on going, through death and decay down to bones. Why did it choose me; why not Sonok?

"I cannot wait," Sonok said. "I have not the patience of a snake." He stepped forward. The snakes watched without a sound as the bear approached, one step every few seconds. "I want to know one solid thing," he called back. "Even if it is whether they eat small furry mascots."

The snakes suddenly bundled backward and started to crawl over each other. Small sucking noises smacked between their bodies. As

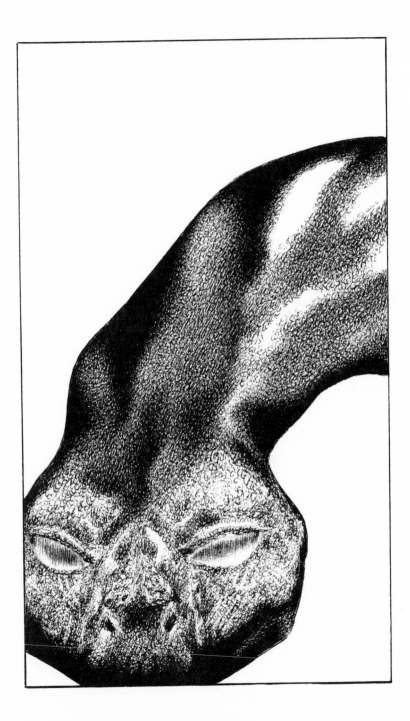

they crossed, the red ovals met and held firm. They assembled and reared into a single mass, cobralike, but flat as a planarian worm. A fringe of snakes weaved across the belly like a caterpillar's idea of Medusa.

Brave Sonok was undone. He swung around and ran past me. I was too shocked to do anything but face the snakes down, neck hairs crawling. I wanted to speak but couldn't. Then, behind me, I heard: *"Sinieux!"*

As I turned, I saw two things, one in the corner of each eye: the snakes fell into a pile, and a man dressed in red and black vanished into a side corridor. The snakes regrouped into a hydra with six tentacles and grasped the hatch's throw-bolts, springing it open and slithering through. The hatch closed, and I was alone.

There was nothing for it but to scream a moment, then cry. I lay back against the wall, getting the fit out of me as loudly and quickly as possible. When I was able to stop, I wiped my eyes with my palms and kept them covered, feeling ashamed. When I looked out again, Sonok was standing next to me.

"We've an Indian on board," he said. "Big, with black hair in three ribbons"—he motioned from crown to neck between his ears—"and a snappy dresser."

"Where is he?" I asked hoarsely.

"Back in place like bridge, I think. He controls snakes?"

I hesitated, then nodded.

"Go look?"

I got up and followed the bear. Sitting on a bench pulled from the wall, the man in red and black watched us as we entered the chamber. He was big—at least two meters tall—and hefty, dressed in a black silk shirt with red cuffs. His cape was black with a red eagle embroidered across the shoulders. He certainly looked Indian—ruddy skin, aristocratic nose, full lips held tight as if against pain.

"Quis la?" he queried.

"I don't speak that," I said. "Do you know English?"

The Indian didn't break his stolid expression. He nodded and turned on the bench to put his hand against a grill. "I was taught in the British school at Nova London," he said, his accent distinctly Oxfordian. "I was educated in Indonesia, and so I speak Dutch, High and

Middle German, and some Asian tongues, specifically Nippon and Tagalog. But at English I am fluent."

"Thank God," I said. "Do you know this room?"

"Yes," he replied. "I designed it. It's for the Sinieux."

"Do you know what's happened to us?"

"We have fallen into hell," he said. "My Jesuit professors warned me of it."

"Not far wrong," I said. "Do you know why?"

"I do not question my punishments."

"We're not being punished—at least, not by God or devils."

He shrugged. It was a moot point.

"I'm from Earth, too," I said. "From *Terre*."

"I know the words for Earth," the Indian said sharply.

"But I don't think it's the same Earth. What year are you from?" Since he'd mentioned Jesuits, he almost had to use the standard Christian Era dating.

"Year of Our Lord 2345," he said.

Sonok crossed himself elegantly. "For me 2290," he added. The Indian examined the bear dubiously.

I was sixty years after the bear, five after the Indian. The limits of the grab bag were less hazy now. "What country?"

"Alliance of Tribal Columbia," he answered, "District Quebec, East Shore."

"I'm from the Moon," I said. "But my parents were born on Earth, in the United States of America."

The Indian shook his head slowly; he wasn't familiar with it.

"Was there—" But I held back the question. Where to begin? Where did the world-lines part? "I think we'd better consider finding out how well this ship is put together. We'll get into our comparative histories later. Obviously you have star drive."

The Indian didn't agree or disagree. "My parents had ancestors from the West Shore, Vancouver," he said. "They were Kwakiutl and Kodikin. The animal, does it have a Russian accent?"

"Some," I said. "It's better than it was a few hours ago."

"I have blood debts against Russians."

"Okay," I said, "but I doubt if you have anything against this one, considering the distances involved. We've got to learn if this ship can take us someplace."

"I have asked," he said.

"Where?" Sonok asked. "A terminal?"

"The ship says it is surrounded by foreign parts and can barely understand them. But it can get along."

"You really don't know what happened, do you?"

"I went to look for worlds for my people and took the Sinieux with me. When I reached a certain coordinate in the sky, far along the arrow line established by my extrasolar pierce, this happened." He lifted his hand. "Now there is one creature, a devil, that tried to attack me. It is dead. There are others, huge black men who wear golden armor and carry gold guns like cannon, and they have gone away behind armored hatches. There are walls like rubber that open onto more demons. And now you—and it." He pointed at the bear.

"I'm not an 'it,'" Sonok said. "I'm an *ours.*"

"Small *ours,*" the Indian retorted.

Sonok bristled and turned away. "Enough," I said. "You haven't fallen into hell, not literally. We've been hit by something called a disrupter. It snatched us from different universes and reassembled us according to our world-lines, our . . . affinities."

The Indian smiled faintly, very condescendingly.

"Listen, do you understand how crazy this is?" I demanded, exasperated. "I've got to get things straight before we all lose our calm. The beings who did this—in my universe they're called 'Aighors.' Do you know about them?"

He shook his head. "I know of no other beings but those of Earth. I went to look for worlds."

"Is your ship a warper ship—does it travel across a geodesic in higher spaces?"

"Yes," he said. "It is not in phase with the crest of the Stellar Sea but slips between the foamy length, where we must struggle to obey all laws."

That was a fair description of translating from status geometry— our universe—to higher geometries. It was more poetic than scientific, but he was here, so it worked well enough. "How long have your people been able to travel this way?"

"Ten years. And yours?"

"Three centuries."

He nodded in appreciation. "You know then what you speak of, and perhaps there aren't any devils, and we are not in hell. Not this time."

"How do you use your instruments in here?"

"I do not, generally. The Sinieux use them. If you will not get upset, I'll demonstrate."

I glanced at Sonok, who was still sulking. "Are you afraid of the snakes?"

The bear shook his head.

"Bring them in," I said. "And perhaps we should know each other's name?"

"Jean Frobish," the Indian said. And I told him mine.

The snakes entered at his whistled command and assembled in the middle of the cabin. There were two sets, each made up of about fifty. When meshed, they made two formidable metaserpents. Frobish instructed them with spoken commands and a language that sounded like birdcalls. Perfect servants, they obeyed faultlessly and without hesitation. They went to the controls at his command and made a few manipulations, then turned to him and delivered, one group at a time, a report in consonantal hisses and claps. The exchange was uncanny and chilling. Jean nodded, and the serpents disassembled.

"Are they specially bred?" I asked.

"Tectonogenetic farming," he said. "They are excellent workers and have no will of their own, since they have no cerebrums. They can remember, and en masse can think, but not for themselves, if you see what I mean." He showed another glimmer of a smile. He was proud of his servants.

"I think I understand. Sonok, were you specially bred?"

"Was mascot," Sonok said. "Could breed for myself, given chance."

The subject was touchy, I could see. I could also see that Frobish and Sonok wouldn't get along without friction. If Sonok had been a big bear—and not a Russian—instead of an ursine dwarf, the Indian might have had more respect for him.

"Jean, can you command the whole ship from here?"

"Those parts that answer."

"Can your computers tell you how much of the ship will respond?"

"What is left of my vessel responds very well. The rest is balky or blank entirely. I was trying to discover the limits when I encountered you."

"You met the people who've been putting in the armored hatches?"

He nodded. "Bigger than Masai," he said.

I now had explanations for some of the things we'd seen and could link them with terrestrial origins. Jean and his Sinieux weren't beyond the stretch of reason, nor was Sonok. The armored hatches weren't quite as mysterious now. But what about the canine? I swallowed. That must have been the demon Frobish killed. And beyond the triplet valves?

"We've got a lot to find out," I said.

"You and the animal, are you together, from the same world?" Frobish asked. I shook my head. "Did you come alone?"

I nodded. "Why?"

"No men, no soldiers?"

I was apprehensive now. "No."

"Good." He stood and approached a blank wall near the grey pillar. "Then we will not have too many to support, unless the ones in golden armor want our food." He put his hand against the wall, and a round opening appeared. In the shadow of the hole, two faces watched with eyes glittering.

"These are my wives," Frobish said. One was dark-haired and slender, no more than fifteen or sixteen. She stepped out first and looked at me warily. The second, stockier and flatter of face, was brown-haired and about twenty. Frobish pointed to the younger first. "This is Alouette," he said. "And this is Mouse. Wives, acquaint with Francis Geneva." They stood one on each side of Frobish, holding his elbows, and nodded at me in unison.

That made four humans, more if the blacks in golden armor were men. Our collage had hit the jackpot.

"Jean, you say your machines can get along with the rest of the ship. Can they control it? If they can, I think we should try to return to Earth."

"To what?" Sonok asked. "Which Earth waits?"

"What's the bear talking about?" Frobish asked.

I explained the situation as best I could. Frobish was a sophisticated engineer and astrogator, but his experience with other continua—theoretical or actual—was small. He tightened his lips and listened grimly, unwilling to admit his ignorance. I sighed and looked to Alouette and Mouse for support. They were meek, quiet, giving all to the stolid authority of Frobish.

"What woman says is we decide where to go," Sonok said. "Depends, so the die is tossed, on whether we like the Earth we would meet."

"You would like my Earth," Frobish said.

"There's no guarantee it'll be your Earth. You have to take that into account."

"You aren't making sense." Frobish shook his head. "My decision is made, nonetheless. We will try to return."

I shrugged. "Try as best you can." We would face the truth later.

"I'll have the Sinieux watch over the machines after I initiate instructions," Frobish said. "Then I would like Francis to come with me to look at the animal I killed." I agreed without thinking about his motives. He gave the metaserpents their orders and pulled down a panel cover to reveal a small board designed for human hands. When he was through programming the computers, he continued his instructions to the Sinieux. His rapport with the animals was perfect—the interaction of an engineer with his tool. There was no thought of discord or second opinions. The snakes, to all intents and purposes, were machines keyed only to his voice. I wondered how far the obedience of his wives extended.

"Mouse will find food for the bear, and Alouette will stand guard with the *fusil. Comprens?*" The woman nodded, and Alouette plucked a rifle from the hideaway. "When we return, we will all eat."

"I will wait to eat with you," Sonok said, standing near me.

Frobish looked the bear over coldly. "We do not eat with tectoes," he said, haughty as a British officer addressing his servant. "But you will eat the same food we do."

Sonok stretched out his arms and made two shivers of anger. "I have never been treated less than a man," he said. "I will eat with all, or not eat." He looked up at me with his small golden eyes and asked in Russian, "Will you go along with him?"

"We don't have much choice," I answered haltingly in kind.

"What do you recommend?"

"Play along for the moment. I understand." I was unable to read his expression behind the black mask and white markings; but if I'd been he, I'd have questioned the understanding. This was no time, however, to instruct the bear in assertion.

Frobish opened the hatch to the wrecked room and let me step in first. He then closed the hatch and sealed it. "I've seen the body already," I said. "What do you want to know?"

"I want your advice on this room," he said. I didn't believe that for an instant. I bent down to examine the creature between the chairs more carefully.

"What did it try to do to you?" I asked.

"It came at me. I thought it was a demon. I shot at it, and it died."

"What caused the rest of this damage?"

"I fired a good many rounds," he said. "I was more frightened then. I'm calm now."

"Thank God for that," I said. "This—he or she—might have been able to help us."

"Looks like a dog," Frobish said. "Dogs cannot help."

For me, that crossed the line. "Listen," I said tightly, standing away from the body. "I don't think you're in touch with what's going on here. If you don't get in touch soon, you might get us all killed. I'm not about to let myself die because of one man's stupidity."

Frobish's eyes widened. "Women do not address men thus," he said.

"This woman does, friend! I don't know what kind of screwy social order you have in your world, but you had damn well better get used to interacting with different sexes, not to mention different species! If you don't, you're asking to end up like this poor thing. It didn't have a chance to say friend or foe, yea or nay! You shot it out of panic, and we can't have any more of that!" I was trembling.

Frobish smiled over grinding teeth and turned to walk away. He was fighting to control himself. I wondered if my own brains were in the right place. The few aspects of this man that were familiar to me couldn't begin to give complete understanding. I was clearly out of my depth, and kicking to stay afloat might hasten death, not slow it.

Frobish stood by the hatch, breathing deeply. "What is the dog-creature? What is this room?"

I turned back to the body and pulled it by one leg from between the chairs. "It was probably intelligent," I said. "That's about all I can tell. It doesn't have any personal effects." The gore was getting to me, and I turned away for a moment. I was tired—oh, so tired I could feel the weary rivers dredging through my limbs. My head hurt abominably. "I'm not an engineer," I said. "I can't tell if any of this equipment is useful to us, or even if it's salvageable. Care to give an opinion?"

Frobish glanced over the room with a slight inclination of one eyebrow. "Nothing of use here."

"Are you sure?"

"I am sure." He looked across the room and sniffed the air. "Too much burned and shorted. You know, there is much that is dangerous here."

"Yes," I said, leaning against the back of a seat.

"You will need protection."

"Oh."

"There is no protection like the bonds of family. You are argumentative, but my wives can teach you our ways. With bonds of family, there will be no uncertainty. We will return, and all will be well."

He caught me by surprise, and I wasn't fast on the uptake. "What do you mean, bonds of family?"

"I will take you to wife and protect you as husband."

"I think I can protect myself, thank you."

"It doesn't seem wise to refuse. Left alone, you will probably be killed by such as this." He pointed at the canine.

"We'll have to get along whether we're family or not. That shouldn't be too hard to understand. And I don't have any inclination to sell myself for security."

"I do not pay money for women!" Frobish said. "Again you ridicule me."

He sounded like a disappointed little boy. I wondered what his wives would think, seeing him butt his head against a wall without sense or sensibility.

"We've got to dispose of the body before it decays," I said. "Help me carry it out of here."

"It isn't fit to touch."

My tiredness took over, and my rationality departed. "You goddamned idiot! Pull your nose down and look at what's going on around you! We're in serious trouble—"

"It isn't the place of a woman to speak thus, I've told you," he said. He approached and raised his hand palm-high to strike. I instinctively lowered my head and pushed a fist into his abdomen. The slap fell like a kitten's paw, and he went over, glancing off my shoulder and twisting my arm into a painful muscle kink. I cursed and rubbed the spot, then sat down on the deck to consider what had happened.

I'd never had much experience with sexism in human cultures. It was disgusting and hard to accept, but some small voice in the back of my mind told me it was no more blameworthy than any other social attitude. His wives appeared to go along with it. At any rate, the situation was now completely shot to hell. There was little I could do except drag him back to his wives and try to straighten things out when he came to. I took him by both hands and pulled him up to the hatch. I unsealed it, then swung him around to take him by the shoulders. I almost retched when one of his shoulders broke the crust on a drying pool of blood and smeared red along the deck.

I miss Jaghit Singh more than I can admit. I think about him and wonder what he'd do in this situation. He is a short, dark man with perfect features and eyes like those in the pictures of Krishna. We formally broke off our relationship three weeks ago, at my behest, for I couldn't see any future in it. He would probably know how to handle Frobish, with a smile and even a spirit of comradeship, but without contradicting his own beliefs. He could make a girl's childhood splinters go back to form the whole log again. He could make these beasts and distortions come together again. Jaghit! Are you anywhere that has seasons? Is it still winter for you? You never did understand the little girl who wanted to play in the snow. Your blood is far too hot and regular to stand up to my moments of indecisive coldness, and you could not—would not—force me to change. I was caught between child and my thirty-year-old form, between spring and winter. Is it spring for you now?

Alouette and Mouse took their husband away from me fiercely, spitting with rage. They weren't talking clearly, but what they shouted in quasi-French made it clear who was to blame. I told Sonok what had happened, and he looked very somber indeed. "Maybe he'll shoot us when he wakes up," he suggested.

To avoid that circumstance, I appropriated the rifle and took it back to my half-room. There was a cabinet intact, and I still had the key. I didn't lock the rifle in, however; better simply to hide it and have easy access to it when needed. It was time to be diplomatic, though all I really wanted for the moment was blessed sleep. My shoulder stung like hell, and the muscles refused to get themselves straight.

When I returned, with Sonok walking point a few steps ahead, Frobish was conscious and sitting in a cot pulled from a panel near the hole. His wives squatted nearby, somber as they ate from metal dishes.

Frobish refused to look me in the eye. Alouette and Mouse weren't in the least reluctant, however, and their gazes threw sparks. They'd be good in a fight, if it ever came down to that. I hoped I wasn't their opposite.

"I think it's time we behaved reasonably," I said.

"There is no reason on this ship," Frobish shot back.

"Aye on that," Sonok said, sitting down to a plate left on the floor. He picked at it, then reluctantly ate, his fingers handling the implements with agility.

"If we're at odds, we won't get anything done," I said.

"That is the only thing which stops me from killing you," Frobish said. Mouse bent over to whisper in his ear. "My wife reminds me you must have time to see the logic of our ways." Were the women lucid despite their anger, or was he maneuvering on his own? "There is also the possibility that you are a leader. I'm a leader, and it's difficult for me to face another leader at times. That is why I alone control this ship."

"I'm not a—" I bit my lip. Not too far, too fast. "We've got to work together and forget about being leaders for the moment."

Sonok sighed and put down the plate. "I have no leader," he said. "That part of me did not follow into this scattershot." He leaned on my leg. "Mascots live best when made whole. So I choose Geneva as my other part. I think my English is good enough now for us to understand."

Frobish looked at the bear curiously. "My stomach hurts," he said after a moment. He turned to me. "You do not hit like a woman. A woman strikes for the soft parts, masculine weaknesses. You go for direct points with knowledge. I cannot accept you as the bear does, but if you will reconsider, we should be able to work together."

"Reconsider the family bond?"

He nodded. To me, he was almost as alien as his snakes. I gave up the fight and decided to play for time.

"I'll have to think about it. My upbringing . . . is hard to overcome," I said.

"We will rest," Frobish said.

"And Sonok will guard," I suggested. The bear straightened perceptibly and went to stand by the hatch. For the moment it looked like a truce had been made, but as cots were pulled out of the walls, I picked up a metal bar and hid it in my trousers.

The Sinieux went to their multilevel cages and lay quiet and still as stone. I slipped into the cot and pulled a thin sheet over myself. Sleep came immediately, and delicious lassitude finally unkinked my arm.

I don't know how long the nap lasted, but it was broken sharply by a screech from Sonok. "They're here! They're here!"

I stumbled out of the cot, tangling one leg in a sheet, and came to a stand only after the Indian family was alert and armed. So much, I thought, for hiding the rifle. "What's here?" I asked, still dopey.

Frobish thrust Sonok away from the hatch with a leg and brought the cover around with a quick arm to slam it shut, but not before a black cable was tossed into the room. The hatch jammed on it, and sparks flew. Frobish stood clear and brought his rifle to his shoulder.

Sonok ran to me and clung to my knee. Mouse opened the cages and let the Sinieux flow onto the deck. Frobish retreated from the hatch as it shuddered. The Sinieux advanced. I heard voices from the other side. They sounded human—like children, in fact.

"Wait a moment," I said. Mouse brought her pistol up and aimed it at me. I shut up.

The hatch flung open, and hundreds of fine cables flew into the room, twisting and seeking, wrapping and binding. Frobish's rifle was plucked from his hands and surrounded like a bacterium with antibodies. Mouse fired her pistol wildly and stumbled, falling into a nest of cables, which jerked and seized. Alouette was almost to the hole, but her ankles were caught and she teetered.

Cables ricocheted from the ceiling and grabbed at the bundles of

Sinieux. The snakes fell apart, some clinging to the cables like insects on a frog's tongue. More cables shot out to hold them all, except for a solitary snake that retreated past me. I was bound rigid and tight, with Sonok strapped to my knee. The barrage stopped, and a small shadowed figure stood in the hatch, carrying a machete. It cleared the entrance of the sticky strands and stepped into the cabin light, looking around cautiously. Then it waved to companions behind, and five more entered.

They were identical, each just under half a meter in height—a little shorter than Sonok—and bald and pink as infants. Their features were delicate and fetal, with large grey-green eyes and thin, translucent limbs. Their hands were stubby-fingered and plump as those on a Rubens baby. They walked into the cabin with long strides, self-assured, nimbly avoiding the cables.

Sonok jerked at a sound in the corridor—a hesitant high-pitched mewing. "With breasts," he mumbled through the cords.

One of the infantoids arranged a ramp over the bottom seal of the hatch. He then stepped aside and clapped to get attention. The others formed a line, pink fannies jutting, and held their hands over their heads as if surrendering. The mewing grew louder. Sonok's trash can with breasts entered the cabin, twisting this way and that like a deranged, obscene toy. It was cylindrical, with sides tapering to a fringed skirt at the base. Three levels of pink and nippled paps ringed it at equal intervals from top to bottom. A low, flat head surmounted the body, tiny black eyes examining the cabin with quick, nervous jerks. It looked like nothing so much as the Diana of Ephesus, *Magna Mater* to the Romans.

One of the infantoids announced something in a piping voice, and the Diana shivered to acknowledge. With a glance around, the same infantoid nodded, and all six stood up to the breasts to nurse.

Feeding over, they took positions around the cabin and examined us carefully. The leader spoke to each of us in turn, trying several languages. None matched our own. I strained to loosen the cords around my neck and jaw and asked Sonok to speak a few of the languages he knew. He did as well as he could through his bonds. The leader listened to him with interest, then echoed a few words and turned to the other five. One nodded and advanced. He spoke to the bear in what sounded like Greek. Sonok stuttered for a moment, then replied in halting fragments.

They moved to loosen the bear's cords, looking up at me apprehensively. The combination of Sonok and six children still at breast hit me deep, and I had to suppress a hysteric urge to laugh.

"I think he is saying he knows what has happened," Sonok said. "They've been prepared for it; they knew what to expect. I think that's what they say."

The leader touched palms with his Greek-speaking colleague, then spoke to Sonok in the same tongue. He held out his plump hands and motioned for the bear to do likewise. A third stepped over rows of crystallized cable to loosen Sonok's arms.

Sonok reluctantly held up his hands, and the two touched. The infantoid broke into shrill laughter and rolled on the floor. His mood returned to utmost gravity in a blink, and he stood as tall as he could, looking us over with an angry expression.

"We are in command," he said in Russian. Frobish and his wives cried out in French, complaining about their bonds. "They speak different?" the infantoid asked Sonok. The bear nodded. "Then my brothers will learn their tongues. What does the other big one speak?"

"English," Sonok said.

The infantoid sighed. "Such diversities. I will learn from her." My cords were cut, and I held out my palms. The leader's hands were cold and clammy, making my arm-hairs crawl.

"All right," he said in perfect English. "Let us tell you what's happened, and what we're going to do."

His explanation of the disruption matched mine closely. "The Alternates have done this to us." He pointed to me. "This big one calls them Aighors. We do not dignify them with a name—we're not even sure they are the same. They don't have to be, you know. Whoever has the secret of disruption, in all universes, is our enemy. We are companions now, chosen from a common pool of those who have been disrupted across a century or so. The choosing has been done so that our natures match closely—we are all from one planet. Do you understand this idea of being companions?"

Sonok and I nodded. The Indians made no response at all.

"But we, members of the Nemi, whose mother is Noctilux, we were prepared. We will take control of the aggregate ship and pilot it to a suitable point, from which we can take a perspective and see what universe we're in. Can we expect your cooperation?"

Again the bear and I agreed, and the others were silent.

"Release them all," the infantoid said with a magnanimous sweep of his hands. "Be warned, however—we can restrain you in an instant, and we are not likely to enjoy being attacked again."

The cords went limp and vaporized with some heat discharge and a slight sweet odor. The Diana rolled over the ramp and left the cabin, with the leader and another infantoid following. The four remaining behind watched us closely, not nervous but intent on our every move. Where the guns had been, pools of slag lay on the floor.

"Looks like we've been overruled," I said to Frobish. He didn't seem to hear me.

In a few hours we were told where we would be allowed to go. The area extended to my cabin and the bathroom, which apparently was the only such facility in our reach. The Nemi didn't seem to need bathrooms, but their recognition of our own requirements was heartening. Within an hour after the takeover, the infantoids had swarmed over the controls in the chamber. They brought in bits and pieces of salvaged equipment, which they altered and fitted with extraordinary speed and skill. Before our next meal, taken from stores in the hole, they understood and controlled all the machinery in the cabin.

The leader then explained to us that the aggregate, or "scatter-shot," as Sonok had called it, was still far from integrated. At least two groups had yet to be brought into the fold. These were the giant blacks in golden armor, and the beings that inhabited the transparent bubble outside the ship. We were warned that leaving the established boundaries would put us in danger.

The sleep period came. The Nemi made certain we were slumbering before they slept, if they slept at all. Sonok lay beside me on the bunk in my room, snukking faint snores and twitching over distant dreams. I stared up into the dark, thinking of the message tank. That was my unrevealed ace. I wanted to get back to it and see what it was capable of telling me. Did it belong to one of the groups we were familiar with, or was it different, perhaps a party in itself?

I tried to bury my private thoughts—disturbing, intricate thoughts—and sleep, but I couldn't. I was deadweight now, and I'd never liked the idea of being useless. Useless things tended to get thrown out. Since joining the various academies and working my way up the line, I'd always assumed I could play some role in any system I was thrust into.

But the infantoids, though tolerant and even understanding, were self-contained. As they said, they'd been prepared, and they knew what to do. Uncertainty seemed to cheer them, or at least draw them together. Of course they were never more than a few meters away from a very impressive symbol of security—a walking breast-bank.

The Nemi had their Diana, Frobish had his wives, and Sonok had me. I had no one. My mind went out, imagined blackness and fields of stars, and perhaps nowhere the worlds I knew, and quickly snapped back. My head hurt, and my back muscles were starting to cramp. I had no access to hormone stabilizers, so I was starting my period. I rolled over, nudging Sonok into grumbly half-waking, and shut my eyes and mind to everything, trying to find a peaceful glade and perhaps Jaghit Singh. But even in sleep all I found was snow and broken grey trees.

The lights came up slowly, and I was awakened by Sonok's movements. I rubbed my eyes and got up from the bunk, standing unsteadily.

In the bathroom Frobish and his wives were going about their morning ablutions. They looked at me but said nothing. I could feel a tension but tried to ignore it. I was irritable, and if I let any part of my feelings out, they might all pour forth—and then where would I be?

I returned to my cabin with Sonok and didn't see Frobish following until he stepped up to the hatchway and looked inside.

"We will not accept the rule of children," he said evenly. "We'll need your help to overcome them."

"Who will replace them?" I asked.

"I will. They've made adjustments to my machines which I and the Sinieux can handle."

"The Sinieux cages are welded shut," I said.

"Will you join us?"

"What could I do? I'm only a woman."

"I will fight, my wives and you will back me up. I need the rifle you took away."

"I don't have it." But he must have seen my eyes go involuntarily to the locker.

"Will you join us?"

"I'm not sure it's wise. In fact, I'm sure it isn't. You just aren't equipped to handle this kind of thing. You're too limited."

"I have endured all sorts of indignities from you. You are a sickness of the first degree. Either you will work with us, or I will cure you now." Sonok bristled, and I noticed the bear's teeth were quite sharp.

I stood and faced him. "You're not a man," I said. "You're a little boy. You haven't got hair on your chest or anything between your legs—just a bluff and a brag."

He pushed me back on the cot with one arm and squeezed up against the locker, opening it quickly. Sonok sank his teeth into the man's calf, but before I could get into action the rifle was out and his hand was on the trigger. I fended the barrel away from me, and the first shot went into the corridor. It caught a Nemi and removed the top of his head. The blood and sound seemed to drive Frobish into a frenzy. He brought the butt down, trying to hammer Sonok, but the bear leaped aside and the rifle went into the bunk mattress, sending Frobish off balance. I hit his throat with the side of my hand and caved in his windpipe.

Then I took the rifle and watched him choking against the cabin wall. He was unconscious and turning blue before I gritted my teeth and relented. I took him by the neck and found his pipe with my thumbs, then pushed from both sides to flex the blockage outward. He took a breath and slumped.

I looked at the body in the corridor. "This is it," I said quietly. "We've got to get out of here." I slung the rifle and peered around the hatch seal. The noise hadn't brought anyone yet. I motioned to Sonok, and we ran down the corridor, away from the Indian's control room and the infantoids.

"Geneva," Sonok said as we passed an armored hatch. "Where do we go?" I heard a whirring sound and looked up. The shielded camera above the hatch was watching us, moving behind its thick grey glass like an eye. "I don't know," I said.

A seal had been placed over the flexible valve in the corridor that led to the bubble. We turned at that point and went past the nook where the message tank had been. It was gone, leaving a few anonymous fixtures behind.

An armored hatch had been punched into the wall several yards beyond the alcove, and it was unsealed. That was almost too blatant an invitation, but I had few other choices. They'd mined the ship like termites. The hatch led into a straight corridor without gravitation. I took Sonok by the arm, and we drifted dreamily down. I saw pieces of familiar equipment studding the walls, and I wondered if people from my world were around. It was an idle speculation. The way I felt now, I doubted I could make friends with anyone. I wasn't the type to establish camaraderie under stress. I was the wintry one.

At the end of the corridor, perhaps a hundred meters down, gravitation slowly returned. The hatch there was armored and open. I brought the rifle up and looked around the seal. No one. We stepped through, and I saw the black in his golden suit, fresh as a ghost. I was surprised; he wasn't. My rifle was up and pointed, but his weapon was down. He smiled faintly.

"We are looking for a woman known as Geneva," he said. "Are you she?"

I nodded. He bowed stiffly, armor crinkling, and motioned for me to follow. The room around the corner was unlighted. A port several meters wide, ribbed with steel beams, opened onto the starry dark. The stars were moving, and I guessed the ship was rolling in space. I saw other forms in the shadows, large and bulky, some human, some apparently not. Their breathing made them sound like waiting predators.

A hand took mine, and a shadow towered over me. "This way."

Sonok clung to my calf, and I carried him with each step I took. He didn't make a sound. As I passed from the viewing room, I saw a blue-and-white curve begin at the top of the port and caught an outline of continent. Asia, perhaps. We were already near Earth. The shapes of the continents could remain the same in countless universes, immobile grounds beneath the thin and pliable paint of living things. What was life like in the distant world-lines where even the shapes of the continents had changed?

The next room was also dark, but a candle flame flickered behind curtains. The shadow that had guided me returned to the viewing room and shut the hatch. I heard the breathing of only one besides myself.

I was shaking. Would they do this to us one at a time? Yes, of course; there was too little food. Too little air. Not enough of anything on this tiny scattershot. Poor Sonok, by his attachment, would go before his proper moment.

The breathing came from a woman, somewhere to my right. I turned to face in her general direction. She sighed. She sounded very old, with labored breath and a kind of pant after each intake.

I heard a dry crack of adhered skin separating, dry lips parting to speak, then the tiny *click* of eyelids blinking. The candle flame wobbled in a current of air. As my eyes adjusted, I could see that the curtains formed a translucent cubicle in the dark.

"Hello," the woman said. I answered weakly. "Is your name Francis Geneva?"

I nodded, then, in case she couldn't see me, and said, "I am."

"I am Junipero," she said, aspirating the *j* as in Spanish. "I was commander of the High-space ship *Callimachus*. Were you a commander on your ship?"

"No," I replied. "I was part of the crew."

"What did you do?"

I told her in a spare sentence or two, pausing to cough. My throat was like parchment.

"Do you mind stepping closer? I can't see you very well."

I walked forward a few steps.

"There is not much from your ship in the way of computers or stored memory," she said. I could barely make out her face as she bent forward, squinting to examine me. "But we have learned to speak your language from those parts that accompanied the Indian. It is not too different from a language in our past, but none of us spoke it until now. The rest of you did well. A surprising number of you could communicate, which was fortunate. And the little children who suckle—the Nemi—they always know how to get along. We've had several groups of them on our voyages."

"May I ask what you want?"

"You might not understand until I explain. I have been through the *mutata* several hundred times. You call it disruption. But we haven't found our home yet, I and my crew. The crew must keep trying, but I won't last much longer. I'm at least two thousand years old, and I can't search forever."

"Why don't the others look old?"

"My crew? They don't lead. Only the top must crumble away to keep the group flexible, only those who lead. You'll grow old, too. But not the crew. They'll keep searching."

"What do you mean, me?"

"Do you know what 'Geneva' means, dear sister?"

I shook my head, no.

"It means the same thing as my name, Junipero. It's a tree that gives berries. The one who came before me, her name was Jenevr, and she lived twice as long as I, four thousand years. When she came, the ship was much smaller than it is now."

"And your men—the ones in armor—"

"They are part of my crew. There are women, too."

"They've been doing this for six thousand years?"

"Longer," she said. "It's much easier to be a leader and die, I think. But their wills are strong. Look in the tank, Geneva."

A light came on behind the cubicle, and I saw the message tank. The murky fluid moved with a continuous swirling flow. The old woman stepped from the cubicle and stood beside me in front of the tank. She held out her finger and wrote something on the glass, which I couldn't make out.

The tank's creatures formed two images, one of me and one of her. She was dressed in a simple brown robe, her peppery black hair cropped into short curls. She touched the glass again, and her image changed. The hair lengthened, forming a broad globe around her head. The wrinkles smoothed. The body became slimmer and more muscular, and a smile came to the lips. Then the image was stable.

Except for the hair, it was me.

I took a deep breath. "Every time you've gone through a disruption, has the ship picked up more passengers?"

"Sometimes," she said. "We always lose a few, and every now and then we gain a large number. For the last few centuries our size has been stable, but in time we'll probably start to grow. We aren't anywhere near the total yet. When that comes, we might be twice as big as we are now. Then we'll have had, at one time or another, every scrap of ship, and every person who ever went through a disruption."

"How big is the ship now?"

"Four hundred kilometers across. Built rather like a volvox, if you know what that is."

"How do you keep from going back yourself?"

"We have special equipment to keep us from separating. When we started out, we thought it would shield us from a *mutata,* but it didn't. This is all it can do for us now: it can keep us in one piece each time we jump. But not the entire ship."

I began to understand. The huge bulk of ship I had seen from the window was real. I had never left the grab bag. I was in it now, riding the aggregate, a tiny particle attracted out of solution to the colloidal mass.

Junipero touched the tank, and it returned to its random flow. "It's a constant shuttle run. Each time we return to the Earth to see who, if any, can find their home there. Then we seek out the ones who have the disrupters, and they attack us—send us away again."

"Out there—is that my world?"

The old woman shook her head. "No, but it's home to one group—three of them. The three creatures in the bubble."

I giggled. "I thought there were a lot more than that."

"Only three. You'll learn to see things more accurately as time passes. Maybe you'll be the one to bring us all home."

"What if I find my home first?"

"Then you'll go, and if there's no one to replace you, one of the crew will command until another comes along. But someone always comes along, eventually. I sometimes think we're being played with, never finding our home, but always having a Juniper to command us." She smiled wistfully. "The game isn't all bitterness and bad tosses, though. You'll see more things, and do more, and be more, than any normal woman."

"I've never been normal," I said.

"All the better."

"If I accept."

"You have that choice."

" 'Junipero,' " I breathed. "Geneva." Then I laughed. "How do you choose?"

The small child, seeing the destruction of its thousand companions with each morning light and the skepticism of the older ones, becomes frightened and wonders if she will go the same way. Someone will raise the shutters and a sunbeam will impale her and she'll phantomize. Or they'll tell her they don't believe *she's* real. So she sits in the dark, shaking. The dark becomes fearful. But soon each day becomes a triumph. The ghosts vanish, but she doesn't, so she forgets the shadows and thinks only of the day. Then she grows older, and the companions are left only in whims and background thoughts. Soon she is whittled away to nothing; her husbands are past, her loves are firm and not potential, and her history stretches away behind her like carvings in crystal. She becomes wrinkled, and soon the daylight haunts her again. Not every day will be a triumph. Soon there will be a final beam of light, slowly piercing her jellied eye, and she'll join the phantoms.

But not now. Somewhere, far away, but not here. All around, the ghosts have been resurrected for her to see and lead. And she'll be resurrected, too, always under the shadow of the tree name.

"I think," I said, "that it will be marvelous."

So it was, thirty centuries ago. Sonok is gone, two hundred years past; some of the others have died, too, or gone to their own Earths. The ship is five hundred kilometers across and growing. You haven't come to replace me yet, but I'm dying, and I leave this behind to guide you, along with the instructions handed down by those before me.

Your name might be Jennifer, or Ginepra, or something else, but you will always be me. Be happy for all of us, darling. We will be forever whole.

MANDALA

THE CITY THAT HAD OCCUPIED MESA CANAAN WAS NOW MARCHING ACROSS the plain. Jeshua watched with binoculars from the cover of the jungle. It had disassembled just before dawn, walking on elephantine legs, tractor treads, and wheels, with living bulkheads upright, dismantled buttresses given new instructions to crawl instead of support; floors and ceilings, transports and smaller city parts, factories and resource centers, all unrecognizable now, like a slime mold soon to gather itself in its new country.

The city carried its plan deep within the living plasm of its fragmented body. Every piece knew its place, and within that scheme there was no room for Jeshua, or for any man.

The living cities had cast them out a thousand years before.

He lay with his back against a tree, binoculars in one hand and an orange in the other, sucking thoughtfully on a bitter piece of rind. No matter how far back he probed, the first thing he remembered was watching a city break into a tide of parts, migrating. He had been three years old, two by the seasons of God-Does-Battle, sitting on his father's shoulders as they came to the village of Bethel-Japhet to live. Jeshua—ironically named, for he would always be chaste—remembered nothing of importance before coming to Bethel-Japhet. Perhaps it had all been erased by the shock of falling into the campfire a month before reaching the village. His body still carried the marks: a circle of scars on his chest, black with the tiny remnants of cinders.

Jeshua was huge, seven feet tall flat on his feet. His arms were as thick as an ordinary man's legs, and when he inhaled, his chest swelled as big as a barrel. He was a smith in the village, a worker of iron and caster of bronze and silver. But his strong hands had also acquired delicate skills to craft ritual and family jewelry. For his trade he had been given the surname Tubal—Jeshua Tubal Iben Daod, craftsman of all metals.

The city on the plain was marching toward the Arat range. It moved with faultless deliberation. Cities seldom migrated more than a hundred miles at a time or more than once in a hundred years, so the legends went; but they seemed more restless now.

He scratched his back against the trunk, then put his binoculars in a pants pocket. His feet slipped into the sandals he'd dropped on the mossy jungle floor, and he stood, stretching. He sensed someone behind him but did not turn to look, though his neck muscles knotted tight.

"Jeshua." It was the chief of the guard and the council of laws, Sam Daniel the Catholic. His father and Sam Daniel had been friends before his father disappeared. "Time for the Synedrium to convene."

Jeshua tightened the straps on his sandals and followed.

Bethel-Japhet was a village of moderate size, with about two thousand people. Its houses and buildings laced through the jungle until no distinct borders remained. The stone roadway to the Synedrium Hall seemed too short to Jeshua, and the crowd within the hearing chamber was far too large. His betrothed, Kisa, daughter of Jake, was not there, but his challenger, Renold Mosha Iben Yitshok, was.

The representative of the seventy judges, the Septuagint, called the gathering to order and asked that the details of the case be presented.

"Son of David," Renold said, "I have come to contest your betrothal to Kisa, daughter of Jake."

"I hear," Jeshua said, taking his seat in the defendant's docket.

"I have reasons for my challenge. Will you hear them?"

Jeshua didn't answer.

"Pardon my persistence. It is the law. I don't dislike you—I remember our childhood, when we played together—but now we are mature, and the time has come."

"Then speak." Jeshua fingered his thick dark beard. His flushed skin was the color of the fine sandy dirt on the riverbanks of the Hebron. He towered a good foot above Renold, who was slight and graceful.

"Jeshua Tubal Iben Daod, you were born like other men but did not grow as we have. You now look like a man, but the Synedrium has records of your development. You cannot consummate a marriage. You cannot give a child to Kisa. This annuls your childhood betrothal. By law and by my wish I am bound to replace you, to fulfill your obligation to her."

Kisa would never know. No one here would tell her. She would come in time to accept and love Renold, and to think of Jeshua as only another man in the Expolis Ibreem and its twelve villages, a man who stayed alone and unmarried. Her slender warm body with skin smooth as the finest cotton would soon dance beneath the man he saw before him. She would clutch Renold's back and dream of the time when humans would again be welcomed into the cities, when the skies would again be filled with ships and God-Does-Battle would be redeemed—

"I cannot answer, Renold Mosha Iben Yitshok."

"Then you will sign this." Renold held out a piece of paper and advanced.

"There was no need for a public witnessing," Jeshua said. "Why did the Synedrium decide my shame was to be public?" He looked around with tears in his eyes. Never before, even in the greatest physical pain, had he cried; not even, so his father said, when he had fallen into the fire.

He moaned. Renold stepped back and looked up in anguish. "I'm sorry, Jeshua. Please sign. If you love either Kisa or myself, or the expolis, sign."

Jeshua's huge chest forced out a scream. Renold turned and ran. Jeshua slammed his fist onto the railing, struck himself on the forehead, and tore out the seams of his shirt. He had had too much. For nine years he had known of his inability to be a whole man, but he had hoped that would change, that his genitals would develop like some tardy flower just beyond normal season, and they had. But not enough. His testicles were fully developed, enough to give him a hairy body, broad shoulders, flat stomach, narrow hips, and all the desires of any young man—but his penis was the small pink dangle of a child's.

Now he exploded. He ran after Renold, out of the hall, bellowing incoherently and swinging his binoculars at the end of their leather strap. Renold ran into the village square and screeched a warning. Children and fowl scattered. Women grabbed their skirts and fled for the wood and brick homes.

Jeshua stopped. He flung his binoculars as high as he could above his head. They cleared the top of the tallest tree in the area and fell a hundred feet beyond. Still bellowing, he charged a house and put his hands against the wall. He braced his feet and heaved. He slammed his shoulder against it. It would not move. More furious still, he turned to a trough of fresh water, picked it up, and dumped it over his head. The cold did not slow him. He threw the trough against the wall and splintered it.

"Enough!" cried the chief of the guard. Jeshua stopped and blinked at Sam Daniel the Catholic. He wobbled, weak with exertion. Something in his stomach hurt.

"Enough, Jeshua," Sam Daniel said softly.

"The law is taking away my birthright. Is that just?"

"Your right as a citizen, perhaps, but not your birthright. You weren't born here, Jeshua. But it is still no fault of yours. There is no telling why nature makes mistakes."

"No!" He ran around the house and took a side street into the market triangle. The stalls were busy with customers picking them over and carrying away baskets filled with purchases. He leaped into the triangle and began to scatter people and shops every which way. Sam Daniel and his men followed.

"He's gone berserk!" Renold shouted from the rear. "He tried to kill me!"

"I've always said he was too big to be safe," growled one of the guard. "Now look what he's doing."

"He'll face the council for it," Sam Daniel said.

"Nay, the Septuagint he'll face, as a criminal, if the damage gets any heavier!"

They followed him through the market.

Jeshua stopped at the base of a hill, near an old gate leading from the village proper. He was gasping painfully, and his face was wine-red. Sweat gnarled his hair. In the thicket of his mind he was searching for a way out, the only way now. His father had told him about it when he was thirteen or fourteen. "The cities were like doctors," his father had said. "They could alter, replace, or repair anything in the

human body. That's what was lost when the cities grew disgusted and cast the people out."

No city would let any real man or woman enter. But Jeshua was different. Real people could sin. He could be a sinner not in fact, but only in thought. In his confusion the distinction seemed important.

Sam Daniel and his men found him at the outskirts of the jungle, walking away from Bethel-Japhet.

"Stop!" the chief of the guard ordered.

"I'm leaving," Jeshua said without turning.

"You can't go without a ruling!"

"I am."

"We'll hunt you!"

"Then I'll hide, damn you!"

There was only one place to hide on the plain, and that was underground, in the places older than the living cities and known collectively as Sheol. Jeshua ran. He soon outdistanced them all.

Five miles ahead he saw the city that had left Mesa Canaan. It had reassembled itself below the mountains of Arat. It gleamed in the sun, as beautiful as anything ever denied mankind. The walls began to glow as the sky darkened, and in the evening silence the air hummed with the internal noises of the city's life. Jeshua slept in a gully, hidden by a lean-to woven out of reeds.

In the soft yellow light of dawn, he looked at the city more closely, lifting his head above the gully's muddy rim. The city began with a ring of rounded outward-leaning towers, like the petals of a monumental lotus. Inward was another ring, slightly taller, and another, rising to support a radiance of buttresses. The buttresses carried a platform with columns atop it, segmented and studded like the branches of a diatom. At the city's summit, a dome like the magnified eye of a fly gave off a corona of diffracted colors. Opal glints of blue and green sparkled in the outside walls.

With the help of the finest architect humanity had ever produced, Robert Kahn, Jeshua's ancestors had built the cities and made them as comfortable as possible. Huge laboratories had labored for decades to produce the right combination of animal, plant, and machine, and to fit them within the proper designs. It had been a proud day when the first cities were opened. The Christians, Jews, and Moslems of God-Does-Battle could boast of cities more spectacular than any that Kahn had built elsewhere, and the builder's works could be found on a hundred worlds.

Jeshua stopped a hundred yards from the glassy steps beneath the outer petals of the city. Broad, sharp spikes rose from the pavement and smooth garden walls. The plants within the garden shrank away at his approach. The entire circuit of paving around the city shattered into silicate thorns and bristled. There was no way to enter. Still, he walked closer.

He faced the tangle of sharp spines and reached to stroke one with a hand. It shuddered at his touch.

"I haven't sinned," he told it. "I've hurt no one, coveted only that which was mine by law." The nested spikes said nothing but grew taller as he watched, until they extended a hundred yards above his head.

He sat on a hummock of grass outside the perimeter and clasped his stomach with his hands to ease the hunger and pressure of his sadness. He looked up at the city's peak. A thin silvery tower rose from the midst of the columns and culminated in a multifaceted sphere. The sunlit side of the sphere formed a crescent of yellow brilliance. A cold wind rushed through his clothes and made him shiver. He stood and began to walk around the city, picking up speed when the wind carried sounds of people from the expolis.

Jeshua knew from long hikes in his adolescence that a large entrance to Sheol yawned two miles farther west. By noon he stood in the cavernous entrance.

The underground passages that made up Sheol had once been service ways for the inorganic cities of twelve centuries ago. All of those had been leveled and their raw material recycled with the completion of the living cities. But the underground causeways would have been almost impossible to destroy, so they had been blocked off and abandoned. Some had filled with groundwater, and some had collapsed. Still others, drawing power from geothermal sources, maintained themselves and acted as if they yet had a purpose. A few became the homes of disgruntled expolitans, not unlike Jeshua.

Many had become dangerous. Some of the living cities, just finished and not completely inspected, had thrown out their human builders during the Exiling, then broken down. Various disembodied parts—servant vehicles, maintenance robots, transports—had left the shambles and crept into the passages of Sheol, ill and incomplete, to avoid the natural cycle of God-Does-Battle's wilderness and the wrath of the exiles. Most had died and disintegrated, but a few had found ways to survive, and rumors about those made Jeshua nervous.

He looked around and found a gnarled sun-blackened vine hard as wood, with a heavy bole. He hefted it, broke off its weak tapering end, and stuck it into his belt where it wouldn't tangle his legs.

Before he scrambled down the debris-covered slope, he looked back. The expolitans from Ibreem were only a few hundred yards away.

He lurched and ran. Sand, rocks, and bits of dead plants had spilled into the wide tunnel. Water dripped off chipped white ceramic walls, plinking into small ponds. Moss and tiered fungus imparted a shaggy veneer to the walls and supports.

The villagers appeared at the lip of the depression and shouted his name. He hid in the shadows for a while until he saw that they weren't following.

A mile into the tunnel, he saw lights. The floor was ankle-deep with muddy water. He had already seen several of God-Does-Battle's native arthropods and contemplated catching one for food, but he had no way to light a fire. He'd left all his matches in Bethel-Japhet, since it was against the law to go into the jungles carrying them unless on an authorized hunt or expedition. He couldn't stand the thought of raw creeper flesh, no matter how hungry he was.

The floor ahead had been lifted up and dropped. A lake had formed within the rimmed depression. Ripples shivered with oily slowness from side to side. Jeshua skirted the water on jagged slabs of concrete. He saw something long and white in the lake, waiting in the shallows, with feelers like the soft feathers of a mulcet branch. It had large grey eyes and a blunt rounded head, with a pocketknife assortment of clippers, grabbers, and cutters branching from arms on each side. Jeshua had never seen anything like it.

God-Does-Battle was seldom so bizarre. It had been a straightforward, slightly dry Earth-like world, which was why humans had colonized in such large numbers thirteen centuries ago, turning the sluggish planet into a grand imitation of the best parts of ten planets. Some of the terraforming had slipped since then, but not drastically.

Water splashed as he stepped on the solid floor of the opposite shore. The undulating feathery nightmare glided swiftly into the depths.

The lights ahead blazed in discrete globes, not the gentle glows of the walls of the living cities. Wiring hissed and crackled in the vicinity of a black metal box. Tracks began at a buffer and ran off around the distant curve. Black strips, faded and scuffed, marked a walkway. Signs in Old English and something akin to the Hebraic hodgepodge spoken in Ibreem warned against deviating from the outlined path. He could read the English more easily than the Hebrew, for Hebraic script had been used. In Ibreem, all writing was in Roman script.

Jeshua stayed within the lines and walked around the curve. Half of the tunnel ahead was blocked by a hulk. It was thirty feet wide and some fifty long, rusting and frozen in its decay. It had been man-operated, not automatic—a seat bucket still rose above a nest of levers, pedals, and a small arched instrument panel. As a smith and designer of tools and motor-driven vehicles, Jeshua thought there were parts of the rail-rider that didn't seem integral. He examined them more closely and saw they hadn't come with the original machine. They were odds and ends of mobile machinery from one of the cities. Part machine, part organism, built with treads and grips, they had joined with the tar-baby rail-rider, trying to find a place on the bigger, more powerful machine. They had found only silence. They were dead now, and what could not rot had long since dusted away. The rest was glazed with rust and decay.

In the tunnel beyond, stalactites of concrete and rusted steel bristled from the ceiling. Fragments of pipes and wiring hung from them on brackets. At one time the entire tunnel must have been filled with them, with room only for rail-riders and maintenance crews walking the same path he was taking. Most of the metal and plastic had been stripped away by scavengers.

Jeshua walked beneath the jagged end of an air duct and heard a susurrus. He cocked his head and listened more closely. Nothing. Then again, almost too faint to make out. The plastic of the air duct was brittle and added a timbre of falling dust to the voices. He found a metal can and stood on it, bringing his ear closer.

"Moobed . . ." the duct echoed.

". . . not 'ere dis me was . . ."

"Bloody poppy-breast!"

"Not'ing . . . do . . ."

The voices stopped. The can crumpled and dropped him to the hard floor, making him yelp like a boy. He stood on wobbly legs and walked farther into the tunnel.

The lighting was dimmer. He walked carefully over the shadow-pocked floor, avoiding bits of tile and concrete, fallen piping, snake wires and loose strapping bands. Fewer people had been this way. Vaguely seen things moved off at his approach: insects, creepers, rodents, some native, some feral. What looked like an overturned drum became, as he bent closer, a snail wide as two handspans, coursing on a shiny foot as long as his calf. The white-tipped eyes glanced up, cat-slits dark with hidden fluids and secret thoughts, and a warm, sickening odor wafted from it. Stuck fast to one side was the rotting body of a large beetle.

A hundred yards on, the floor buckled again. The rutted underground landscape of pools, concrete, and mud smelled foul and felt more foul to his sandaled feet. He stayed away from the bigger pools, which were surrounded by empty larvae casings and filled with snorkeling insect young.

He regretted his decision. He wondered how he could return to the village and face his punishment. To live within sight of Kisa and Renold. To repair the water trough and do labor penance for the stall owners.

He stopped to listen. Water fell in a cascade ahead. The sound drowned out anything more subtle, but something of a squabbling nature rose above. Men were arguing and coming closer.

Jeshua moved back from the middle of the tunnel and hid behind a fallen pipe.

Someone ran from block to block, dancing agilely in the tunnel, arms held out in balance and hands gesturing like wing tips. Four others followed, knife blades gleaming in the half-light. The fleeing man ran past, saw Jeshua in the shadows, and stumbled off into black mud. Jeshua pushed against the pipe as he stood and turned to run. He felt a tremor through his hand on the wall. A massive presence of falling rock and dirt knocked him over and tossed debris around him. Four shouts were severed. He choked on the dust, waving his arms and crawling.

The lights were out. Only a putrid blue-green swamp glow remained. A shadow crossed the ghost of a pond. Jeshua stiffened and waited for the attacking blow.

"Who?" the shadow said. "Go, spek. Shan hurt."

The voice sounded like it might come from an older boy, perhaps eighteen or nineteen. He spoke a sort of English. It wasn't the tongue Jeshua had learned while visiting Expolis Winston, but he could understand some of it. He thought it might be Chaser English, but there weren't supposed to be chasers in Expolis Ibreem. They must have followed the city. . . .

"I'm running, like you," Jeshua said in Winston dialect.

"Dis me," said the shadow. "Sabed my ass, you did. Quartie ob toms, lie dey t'ought I spek. Who appel?"

"What?"

"Who name? You."

"Jeshua," he said.

"Jeshoo-a. Iberhim."

"Yes, Expolis Ibreem."

"No' far dis em. Stan' an' clean. Takee back."

"No, I'm not lost. I'm running."

"No' good t'stay. Bugga bites mucky, bugga bites you more dan dey bites dis me."

Jeshua slowly wiped mud from his pants with broad hands. Dirt and pebbles scuttled down the hill where the four lay tombed.

"Slow," the boy said. "Slow, no? Brainsick?" The boy advanced. "Dat's it. Slow, you."

"No, tired," Jeshua said. "How do we get out of here?"

"Dat, dere an' dere. See?"

"Can't see," Jeshua said. "Not very well."

The boy advanced again and laid a cool, damp hand on his forearm. "Big, you. Skeez, maybe tight." The hand gripped and tested. Then the shadow backed off. Jeshua's eyes were adjusting, and he could see the boy's thinness.

"What's your name?" he asked.

"No' matta. Go 'long wi' dis me now."

The boy led him to the hill of debris and poked around in the pitchy black to see if they could pass. "Allry. Dis way." Jeshua climbed up the rubble and pushed through the hole at the top with his back scraping the ceramic roof. The other side of the tunnel was dark. The boy cursed under his breath. "Whole tube," he said. "Ginger walk, now."

The pools beyond were luminous with the upright glows of insect larvae. Some were a foot long and solitary; others were smaller and grouped in hazes of meager light. Always there was a soft sucking sound and thrash of feelers, claws, legs. Jeshua's skin crawled, and he shivered in disgust.

"Sh," the boy warned. "Skyling here, sout' go, tro sound."

Jeshua caught none of the explanation but stepped more lightly. Dirt and tiles dropped in the water, and a chitinous chorus complained.

"Got dur here," the boy said, taking Jeshua's hand and putting it against a metal hatch. "Ope', den go. Compree?"

The hatch slid open with a drawn-out squeal, and blinding glare filled the tunnel. Things behind hurried for shadows. Jeshua and the boy stepped from the tunnel into a collapsed anteroom open to the last light of day. Vegetation had swarmed into the wet depression, decorating hulks of pipe valves and electric boxes. As the boy closed the hatch, Jeshua scraped at a metal cube with one hand and drew off a layered clump of moss. Four numbers were engraved beneath: "2278."

"Don' finga," the boy warned. He had wide grey eyes and a pinched, pale face. A grin spread between narcissus-white cheeks. He was tight-sewn, tense, with wide knees and elbows and little flesh to cover his long limbs. His hair was rusty orange and hung in strips across his forehead and ears. Beneath a ragged vest, his chest bore a tattoo. The boy rubbed his hand across it, seeing Jeshua's interest, and left a smear of mud behind.

"My bran'," the boy said. The "brand" was a radiant circle in orange and black, with a central square divided by diagonals. Triangles diminished to points in each division, creating a vibrant skewedness. "Dat put dere, long 'go, by Mandala."

"What's that?"

"De gees run me, you drop skyling on, woodna dey lissen wen I say, say dis me, dat de polis, a dur go up inna." He laughed. "Dey say, 'Nobod eba go in polis, no mo' eba.'"

"Mandala's a city, a polis?"

"Ten, fi'teen lees fr' 'ere."

"Lees?"

"Kileemet'. Lee."

"You speak anything else?" Jeshua asked, his face screwed up with the strain of turning instant linguist.

"You, 'Ebra spek, bet. But no good dere. I got better Englise, tone up a bit?"

"Hm?"

"I can . . . try . . . this, if it betta." He shook his head. "Blow me ou' to keep up long, do."

"Maybe silence is best," Jeshua said. "Or you just nod yes or no if you understand. You've found a way to get into a polis?"

Nod.

"Named Mandala. Can you get back there, take me with you?"

Shake, no. Smile.

"Secret?"

"No secret. Dey big machee . . . machine dat tell dis me neba retourn. Put dis on my bod." He touched his chest. "Tro me out."

"How did you find your way in?"

"Dur? Dis big polis, it creep affa exhaus'—sorry, moob afta run outta soil das good to lib on, many lee fro' 'ere, an' squat on top ob place where tube ope' ri' middle ob undaside. I know dat way, so dis me go in, an' out soon afta . . . after. On my—" He slapped his butt. "Coupla bounce, too."

The collapsed ceiling of the anteroom—or skyling, as the boy called it—formed a convenient staircase from the far wall to the surface. They climbed and stood on the edge, looking each other over uncertainly. Jeshua was covered with dark green mud. He picked at the caked rings with his hands, but the mud clung to his skin fiercely.

"Maybe, come fine a ob wet to slosh in."

A branch of the Hebron River, flowing out of the Arat range, showed itself by a clump of green reeds a half mile from the tunnel exit. Jeshua drew its muddy water up in handfuls and poured it over his head. The boy dipped and wallowed and spumed it from puffed cheeks, then grinned like a terrier at the Ibreemite, mud streaming down his face.

"Comes off slow," Jeshua said, scraping at his skin with clumped silkreeds.

"Why you interest' in place no man come?"

Jeshua shook his head and didn't answer. He finished with his torso and kneeled to let his legs soak. The bottom of the stream was rocky and sandy and cool. He looked up and let his eyes follow the spine of a peak in Arat, outlined in sunset glow. "Where is Mandala?"

"No," the boy said. "My polis."

"It kicked you out," Jeshua said. "Why not let somebody else try?"

"Somebod' alread' tried," the boy informed him with a narrowed glance. "Dat dey tried, and got in, but dey didna t'rough my dur go. Dey—shee—one gol, dat's all—got in widout de troub' we aw ekspek. Mandala didna sto' 'er."

"I'd like to try that."

"Dat gol, she special, she up an' down legen' now. Was a year ago she went and permissed to pass was. You t'ink special you might be?"

"No," Jeshua admitted. "Mesa Canaan's city wouldn't let me in."

"One it wander has, just early yes'day?"

"Hm?"

"Wander, moob. Dis Mase Cain' you mumbur 'bout."

"I know."

"So't don' let dis you in, why Mandala an' differs?"

Jeshua climbed from the river, frowning. "Appel?" he asked.

"Me, m'appel, not true appel or you got like hair by demon grab, m'appel for you is Thinner."

"Thinner, where do you come from?"

"Same as de gol, we follow the polis."

"City chasers?" By Ibreem's estimation, that made Thinner a ruthless savage. "Thinner, you don't want to go back to Mandala, do you? You're afraid."

"Cumsay, afraid? Like terrafy?"

"Like tremble in your bare feet in the dirtafy."

"No' possible for Thinner. Lead'er like, snake-skin, poke an' I bounce, no' go t'rough."

"Thinner, you're a faker." Jeshua reached out and lifted him from the water. "Now stop with the nonsense and give me straight English. You speak it—out!"

"No!" the boy protested.

"Then why do you drop all 'thu's' but in your name and change the word order every other sentence? I'm no fool. You're a fake."

"If Thinner lie, feet may curl up an' blow! Born to spek dis odd inflek, an' I spek differs by your ask! Dis me, no fake! Drop!" Thinner kicked Jeshua on the shin but only bent his toe. He squalled, and Jeshua threw him back like a fingerling. Then he turned to pick up his clothes and lumbered up the bank to leave.

"Nobod dey neba treat Thinner dis way!" the boy howled.

"You're lying to me," Jeshua said.

"No! Stop." Thinner stood in the river and held up his hands. "You're right."

"I know I am."

"But not completely. I'm from Winston, and I'm speaking like a city chaser for a reason. And speaking accurately, mind you."

Jeshua frowned. The boy no longer seemed a boy. "Why fool me, or try to?" he asked.

"I'm a free-lance tracker. I'm trying to keep tabs on the chasers. They've been making raids on the farmlands outside of Winston. I was almost caught by a few of them, and I was trying to convince them I was part of a clan. When they were buried, I thought you might have been another, and after speaking to you like that—well, I have an instinct to keep a cover in a tight spot."

"No Winstoner has a tattoo like yours."

"That part's the truth, too. I did find a way into the city, and it did kick me out."

"Do you still object to taking me there?"

Thinner sighed and crawled out of the stream. "It's not part of my trip. I'm heading back for Winston."

Jeshua watched him cautiously as he dried himself. "You don't think it's odd that you even got into a city at all?"

"No. I did it by trick."

"Men smarter than you or I tried for centuries before they all gave up. Now you've succeeded, and you don't even feel special?"

Thinner put on his scrappy clothes. "Why do you want to go?"

"I've got reasons."

"Are you a criminal in Ibreem?"

Jeshua shook his head. "I'm sick," he said. "Nothing contagious. But I was told a city might cure me, if I could find a way in."

"I've met your kind before," Thinner said. "But they've never made it. A few years ago Winston sent a whole pilgrimage of sick and wounded to a city. Bristled its barbs like a fighting cat. No mercy there, you can believe."

"But you have a way, now."

"Okay," Thinner said. "We can go back. It's on the other side of Arat. You've got me a little curious now. And besides, I think I might like you. You look like you should be dumb as a creeper, but you're smart. Sharp. And besides, you've still got that club. Are you desperate enough to kill?"

Jeshua thought about that for a moment, then shook his head.

"It's almost dark," Thinner said. "Let's camp and start in the morning."

In the far valley at the middle of Arat, the Mesa Canaan city—now probably to be called the Arat city—was warm and sunset-pretty, like a diadem. Jeshua made a bed from the reeds and watched Thinner as he hollowed out the ground and made his own nest. Jeshua slept lightly that evening and came awake with dawn. He opened his eyes to a small insect on his chest, inquiring its way with finger-long antennae. He flicked it off and cleared his throat.

Thinner jack-in-the-boxed from his nest, rubbed his eyes, and stood.

"I'm amazed," he said. "You didn't cut my throat."

"Wouldn't do me any good."

"Work like this rubs down a man's trust."

Jeshua returned to the river and soaked himself again, letting the chill wallop his face and back in heavy hand-loads. The pressure in his groin was lighter this morning than most, but it still made him grit his teeth. He wanted to roll in the reeds and groan, rut the earth, but it would do him no good. Only the impulse existed.

They agreed on which pass to take through the Arat peaks and set out.

Jeshua had spent most of his life within sight of the villages of the Expolis Ibreem and found himself increasingly nervous the farther he hiked. They crawled up the slope, and Thinner's statement about having tough soles proved itself. He walked barefoot over all manner of jagged rocks without complaining.

At the crest of a ridge, Jeshua looked back and saw the plain of reeds and the jungle beyond. With some squinting and hand-shading, he could make out the major clusters of huts in two villages and the Temple Josiah on Mount Miriam. All else was hidden.

In two days they crossed Arat and a rilled terrain of foothills beyond. They walked through fields of wild oats. "This used to be called Agripolis," Thinner said. "If you dig deep enough here, you'll come across irrigation systems, automatic fertilizing machines, harvesters, storage bins—the whole works. It's all useless now. For nine hundred years it wouldn't let any human cross these fields. It finally broke down, and those parts that could move, did. Most died."

Jeshua knew a little concerning the history of the cities around Arat and told Thinner about the complex known as Tripolis. Three cities had been grouped on one side of Arat, about twenty miles north of where they were standing. After the Exiling, one had fragmented and died. Another had moved successfully and had left the area. The third had tried to cross the Arat range and failed. The major bulk of its wreckage lay in a disorganized mute clump not far from them.

They found scattered pieces of it on the plain of Agripolis. As they walked, they saw bulkheads and buttresses, most hardy of a city's larger members, still supported by desiccated legs. Some were fifty to sixty yards long and twenty feet across, mounted on organic wheel movements. Their metal parts had corroded badly. The organic parts had disappeared, except for an occasional span of silicate wall or internal skeleton of colloid.

"They're not all dead, though," Thinner said. "I've been across here before. Some made the walk a little difficult."

In the glare of afternoon they hid from a wheeled beast armored like a great translucent tank. "That's something from deep inside a city—a mover or loader," Thinner said. "I don't know anything about the temper of a feral city part, but I'm not going to aggravate it."

When the tank thing passed, they continued. There were creatures less threatening, more shy, which they ignored. Most of them Jeshua couldn't fit into a picture of ancient city functions. They were queer, dreamy creatures: spinning tops, many-legged browsers, things with bushes on their backs, bowls built like dogs but carrying water—insane, confusing fragments.

By day's end they stood on the outskirts of Mandala. Jeshua sat on a stone to look at the city. "It's different," he said. "It isn't as pretty." Mandala was more square, less free and fluid. It had an ungainly zigguratlike pear shape. The colors that were scattered along its walls and light-banners—black and orange—didn't match well with the delicate blues and greens of the city substance.

"It's older," Thinner said. "One of the first, I think. It's an old tree, a bit scabrous, not like a young sprout."

Jeshua looped his belt more tightly about his club and shaded his eyes against the sun. The young of Ibreem had been taught enough about cities to identify their parts and functions. The sunlight-absorbing banners that rippled near Mandala's peak were like the leaves of a tree and also like flags. Designs on their surfaces formed a language conveying the city's purpose and attitude. Silvery reflectors cast shadows below the banners. By squinting, he could see the gardens and fountains and crystalline recreation buildings of the uppermost promenade, a mile above them. Sunlight illuminated the green walls and showed their mottled innards, pierced the dragonfly buttresses whose wings with slow in-out beats kept air moving, and crept back and forth through the halls, light wells, and living quarters, giving all of Mandala an interior luminosity. Despite the orange and black of the colored surfaces, the city had an innate glory that made Jeshua's chest ache with desire.

"How do we get in?" he asked.

"Through a tunnel, about a mile from here."

"You mentioned a girl. Was that part of the cover?"

"No. She's here. I met her. She has the liberty of the city. I don't think she has to worry about anything, except loneliness." He looked at Jeshua with an uncharacteristic wry grin. "At least she doesn't have to worry about where the next meal comes from."

"How did she get in? Why does the city let her stay?"

"Who can judge the ways of a city?"

Jeshua nodded thoughtfully. "Let's go."

Thinner's grin froze and he stiffened, staring over Jeshua's shoulder. Jeshua looked around and surreptitiously loosened his club in his belt. "Who are they?" he asked.

"The city chasers. They usually stay in the shadow. Something must be upsetting them today."

At a run through the grass, twenty men dressed in rough orange-and-black rags advanced on them. Jeshua saw another group coming from the other side of the city perimeter. "We'll have to take a stand," he said. "We can't outrun them."

Thinner looked distressed. "Friend," he said. "It's time I dropped another ruse. We can get into the city here, but they can't."

Jeshua ignored the non sequitur. "Stand to my rear," he said. Jeshua swung his club up and took a stance, baring his teeth and hunkering low as his father had taught him to do when facing wild beasts. The bluff was the thing, especially when backed by his bulk. Thinner pranced on his bandy legs for a second, panic tightening his face. "Follow me, or they'll kill us," he said.

He broke for the glassy gardens within the perimeter. Jeshua turned and saw the polis chasers were forming a circle, concentrating on him, aiming spears for a throw. He ducked and lay flat as the metal-tipped shafts flew over, thunking into the grass. He rose, and a second flight shot by, one grazing him painfully on the shoulder. He heard Thinner rasp and curse. A chaser held him at arm's length, repeatedly slashing his chest with a knife. Jeshua stood tall and ran for the circle, club held out before him. Swords came up and out, dull grey steel spotted with blood-rust. He blocked a thrust and cut it aside with the club, then killed the man with a downward swing.

"Stop it, you goddamn idiots!" someone shouted. One of the chasers shrieked, and the others backed away from Jeshua. Thinner's attacker held a head, severed from the boy's body. It was trailing green. Though decapitated, Thinner was shouting invective in several languages, including Hebrew and Chaser English. The attackers abandoned their weapons before the oracular monster and ran pale and stumbling. The petrified man who held the head dropped it and fell over.

Jeshua stood his ground, bloody club trembling in his loosening hand.

"Hey," said the muffled voice in the grass. "Come here and help!"

Jeshua spotted six points on his forehead and drew two meshed triangles between. He walked slowly through the grass.

"El and hell," Thinner's head cried out. "I'm chewing grass. Pick me up."

He found the boy's body first. He bent over and saw the red, bleeding skin on the chest, pulpy green below that, and the pale colloid ribs that supported. Deeper still, glassy machinery and pale blue fluids in filigree tubes surrounded glints of organic circuit and metal. The chaser nearby had fainted from shock.

He found Thinner's head facedown, jaw working and hair standing on end. "Lift me out," the head said. "By the hair, if you're squeamish, but lift me out."

Jeshua reached down and picked the head up by the hair. Thinner stared at him above green-leaking nose and frothed lips. The eyes blinked. "Wipe my mouth with something." Jeshua picked up a clump of grass and did so, leaving bits of dirt behind, but getting most of the face clean. His stomach squirmed, but Thinner was obviously no mammal, nor a natural beast of any form, so he kept his reactions in check.

"I wish you'd listened to me," the head said.

"You're from the city," Jeshua said, twisting it this way and that.

"Stop that—I'm getting dizzy. Take me inside Mandala."

"Will it let me in?"

"Yes, dammit. I'll be your passkey."

"If you're from the city, why would you want me or anyone else to go inside?"

"Take me in, and you'll discover."

Jeshua held the head at arm's length and inspected it with half-closed eyes. Then, slowly, he lowered it, looked at the tiled gardens within the perimeter, and took his first step. He stopped, shaking.

"Hurry," the head said. "I'm dripping."

At any moment Jeshua expected the outskirts to splinter and bristle, but no such thing happened. "Will I meet the girl?" he asked.

"Walk, no questions."

Eyes wide and stomach tense as rock, Jeshua entered the city of Mandala.

"There, that came more easily than you expected, didn't it?" the head asked.

Jeshua stood in a cyclopean green mall, light bright but filtered, like the bottom of a shallow sea, surrounded by the green of thick glass and botanic fluids. Tetrahedral pylons and slender arches rose all around and met high above in a circular design of orange and black, similar to the markings on Thinner's chest. The pylons supported four floors opening onto the court. The galleries were empty.

"You can put me down here," Thinner said. "I'm broken. Something will come along to fix me. Wander for a while if you want. Nothing will hurt you. Perhaps you'll meet the girl."

Jeshua looked around apprehensively. "Would do neither of us any good," he said. "I'm afraid."

"Why, because you're not a whole man?"

Jeshua dropped the head roughly on the hard floor, and it bounced, screeching.

"How did you know?" he asked loudly, desperately.

"Now you've made me confused," the head said. "What did I say?" It stopped talking, and its eyes closed. Jeshua touched it tentatively with his boot. It did nothing. He straightened up and looked for a place to run. The best way would be out. He was a sinner now, a sinner by anger and shame. The city would throw him out violently. Perhaps it would brand him, as Thinner had hinted earlier. Jeshua wanted the familiarity of the grasslands and tangible enemies like the city chasers.

The sunlight through the entrance arch guided him. He ran for the glassy walkway and found it rising to keep him in. Furious with panic, he raised his club and struck at the spines. They sang with the blows but did not break.

"Please," he begged. "Let me out, let me out!"

He heard a noise behind him and turned. A small wheeled cart gripped Thinner's head with gentle mandibles and lifted its segmented arms to send the oracle down a chute into its back. It rolled from the mall into a corridor.

Jeshua lifted his slumped shoulders and expanded his chest. "I'm afraid!" he shouted at the city. "I'm a sinner! You don't want me, so let me go!"

He squatted on the pavement with club in hand, trembling. The hatred of the cities for man had been deeply impressed in him. His breathing slowed until he could think again, and the fear subsided.

Why had the city let him in, even with Thinner? He stood and slung the club in his belt. There was an answer someplace. He had little to lose—at most, a life he wasn't particularly enjoying.

And in a city there was the possibility of healing arts now lost to the expolitans.

"Okay," he said. "I'm staying. Prepare for the worst."

He walked across the mall and took a corridor beyond. Empty rooms with hexagonal doors waited silent on either side. He found a fountain of refreshing water in a broad cathedral-nave room and drank from it. Then he spent some time studying the jointing of the arches that supported the vault above, running his fingers over the grooves.

A small anteroom had a soft couchlike protrusion, and he rested there, staring blankly at the ceiling. For a short while he slept. When he awoke, both he and his clothes were clean. A new pair had been laid out for him—standard Ibreem khaki shirt and short pants and a twine belt, more delicately knitted than the one he was wearing. His club hadn't been removed. He lifted it. It had been tampered with—and improved. It fitted his grip better now and was weighted to balance well. A table was set with dishes of fruit and what looked like bread-gruel. He had been accommodated in all ways, more than he deserved from any city. It almost gave him the courage to be bold. He took off his ragged clothes and tried on the new set. They fit admirably, and he felt less disreputable. His sandals had been stitched up but not replaced. They were comfortable, as always, but sturdier.

"How can I fix myself here?" he asked the walls. No answer came. He drank water from the fountain again and went to explore further.

The ground plan of Mandala's lowest level was relatively simple. It consisted mostly of trade and commerce facilities, with spacious corridors for vehicle traffic, large warehouse areas, and dozens of conference rooms. Computing facilities were also provided. He knew a little about computers—the trade office in Bethel-Japhet still had an ancient pocket model taken from a city during the Exiling. The access terminals in Mandala were larger and clumsier, but recognizable. He came across a room filled with them. Centuries of neglect had made them irregular in shape, their plastic and thin metal parts warping. He wondered what portions of them, if any, were alive.

Most of the rooms on the lowest level maintained the sea-floor green motif. The uniformity added to Jeshua's confusion, but after several hours of wandering, he found the clue that provided guidance. Though nothing existed in the way of written directions or graphic signs or maps, by keeping to the left he found he tended to the center; and to the right, the exterior. A Mandalan of ten centuries ago would have known the organization of each floor by education, and perhaps by portable guidebooks or signalers. Somewhere, he knew, there had to be a central elevator system.

He followed all left-turning hallways. Avoiding obvious dead ends, he soon reached the base of a hollow shaft. The floor was tiled with a changing design of greens and blues, advancing and flowing beneath his feet like a cryptic chronometer. He craned his neck back and looked up through the center of Mandala. High above he saw a bluish circle, the waning daytime sky. Wind whistled down the shaft.

Jeshua heard a faint hum from above. A speck blocked out part of the skylight and grew as it fell, spiraling like a dropped leaf. It had wings, a thick body for passengers, and an insect head, like the dragonfly buttresses that provided ventilation on Mandala's exterior. Slowing its descent, it lifted its nose and came to a stop in front of him, still several feet above the floor. The bottoms of its unmoving transparent wings reflected the changing design of the floor.

Then he saw that the floor was coming to a conclusion, like an assembled puzzle. It formed a mosaic triskelion, a three-winged symbol outlined in red.

The glider waited for him. In its back there was room for at least five people. He chose the front seat. The glider trembled and moved forward. The insect-head tilted back, cocked sideways, and inspected its ascent. Metallic antennae emerged from the front of the body. A tingling filled the air. And he began to fly.

The glider slowed some distance above the floor and came to a stop at a gallery landing. Jeshua felt his heartbeat race as he looked over the black railing, down the thousand feet or so to the bottom of the shaft.

"This way, please."

He turned, expecting to see Thinner again. Instead there waited a device like a walking coat-tree, with a simple vibration speaker mounted on its thin neck, a rod for a body, and three appendages jointed like a mantis's front legs. He followed it.

Transparent pipes overhead pumped bubbling fluids like exposed arteries. He wondered whether dissenting citizens in the past could have severed a city's lifelines by cutting such pipes—or were these mere ornaments, symbolic of deeper activities? The coat-tree clicked along in front of him, then stopped at a closed hexagonal door and tapped its round head on a metal plate. The door opened. "In here."

Jeshua entered. Arranged in racks and rows in endless aisles throughout the huge room were thousands of constructions like Thinner. Some were incomplete, with their machinery and sealed-off organic connections hanging loose from trunks, handless arms, headless necks. Some had gaping slashes, broken limbs, squashed torsos. The coat-tree hurried off before he could speak, and the door closed behind.

He was beyond anything but the most rudimentary anxiety now. He walked down the central aisle, unable to decide whether this was a workshop or a charnel house. If Thinner was here, it might take hours to find him.

He stared straight ahead and stopped. There was someone not on the racks. At the far end of the room, it stood alone, too distant to be discerned in detail. Jeshua waited, but the figure did not move. It was a stalemate.

He made the first step. The figure darted to one side like a deer. He automatically ran after it, but by the time he'd reached the end of the aisle, it was nowhere to be seen.

"Hide and seek," he murmured. "For God's sake, hide and seek."

He rubbed his groin abstractedly, trying to still the flood of excitement rushing into his stomach and chest. His fantasies multiplied, and he bent over double, grunting. He forced himself to straighten up, held out his arms, and concentrated on something distracting.

He saw a head that looked very much like Thinner's. It was wired to a board behind the rack, and fluids pulsed up tubes into its neck. The eyes were open but glazed, and the flesh was ghostly. Jeshua reached out to touch it. It was cold, lifeless.

He examined other bodies more closely. Most were naked, complete in every detail. He hesitated, then reached down to touch the genitals of a male. The flesh was soft and flaccid. He shuddered. His fingers, as if working on their own, went to the pubic mound of a female figure. He grimaced and straightened, rubbing his hand on his pants with automatic distaste. A tremor jerked up his back. He was spooked now, having touched the lifeless forms, feeling what seemed dead flesh.

What were they doing here? Why was Mandala manufacturing thousands of surrogates? He peered around the racks of bodies, this way and behind, and saw open doors far beyond. Perhaps the girl— it must have been the girl—had gone into one of those.

He walked past the rows. The air smelled like cut grass and broken reed stems, with sap leaking. Now and then it smelled like fresh slaughtered meat, or like oil and metal.

Something made a noise. He stopped. One of the racks. He walked slowly down one aisle, looking carefully, seeing nothing but stillness, hearing only the pumping of fluids in thin pipes and the clicks of small valves. Perhaps the girl was pretending to be a cyborg. He mouthed the word over again. Cyborg. He knew it from his schooling. The cities themselves were cybernetic organisms.

He heard someone running. The footsteps were going away from him, slap of bare feet on floor. He paced evenly past the rows, look-ing down each aisle, nothing, nothing, stillness, there! The girl was at the opposite end, laughing at him. An arm waved. Then she vanished.

He decided it was wise not to chase anyone who knew the city better than he did. Best to let her come to him. He left the room through an open door.

A gallery outside adjoined a smaller shaft. This one was red and only fifty or sixty feet in diameter. Rectangular doors opened off the galleries, closed but unlocked. He tested the three doors on his level, opening them one at a time with a push. Each room held much the same thing—a closet filled with dust, rotting and collapsed furni-ture, emptiness and the smell of old tombs. Dust drifted into his nostrils, and he sneezed. He went back to the gallery and the hexag-onal door. Looking down, he swayed and felt sweat start. The view was dizzying and claustrophobic.

A singing voice came down to him from above. It was feminine, sweet, and young, a song in words he did not completely catch. They resembled Thinner's chaser dialect, but echoes broke the meaning. He leaned out over the railing as far as he dared and looked up. It was definitely the girl—five, six, seven levels up. The voice sounded almost childish. Some of the words reached him clearly with a puff of direct breeze:

"Dis em, in solit lib, dis em . . . Clo'ed in clo'es ob dead . . ."

The red shaft vanished to a point without skylight. The unfamiliar glare hurt his eyes. He shaded them to see more clearly. The girl backed away from the railing and stopped singing.

He knew by rights he should be angry, that he was being teased. But he wasn't. Instead he felt a loneliness too sharp to sustain. He turned away from the shaft and looked back at the door to the room of cyborgs.

Thinner stared back at him, grinning crookedly. "Didn't have chance to welcome," he said in Hebrew. His head was mounted on a metal snake two feet long, his body was a rolling green car with three wheels, a yard long and half a yard wide. It moved silently. "Have any difficulty?"

Jeshua looked him over slowly, then grinned. "It doesn't suit you," he said. "Are you the same Thinner?"

"Doesn't matter, but yes, to make you comfortable."

"If it doesn't matter, then who am I talking to? The city computers?"

"No, no. They can't talk. Too concerned with maintaining. You're talking with what's left of the architect."

Jeshua nodded slowly, though he didn't understand.

"It's a bit complicated," Thinner said. "Go into it with you later. You saw the girl, and she ran away from you."

"I must be pretty frightening. How long has she been here?"

"A year."

"How old is she?"

"Don't know for sure. Have you eaten for a while?"

"No. How did she get in?"

"Not out of innocence, if that's what you're thinking. She was already married before she came here. The chasers encourage marriage early."

"Then I'm not here out of innocence, either."

"No."

"You never saw me naked," Jeshua said. "How did you know what was wrong with me?"

"I'm not limited to human senses, though El knows what I do have are bad enough. Follow me, and I'll find suitable quarters for you."

"I may not want to stay."

"As I understand it, you've come here to be made whole. That can be done, and I can arrange it. But patience is always a virtue."

Jeshua nodded at the familiar homily. "She speaks Chaser English. Is that why you were with the chasers, to find a companion for her?"

The Thinner-vehicle turned away from Jeshua without answering. It rolled through the cyborg chamber, and Jeshua followed. "It would be best if someone she was familiar with would come to join her, but none could be persuaded."

"Why did she come?"

Thinner was silent again. They took a spiral moving walkway around the central shaft, going higher. "It's the slow, scenic route," Thinner said, "but you'll have to get used to the city and its scale."

"How long am I going to stay?"

"As long as you wish."

They disembarked from the walkway and took one of the access halls to an apartment block on the outer wall of the city. The construction and colors here were more solid. The bulkheads and doors were opaque and brightly colored in blue, burnt orange, and purple. The total effect reminded Jeshua of a sunset. A long balcony in the outer wall gave a spectacular view of Arat and the plains, but Thinner allowed him no time to sightsee. He took Jeshua into a large apartment and made him familiar with the layout.

"It's been cleaned up and provided with furniture you should be used to. You can trade it in for somewhere else whenever you want. But you'll have to wait until you've been seen to by the medical units. You've been scheduled for work in this apartment." Thinner showed him a white-tile and stainless-steel kitchen, with food dispensers and basic utensils. "Food can be obtained here. There's enough material to customize whatever comes out of the dispensers. Sanitary units are in here and should explain themselves—"

"They talk?"

"No. I mean their use should be self-evident. Very few things talk in the city."

"We were told the cities were commanded by voice."

"Not by most of the citizens. The city itself does not talk back.

Only certain units, not like myself—none of the cyborgs were here when humans were. That's a later development. I'll explain in time. I'm sure you're more used to books and scrolls than tapes or tridvee experiences, so I've provided some offprints for you on these shelves. Over here—"

"Seems I'm going to be here for a long time."

"Don't be worried by the accommodations. This may be fancy by your standards, but it certainly isn't by Mandala's. These used to be apartments for those of an ascetic temper. If there's anything you want to know when I'm not here, ask the information desk. It's hooked to the same source I am."

"I've heard of the city libraries. Are you part of them?"

"No. I've told you, I'm part of the architect. Avoid library outlets for the moment. In fact, for the next few days, don't wander too far. Too much too soon, and all that. Ask the desk, and it will give you safe limits. Remember, you're more helpless than a child here. Mandala is not out-and-out dangerous, but it can be disturbing."

"What do I do if the girl visits me?"

"You anticipate it?"

"She was singing to me, I think. But she didn't want to show herself directly. She must be lonely."

"She is." Thinner's voice carried something more than a tone of crisp efficiency. "She's been asking a lot of questions about you, and she's been told the truth. But she's lived without company for a long time, so don't expect anything soon."

"I'm confused," Jeshua said.

"In your case, that's a healthy state of mind. Relax for a while; don't let unknowns bother you."

Thinner finished explaining about the apartment and left. Jeshua went out the door to stand on the terrace beyond the walkway. Light from God-Does-Battle's synchronous artificial moons made the snows of Arat gleam like dull steel in the distance. Jeshua regarded the moons with an understanding he'd never had before. Humans had brought them from the orbit of another world, to grace God-Does-Battle's nights. The thought was staggering. People used to live there, a thousand years ago. What had happened to them when the cities had exiled their citizens? Had the lunar cities done the same thing as the cities of God-Does-Battle?

He went to his knees for a moment, feeling ashamed and primitive, and prayed to El for guidance. He was not convinced his confusion was so healthy.

He ate a meal that came as close as amateur instructions could make it to the simple fare of Bethel-Japhet. He then examined his bed, stripped away the covers—the room was warm enough—and slept.

Once, long ago, if his earliest childhood memories were accurate, he had been taken from Bethel-Japhet to a communion in the hills of Kebal. That had been years before the Synedrium had stiffened the separation laws between Catholic and Habiru rituals. His father and most of his acquaintances had been Habiru and spoke Hebrew. But prominent members of the community, such as Sam Daniel, had by long family tradition worshiped Jesus as more than a prophet, according to established creeds grouped under the title of Catholicism. His father had not resented the Catholics for their ideas.

At that communion, not only had Habiru and Catholic worshiped, but also the now-separate Muslims and a few diverse creeds best left forgotten. Those had been difficult times, perhaps as hard as the times just after the Exiling. Jeshua remembered listening to the talk between his father and a group of Catholics—relaxed, informal talk, without the stiffness of ceremony that had grown up since. His father had mentioned that his young son's name was Jeshua, which was a form of Jesus, and the Catholics had clustered around him like fathers all, commenting on his fine form as a six-year-old and his size and evident strength. "Will you make him a carpenter?" they asked jokingly.

"He will be a cain," his father answered.

They frowned, puzzled.

"A maker of tools."

"It was the making of tools that brought us to the Exiling," Sam Daniel said.

"Aye, and raised us from beasts," his father countered.

Jeshua remembered the talk that followed in some detail. It had stuck with him and determined much of his outlook as an adult, after the death of his father in a mining accident.

"It was the shepherd who raised us above the beasts by making us their masters," another said. "It was the maker of tools and tiller of the soil who murdered the shepherd and was sent to wander in exile."

"Yes," his father said, eyes gleaming in the firelight. "And later it was the shepherd who stole a birthright from his nomad brother—or have we forgotten Jacob and Esau? The debt, I think, was even."

"There's much that is confusing in the past," Sam Daniel admitted. "And if we use our eyes and see that our exile is made less difficult by the use of tools, we should not condemn our worthy cains. But those who built the cities that exiled us were also making tools, and the tools turned against us."

"But why?" his father asked. "Because of our degraded state as humans? Remember, it was the Habirus and Catholics—then Jews and Christians—who commissioned Robert Kahn to build the cities for God-Does-Battle and to make them pure cities for the best of mankind, the final carriers of the flame of Jesus and the Lord. We were self-righteous in those days and wished to leave behind the degraded ways of our neighbors. How was it that the best were cast out?"

"Hubris," chuckled a Catholic. "A shameful thing, anyway. The histories tell us of many shameful things, eh, lad?" He looked at Jeshua. "You remember the stories of the evil that men did."

"Don't bother the child," his father said angrily.

Sam Daniel put his arm around the shoulder of Jeshua's father. "Our debater is at it again. Still have the secret for uniting us all?"

Half-asleep, he opened his eyes and tried to roll over on the bed.

Something stopped him, and he felt a twinge at the nape of his neck. He couldn't see well—his eyes were watering and everything was blurred. His nose tickled and his palate hurt vaguely, as if something were crawling through his nostrils into the back of his throat. He tried to speak but couldn't. Silvery arms weaved above him, leaving grey trails of shadow behind, and he thought he saw wires spinning over his chest. He blinked. Liquid drops hung from the wires like dew from a web. When the drops fell and touched his skin, waves of warmth and numbness radiated.

He heard a whine, like an animal in pain. It came from his own throat. Each time he breathed, the whine escaped. Again the metal things bobbed above him, this time unraveling the wires. He blinked, and it took a long time for his eyelids to open again. There was a split in the ceiling, and branches grew down from it, one coming up under his vision and reaching into his nose, others holding him gently on the bed, another humming behind his head, making his scalp prickle. He searched for the twinge below his neck. It felt as if a hair was being pulled from his skin or a single tiny ant was pinching him. He was aloof, far above it, not concerned; but his hand still wanted to scratch and a branch prevented it from moving. His vision cleared for an instant, and he saw green enameled tubes, chromed grips, pale blue ovals being handed back and forth.

"A anna eh uh," he tried to say. "Eh ee uh." His lips wouldn't move. His tongue was playing with something sweet. He'd been given candy. Years ago he'd gone for a mouth examination—with a clean bill of health—and he'd been given a roll of sugar gum to tongue on the way home.

He sank back into his skull to listen to the talk by the fireside again. "Hubris," chuckled a Catholic.

"Habirus," he said to himself. "Hubris."

"A shameful thing, anyway—"

"Our debater is at it again. Still have the secret for uniting us all?"

"And raised us from beasts."

Deep, and sleep.

He opened his eyes and felt something in the bed with him. He moved his hand to his crotch. It felt as if a portion of the bed had gotten loose and was stuck under his hip, in his shorts. He lifted his hips and pulled down the garment, then lay back, a terrified look coming into his face. Tears streamed from his eyes.

"Thanks to El," he murmured. He tried to back away from the vision, but it went with him, was truly a part of him. He hit the side of his head to see if it was still a time for dreams. It was real.

He climbed off the bed and stripped away his shirt, standing naked by the mirror to look at himself. He was afraid to touch it, but of itself it jerked and nearly made him mad with desire. He reached up and hit the ceiling with his fists.

"Great El, magnificent Lord," he breathed. He wanted to rush out the door and stand on the balcony, to show God-Does-Battle he was now fully a man, fully as capable as anyone else to accomplish any

task given to him, including—merciful El!—founding and fathering a family.

He couldn't restrain himself. He threw open the door of the apartment and ran naked outside.

"BiGod!"

He stopped, his neck hair prickling, and turned to look.

She stood by the door to the apartment, poised like a jacklighted animal. She was only fourteen or fifteen, at the oldest, and slender, any curves hidden beneath a sacky cloth of pink and orange. She looked at him as she might have looked at a ravening beast. He must have seemed one. Then she turned and fled.

Devastated in the midst of his triumph, he stood with shoulders drooped, hardly breathing, and blinked at the afterimage of brown hair and naked feet. His erection subsided into a morning urge to urinate. He threw his hands up in the air, returned to the apartment, and went into the bathroom.

After breakfast he faced the information desk, squatting uncomfortably on a small stool. The front of the desk was paneled with green slats, which opened as he approached. Sensor cells peered out at him.

"I'd like to know what I can do to leave," he said.

"Why do you want to leave?" The voice was deeper than Thinner's, but otherwise much the same.

"I've got friends elsewhere, and a past life to return to. I don't have anything here."

"You have all of the past here, an infinite number of things to learn."

"I really just want out."

"You can leave anytime."

"How?"

"This is a problem. Not all of Mandala's systems cooperate with this unit—"

"Which unit?"

"I am the architect. The systems follow schedules set up a thousand years ago. You're welcome to try to leave—we certainly won't do anything to stop you—but it could be difficult."

Jeshua drummed his fingers on the panel for a minute. "What do you mean, the architect?"

"The unit constructed to design and coordinate the building of the cities."

"Could you ask Thinner to come here?"

"Thinner unit is being reassembled."

"Is he part of the architect?"

"Yes."

"Where are you?"

"If you mean, where is my central position, I have none. I am part of Mandala."

"Does the architect control Mandala?"

"No. Not all city units respond to the architect. Only a few."

"The cyborgs were built by the architect," Jeshua guessed.

"Yes."

Jeshua drummed his fingers again, then backed away from the desk and left the apartment. He stood on the terrace, looking across the plains, working his teeth in frustration. He seemed to be missing something terribly important.

"Hey."

He looked up. The girl was on a terrace two levels above him, leaning with her elbows on the rail.

"I'm sorry I scared you," he said.

"Dis me, no' terrafy. Li'l shock, but dat all mucky same-same 'ereber dis em go now. Hey, do, I got warns fo' you."

"What? Warnings?"

"Dey got probs here, 'tween Mandala an' dey 'oo built."

"I don't understand."

"No' compree? Lissy dis me, close, like all dis depen' on't: Dis em, was carry by polis 'en dis dey moob, week 'r two ago. Was no' fun. Walk an' be carry, was I. No' fun."

"The city moved? Why?"

"To leeb behine de part dis dey call builder."

"The architect? You mean, Thinner and the information desks?"

"An' too de bods 'ich are hurt."

Jeshua began to understand. There were at least two forces in Mandala that were at odds with each other—the city and something within the city that called itself the architect.

"How can I talk to the city?"

"De polis no' talk."

"Why does the architect want us here?"

"Don' know."

Jeshua messaged his neck to stop a cramp. "Can you come down here and talk?"

"No' now dis you are full a man. . . . Too mucky for dis me, too cashin' big."

"I won't hurt you. I've lived with it for all my life—can live a while longer."

"Oop!" She backed away from the rail.

"Wait!" Jeshua called. He turned and saw Thinner, fully corporeal now, leaning on the rounded corner of the access hall.

"So you've been able to talk to her," Thinner said.

"Yes. Made me curious, too. And the information desk."

"We expected it."

"Then can I have some sound answers?"

"Of course."

"Why was I brought here—to mate with the girl?"

"El! Not at all." Thinner gestured for him to follow. "I'm afraid you're in the middle of a pitched battle. The city rejects all humans. But the architect knows a city needs citizens. Anything else is a farce."

"We were kicked out for our sins," Jeshua said.

"That's embarrassing, not for you so much as for us. The architect designed the city according to the specifications given by humans— but any good designer should know when a program contains an incipient psychosis. I'm afraid it's set this world back quite a few centuries. The architect was made to direct the construction of the cities. Mandala was the first city, and we were installed here to make it easier to supervise construction everywhere. But now we have no control elsewhere. After a century of building and successful testing, we put community control into the city maintenance computers. We tore down the old cities when there were enough of the new to house the people of God-Does-Battle. Problems didn't develop until all the living cities were integrated on a broad plan. They began to compare notes, in a manner of speaking."

"They found humanity wanting."

"Simply put. One of the original directives of the city was that socially destructive people—those who did not live their faith as Jews or Christians—would be either reformed or exiled. The cities were constantly aware of human activity and motivation. After a few decades they decided everybody was socially destructive in one way or another."

"We are all sinners."

"This way," Thinner directed. They came to the moving walkway around the central shaft and stepped onto it. "The cities weren't capable of realizing human checks and balances. By the time the problem was discovered, it was too late. The cities went on emergency systems and isolated themselves, because each city reported that it was full of antisocials. They were never coordinated again. It takes people to reinstate the interurban links."

Jeshua looked at Thinner warily, trying to judge the truth of the story. It was hard to accept—a thousand years of self-disgust and misery because of bad design! "Why did the ships leave the sky?"

"This world was under a colony contract and received support only so long as it stayed productive. Production dropped off sharply, so there was no profit, and considerable expense and danger in keeping contact. There were tens of millions of desperate people here then. After a time, God-Does-Battle was written off as a loss."

"Then we are not sinners, we did not break El's laws?"

"No more than any other living thing."

Jeshua felt a slow hatred begin inside. "There are others who must learn this," he said.

"Sorry," Thinner said. "You're in it for the duration. We'll get off here."

"I will not be a prisoner," Jeshua said.

"It's not a matter of being held prisoner. The city is in for another move. It's been trying to get rid of the architect, but it can't—it never will. It would go against a directive for city cohesion. And so would you if you try to leave now. Whatever is in the city just before a move is cataloged and kept careful track of by watcher units."

"What can any of you do to stop me?" Jeshua asked, his face set as if he'd come across a piece of steel difficult to hammer. He walked away from the shaft exit, wondering what Thinner would try.

The floor rocked back and forth and knocked him on his hands and knees. Streamers of brown and green crawled over a near wall, flexing and curling. The wall came away, shivered as if in agony, then fell on its side. The sections around it did likewise until a modular room had been disassembled. Its contents were neatly packed by scurrying coat-trees, each with a fringe of arms and a heavier frame for loads. All around the central shaft, walls were being plucked out and rooms dismantled. Thinner kneeled next to Jeshua and patted him on the shoulder.

"Best you come with this unit and avoid the problems here. I can guarantee safe passage until the city has reassembled."

Jeshua hesitated, then looked up and saw a cantilever arch throwing out green fluid ropes like a spider spinning silk. The ropes caught on opposite bracings and allowed the arch to lower itself. Jeshua stood up on the uncertain flooring and followed Thinner.

"This is only preliminary work," Thinner said as he took him into the cyborg room. "In a few hours the big structural units will start to come down, then the bulkheads, ceiling, and floor pieces, then the rest. By this evening, the whole city will be mobile. The girl will be here in a few minutes—you can travel together if you want to. This unit will give you instructions on how to avoid injury during reassembly."

But Jeshua had other plans. He did as Thinner told him, resting on one of the racks like a cyborg, stiffening as the girl came in from another door and positioned herself several aisles down. He was sweating profusely, and the smell of his fear nauseated him.

The girl looked at him cautiously. "You know 'at dis you in fo'?" she asked.

He shook his head.

The clamps on the rack closed and held him comfortably but securely. He didn't try to struggle. The room was disassembling itself. Panels beneath the racks retracted, and wheels jutted out. Shivering with their new energy, the racks elevated and wheeled out their charges.

The racks formed a long train down a hall crowded with scurrying machines. Behind them, the hall took itself apart with spewed ropes, fresh-sprouted grasping limbs and feet, wheels and treads.

It was a dance. With the precision of a bed of flowers closing for the night, the city shrank, drew in, pulled itself down from the top, and packed itself onto wide-tread beasts with unfathomable jade eyes. The racks were put on the backs of a trailer like a flat-backed spider, long multiple legs pumping up and down smoothly. A hundred spiders like it carried the remaining racks, and thousands of other choreographed tractors, robots, organic cranes, cyborg monsters, waited in concentric circles around Mandala. A storm gathered to the south about Arat's snowy peaks. As the day went on and the city diminished, the grey front swept near, then over. A mantle of cloud hid the disassembly of the upper levels. Rain fell on the ranks of machines and half-machines, and the ground became dark with mud and trampled vegetation. Transparent skins came up over the backs of the spider-trailers, hanging from rigid foam poles. Thinner crawled between the racks and approached Jeshua, who was stiff and sore by now.

"We've let the girl loose," Thinner said. "She has no place to go but with us. Will you try to leave?"

Jeshua nodded.

"It'll only mean trouble for you. But I don't think you'll get hurt." Thinner tapped the rack, and the clamps backed away. Night was coming down over the storm. Through the trailer skin, Jeshua could see the city's parts and vehicles switch on interior glows. Rain streaks distorted the lights into ragged splashes and bars. He stretched his arms and legs and winced.

A tall tractor unit surmounted by a blunt-nosed cone rumbled up to the trailer and hooked itself on. The trailer lurched and began to move. The ride on the pumping man-thick legs was surprisingly smooth. Mandala marched through the rain and dark.

By morning, the new site had been chosen.

Jeshua lifted the trailer skin and jumped into the mud. He had slept little during the trek, thinking about what had happened and what he had been told. He was no longer meek and ashamed.

The cities were no longer lost paradises to him. They now had an air of priggishness. They were themselves flawed. He spat into the mud.

But the city had made him whole again. Who had been more responsible: the architect or Mandala itself? He didn't know and hardly cared. He had been taken care of as any unit in Mandala would have been, automatically and efficiently. He coveted his new wholeness, but it didn't make him grateful. It should have been his by a birthright of ten centuries. It had been denied by incompetence—and whatever passed as willful blindness in the cities.

He could not accept it as perpetual error. His people tended to think in terms of will and responsibility.

The maze of vehicles and city parts was quiet now, as if resting before the next effort of reassembly. The air was misty and grey with a heaviness that lowered his spirits.

" 'Ere dis you go?"

He turned back to the trailer and saw the girl peering under the skin. "I'm going to try to get away," he said. "I don't belong here. Nobody does."

"Lissy. I tol' de one, T-*Thi*nner to teach dis me . . . teach me how to spek li' dis you. When you come back, I know by den."

"I don't plan on coming back." He looked at her closely. She was wearing the same shift she wore when he first saw her, but a belt had tightened it around her waist. He took a deep breath and backed away a step, his sandals sinking in the mud.

"I don' know 'oo you are . . . who you are . . . but if Th-Thinner brought you, you must be a good person."

Jeshua widened his eyes. "Why?"

She shrugged. "Dis me just know." She jumped down from the trailer, swinging from a rain-shiny leg. Mud splattered up her bare white calves.

"If you, dis me, t'ought . . . thought you were bad, I'd expec' you to brute me right now. But you don'. Even though you neba—never have a gol before." Her strained speech started to crack, and she laughed nervously. "I was tol' abou' you 'en you came. About your prob—lem." She looked at him curiously. "How do you feel?"

"Alive. And I wouldn't be too sure I'm not a danger. I've never had to control myself before."

The girl looked him over coquettishly.

"Mandala, it isn't all bad, no good," she said. "It took care ob you. Dat's good, is it no?"

"When I go home," Jeshua said, drawing a breath, "I'm going to tell my people we should come and destroy the cities."

The girl frowned. "Li' take down?"

"Piece by piece."

"Too much to do. Nobod can do dat."

"Enough people can."

"No' good to do in firs' place. No' tall."

"It's because of them we're like savages now."

The girl shimmied up the spider's leg again and motioned for him to follow. He lifted himself and stood on the rounded lip of the back, watching her as she walked with arms balancing to the middle of the vehicle. "Look dis," she said. She pointed to the ranked legions of Mandala. The mist was starting to burn off. Shafts of sunlight cut through and brightened wide circles of the plain. "De polis, dey are li' not'ing else. Dey are de . . ." She sighed at her lapses. "They are the fines' thing we eba put together. We should try t'save dem."

But Jeshua was resolute. His face burned with anger as he looked out over the disassembled city. He jumped from the rim and landed in the pounded mud. "If there's no place for people in them, they're useless. Let the architect try to reclaim. I've got more immediate things to do."

The girl smiled slowly and shook her head. Jeshua stalked off between the vehicles and city parts.

Mandala, broken down, covered at least thirty square miles of the plain. Jeshua took his bearings from a tall rock pinnacle, chose the shortest distance to the edge, and sighted on a peak in Arat. He walked without trouble for a half hour and found himself approaching an attenuated concentration of city fragments. Grass grew up between flattened trails. Taking a final sprint, he stood on the edge of Mandala. He took a deep breath and looked behind to see if anything was following.

He still had his club. He held it in one hand, hefted it, and examined it closely, trying to decide what to do with it if he was bothered. He put it back in his belt, deciding he would need it for the long trip back to his expolis. Behind him, the ranks of vehicles and parts lurched and began to move. Mandala was beginning reconstruction. It was best to escape now.

He ran. The long grass made speed difficult, but he persisted until he stumbled into a burrow and fell over. He got up, rubbed his ankle, decided he was intact, and continued his clumsy springing gait.

In an hour he rested beneath the shade of a copse of trees and laughed to himself. The sun beat down heavily on the plain, and the grass shimmered with a golden heat. It was no time for travel. There was a small puddle held in the cup of a rock, and he drank from that, then slept for a while.

He was awakened by a shoe gently nudging him in the ribs.

"Jeshua Tubal Iben Daod," a voice said.

He rolled from his stomach and looked into the face of Sam Daniel the Catholic. Two women and another man, as well as three young children, were behind him jockeying for positions in the coolest shade.

"Have you calmed yourself in the wilderness?" the Catholic asked. Jeshua sat up and rubbed his eyes. He had nothing to fear. The chief of the guard wasn't acting in his professional capacity—he was traveling, not searching. And besides, Jeshua was returning to the expolis.

"I am calmer, thank you," Jeshua said. "I apologize for my actions."

"It's only been a fortnight," Sam Daniel said. "Has so much changed since?"

"I . . ." Jeshua shook his head. "I don't think you would believe."

"You came from the direction of the traveling city," the Catholic said, sitting on the soft loam. He motioned for the rest of the troop to rest and relax. "Meet anything interesting there?"

Jeshua nodded. "Why have you come this far?"

"For reasons of health. And to visit the western limb of Expolis Canaan, where my parents live now. My wife has a bad lung ailment —I think an allergic reaction to the new strain of sorghum being planted in the ridge paddies above Bethel-Japhet. We will stay away until the harvest. Have you stayed in other villages near here?"

Jeshua shook his head. "Sam Daniel, I have always thought you a man of reason and honor. Will you listen with an open mind to my story?"

The Catholic considered, then nodded.

"I have been inside a city."

He raised his eyebrows. "The one on the plain?"

Jeshua told him most of the story. Then he stood. "I'd like you to follow me. Away from the rest. I have proof."

Sam Daniel followed Jeshua behind the rocks, and Jeshua shyly revealed his proof. Sam Daniel stared. "It's real?" he asked. Jeshua nodded.

"I've been restored. I can go back to Bethel-Japhet and become a regular member of the community."

"No one has ever been in a city before. Not for as long as any remember."

"There's at least one other, a girl. She's from the city chasers."

"But the city took itself apart and marched. We had to change our course to go around it or face the hooligans following. How could anyone live in a rebuilding city?"

"I survived its disassembly. There are ways." And he told about the architect and its extensions. "I've had to twist my thoughts to understand what I've experienced," he said. "But I've reached a conclusion. We don't belong in the cities, any more than they deserve to have us."

"Our shame lies in them."

"Then they must be destroyed."

Sam Daniel looked at him sharply. "That would be blasphemous. They serve to remind us of our sins."

"We were exiled not for our sins, but for what we are—human beings! Would you kick a dog from your house because it dreams of hunting during Passover—or Lent? Then why should a city kick its citizens out because of their inner thoughts? Or because of a minority's actions? They were built with morals too rigid to be practical. They are worse than the most callous priest or judge, like tiny children in their self-righteousness. They've caused us to suffer needlessly. And as long as they stand, they remind us of an inferiority and shame that is a lie! We should tear them down to their roots and sow the ground with salt."

Sam Daniel rubbed his nose thoughtfully between two fingers. "It goes against everything the expolises stand for," he said. "The cities are perfect. They are eternal, and if they are self-righteous, they deserve to be. You of all should know that."

"You haven't understood," Jeshua said, pacing. "They are not perfect, not eternal. They were made by men—"

"Papa! Papa!" a child screamed. They ran back to the group. A black tractor-mounted giant with an angular birdlike head and five arms sat ticking quietly near the trees. Sam Daniel called his family back near the center of the copse and looked at Jeshua with fear and anger. "Has it come for you?"

He nodded.

"Then go with it."

Jeshua stepped forward. He didn't look at the Catholic as he said, "Tell them what I've told you. Tell them what I've done, and what I know we must do."

A boy was moaning softly.

The giant picked Jeshua up delicately with a mandibled arm and set him on its back. It spun around with a spew of dirt and grass, then moved quietly back across the plain to Mandala.

When they arrived, the city was almost finished rebuilding. It looked no different from when he'd first seen it, but its order was ugly to him now. He preferred the human asymmetry of brick homes and stone walls. Its noises made him queasy. His reaction grew like steam pressure in a boiler, and his muscles felt tense as a snake about to strike.

The giant set him down in the lowest level of the city. Thinner met him there. Jeshua saw the girl waiting on a platform near the circular design in the shaft.

"If it makes any difference to you, we had nothing to do with bringing you back," Thinner said.

"If it makes any difference to you, I had nothing to do with returning. Where will you shut me in tonight?"

"Nowhere," Thinner said. "You have the run of the city."

"And the girl?"

"What about her?"

"What does she expect?"

"You don't make much sense," Thinner said.

"Does she expect me to stay and make the best of things?"

"Ask her. We don't control her, either."

Jeshua walked past the cyborgs and over the circular design, now disordered again. The girl watched him steadily as he approached. He stopped below the platform and looked up at her, hands tightly clenched at his waist.

"What do you want from this place?" he asked.

"Freedom," she said. "The choice of what to be, where to live."

"But the city won't let you leave. You have no choice."

"Yes, the city, I can leave it whenever I want."

Thinner called from across the mall. "As soon as the city is put together, you can leave, too. The inventory is policed only during a move."

Jeshua's shoulders slumped, and his bristling stance softened. He had nothing to fight against now, not immediately. He kept his fists clenched, even so.

"I'm confused," he said.

"Stay for the evening," she suggested. "Then will you make thought come clear of confusion."

He followed her to his room near the peak of the city. The room hadn't been changed. Before she left him there, he asked what her name was.

"Anata," she said. "Anata Leucippe."

"Do you get lonely in the evenings?" he asked, stumbling over the question like a child in a field of corn stubble.

"Never," she said. She laughed and turned half-away from him. "An' now certes am dis em, you no' trustable!"

She left him by the door. "Eat!" she called from the corner of the access hall. "I be back, around mid of the evening."

He smiled and shut his door, then turned to the kitchen to choose what he was going to eat.

Being a whole man, he now knew, did not stop the pain and fear of loneliness. The possibility of quenching was, in fact, a final turn of the thumbscrew. He paced like a caged bear, thinking furiously and reaching no conclusions.

By midnight he was near an explosion. He waited in the viewing area of the terrace, watching the moonlight bathe God-Does-Battle like milk, gripping the railing with strength that could have crushed wood. He listened to the noise of the city. It was less soothing than he remembered, neither synchronous nor melodic.

Anata came for him half an hour after she said she would. Jeshua had gone through so many ups and downs of despair and aloofness that he was exhausted. She took his hand and led him to the central shaft on foot. They found hidden curved stairwells and went down four levels to a broad promenade that circled a widening in the shaft. "The walkway, it doesn't work yet," she told him. "My tongue, I'm getting it down. I'm studying."

"There's no reason you should speak like me," he said.

"It is difficult at times. Dis me—I cannot cure a lifetime ob—of talk."

"Your own language is pretty," he said, half-lying.

"I know. Prettier. Alive-o. But—" She shrugged.

Jeshua thought he couldn't be more than five or six years older than she was, by no means an insurmountable distance. He jerked as the city lights dimmed. All around, the walls lost their bright glow and produced in its stead a pale lunar gleam, like the night outside.

"This is what I brough' you here for," she said. "To see."

The ghost-moon luminescence made him shiver. Bits of the walls and floor passed threads of light between them, and from the threads grew spirits, shimmering first like mirages, then settling into translucent steadiness. They began to move.

They came in couples, groups, crowds, and with them were children, animals, birds, and things he couldn't identify. They filled the promenade and terraces and walked, talking in tunnel-end whispers he couldn't make out, laughing and looking and being alive, but not in Jeshua's time.

They were not solid, not robots or cyborgs. They were spirits from ten centuries past, and he was rapidly losing all decorum watching them come to form around him.

"Sh!" Anata said, taking his arm to steady him. "They don't hurt anybody. They're no' here. They're dreams."

Jeshua clasped his hands tight and forced himself to be calm.

"This is the city, what it desires," Anata said. "You want to kill the polis, the city, because it keeps out the people, but look—it hurts, too. It wants. What's a city without its people? Just sick. No' bad. No' evil. Can't kill a sick one, can you?"

Each night, she said, the city reenacted a living memory of the past, and each night she came to watch.

Jeshua saw the pseudolife, the half-silent existence of a billion recorded memories, and his anger slowly faded. His hands loosened their grip on each other. He could never sustain hatred for long. Now, with understanding just out of reach, but obviously coming, he could only resign himself to more confusion for the moment.

"It'll take me a long, long time to forgive what happened," he said.

"This me, too." She sighed. "When I was married, I found I could not have children. This my husband could not understand. All the others of the women in the group could have children. So I left in shame and came to the city we had always worshiped. I thought it would be, the city, the only one to cure. But now I don't know. I do not want another husband, I want to wait for this to go away. It is too beautiful to leave while it is still here."

"Go away?"

"The cities, they get old and they wander," she said. "Not all things work good here now. Pieces are dying. Soon it will all die. Even such as Thinner, they die. The room is full of them. And no more are being made. The city is too old to grow new. So I wait until the beauty is gone."

Jeshua looked at her more closely. There was a whitish cast in her left eye. It had not been there a few hours ago.

"It is time to go to sleep," she said. "Very late."

He took her gently by the hand and led her through the phantoms, up the empty but crowded staircases, asking her where she lived.

"I don't have any one room," she said. "Sleep in all of them at some time or another. But we can't go back dere." She stopped. "There. Dere. Can't go back." She looked up at him. "Dis me, canno' spek mucky ob—" She held her hand to her mouth. "I forget. I learned bu' now—I don't know . . ."

He felt a slow horror grind in his stomach.

"Something is going wrong," she said. Her voice became deeper, like Thinner's, and she opened her mouth to scream but could not. She tore away from him and backed up. "I'm doing something wrong."

"Take off your shirt," Jeshua said.

"No." She looked offended.

"It's all a lie, isn't it?" he asked.

"No."

"Then take off your shirt."

She began to remove it. Her hands hesitated.

"Now."

She peeled it over her head and stood naked, with her small breasts outthrust, narrow hips square and bonily dimpled, genitals flossed in feathery brown. A pattern of scars on her chest and breasts formed a circle. Bits of black remained like cinders, like the cinders on his own chest—from a campfire that had never been. Once, both of them had been marked like Thinner, stamped with the seal of Mandala.

She turned away from him on the staircase, phantoms drifting past her and through her. He reached out to stop her but wasn't quick enough. Her foot spasmed and she fell, gathering into a twisted ball, down the staircase, up against the railings, to the bottom.

He stood near the top and saw her pale blue fluid and red skin-blood and green tissue leaking from a torn leg. He felt he might go insane.

"*Thinner!*" he screamed. He kept calling the name. The lunar glow brightened, and the phantoms disappeared. The halls and vaults echoed with his braying cry.

The cyborg appeared at the bottom of the staircase and knelt down to examine the girl.

"Both of us," Jeshua said. "Both lies."

"We don't have the parts to fix her," Thinner said.

"Why did you bring us back? Why not let us stay? And why not just tell us what we are?"

"Until a few years ago there was still hope," Thinner said. "The city was still trying to correct the programs, still trying to get back its citizens. Sixty years ago it gave the architect more freedom to try to find out what went wrong. We built ourselves—you, her, the others—to go among the humans and see what they were like now, how the cities could accommodate. And if we had told you this, would you have believed? As humans, you were so convincing you couldn't even go into cities except your own. Then the aging began, and the sickness. The attempt finally died."

Jeshua felt the scars on his chest and shut his eyes, wishing, hoping it was all a nightmare.

"David the smith purged the mark from you when you were a young cyborg, that you might pass for human. Then he stunted your development that you might someday be forced to come back."

"My father was like me."

"Yes. He carried the scar, too."

Jeshua nodded. "How long do we have?"

"I don't know. The city is running out of memories to repeat. Soon it will have to give up . . . less than a century. It will move like the others and strand itself someplace."

Jeshua walked away from Thinner and the girl's body and wandered down an access hall to the terraces on the outer wall of the city. He shaded his eyes against the rising sun in the east and looked toward Arat. There, he saw the city that had once occupied Mesa Canaan. It had disassembled and was trying to cross the mountains.

"Kisa," he said.

HARDFOUGHT

In the Han Dynasty, historians were appointed by royal edict to write the history of Imperial China. They alone were the arbiters of what would be recorded. Although various emperors tried, none could gain access to the ironbound chest in which each document was placed after it was written. The historians preferred to suffer death rather than betray their trust.

At the end of each reign the box would be opened and the documents published, perhaps to benefit the next emperor. But for these documents, Imperial China, to a large extent, has no history.

The thread survives by whim.

HUMANS CALLED IT THE MEDUSA. ITS LONG TWISTED RIBBONS OF GAS STRAYED across fifty parsecs, glowing blue, yellow, and carmine. Its central core was a ghoulish green flecked with watery black. Half a dozen protostars circled the core, and as many more dim conglomerates pooled in dimples in the nebula's magnetic field. The Medusa was a huge womb of stars—and disputed territory.

Whenever Prufrax looked at it in displays or through the ship's ports, it seemed malevolent, like a zealous mother displaying an ominous face to protect her children. Prufrax had never had a mother, but she had seen them in some of the fibs.

At five, Prufrax was old enough to know the *Mellangee*'s mission and her role in it. She had already been through four ship-years of indoctrination. Until her first battle she would be educated in both the Know and the Tell. She would be exercised and trained in the Mocks; in sleep she would dream of penetrating the huge red-and-white

Senexi seedships and finding the brood mind. "Zap, Zap," she went with her lips, silent so the tellman wouldn't think her thoughts were straying.

The tellman peered at her from his position in the center of the spherical classroom. Her mates stared straight at the center, all focusing somewhere around the tellman's spiderlike teaching desk, waiting for the trouble, some fidgeting. "How many branch individuals in the Senexi brood mind?" he asked. He looked around the classroom. Peered face by face. Focused on her again. "Pru?"

"Five," she said. Her arms ached. She had been pumped full of moans the wake before. She was already three meters tall, in elf-state, with her long, thin limbs not nearly adequately fleshed out and her fingers still crisscrossed with the surgery done to adapt them to the gloves.

"What will you find in the brood mind?" the tellman pursued, his impassive face stretched across a hammerhead as wide as his shoulders. Some of the fems thought tellmen were attractive. Not many—and Pru was not one of them.

"Yoke," she said.

"What is in the brood-mind yoke?"

"Fibs."

"More specifically? And it really isn't all fib, you know."

"Info. Senexi data."

"What will you do?"

"Zap," she said, smiling.

"Why, Pru?"

"Yoke has team gens-memory. Zap yoke, spill the life of the team's five branch inds."

"Zap the brood, Pru?"

"No," she said solemnly. That was a new instruction, only in effect since her class's inception. "Hold the brood for the supreme overs." The tellman did not say what would be done with the Senexi broods. That was not her concern.

"Fine," said the tellman. "You tell well, for someone who's always half-journeying."

Brainwalk, Prufrax thought to herself. Tellman was fancy with the words, but to Pru, what she was prone to do during Tell was brainwalk, seeking out her future. She was already five, soon six. Old. Some saw Senexi by the time they were four.

"Zap, Zap," she went with her lips.

Aryz skidded through the thin layer of liquid ammonia on his broadest pod, considering his new assignment. He knew the Medusa by another name, one that conveyed all the time and effort the Senexi had invested in it. The protostar nebula held few mysteries for him. He and his four branch-mates, who along with the all-important brood mind comprised one of the six teams aboard the seedship, had patrolled the nebula for ninety-three orbits, each orbit —including the timeless periods outside status geometry—taking some one hundred and thirty human years. They had woven in and out of the tendrils of gas, charting the infalling masses and exploring the rocky accretion disks of stars entering the main sequence. With each measure and update, the brood minds refined their view of the nebula as it would be a hundred generations hence when the Senexi plan would finally mature.

The Senexi were nearly as old as the galaxy. They had achieved spaceflight during the time of the starglobe when the galaxy had been a sphere. They had not been a quick or brilliant race. Each great achievement had taken thousands of generations, and not just because of their material handicaps. In those times elements heavier than helium had been rare, found only around stars that had greedily absorbed huge amounts of primeval hydrogen, burned fierce and blue and exploded early, permeating the ill-defined galactic arms with carbon and nitrogen, lithium and oxygen. Elements heavier than iron had been almost nonexistent. The biologies of cold gas-giant worlds had developed with a much smaller palette of chemical combinations in producing the offspring of the primary Population II stars.

Aryz, even with the limited perspective of a branch ind, was aware that, on the whole, the humans opposing the seedship were more adaptable, more vital. But they were not more experienced. The Senexi with their billions of years had often matched them. And Aryz's perspective was expanding with each day of his new assignment.

In the early generations of the struggle, Senexi mental stasis and cultural inflexibility had made them avoid contact with the Population I species. They had never begun a program of extermination of the younger, newly life-forming worlds; the task would have been monumental and probably useless. So when spacefaring cultures developed, the Senexi had retreated, falling back into the redoubts of old stars even before engaging with the new kinds. They had retreated for three generations, about thirty thousand human years, raising their broods on cold nestworlds around red dwarfs, conserving, holding back for the inevitable conflicts.

As the Senexi had anticipated, the younger Population I races had found need of even the aging groves of the galaxy's first stars. They had moved in savagely, voraciously, with all the strength and mutability of organisms evolved from a richer soup of elements. Biology had, in some ways, evolved in its own right and superseded the Senexi.

Aryz raised the upper globe of his body, with its five silicate eyes arranged in a cross along the forward surface. He had memory of those times, and times long before, though his team hadn't existed then. The brood mind carried memories selected from the total store of nearly twelve billion years' experience; an awesome amount of knowledge, even to a Senexi. He pushed himself forward with his rear pods.

Through the brood mind Aryz could share the memories of a hundred thousand past generations, yet the brood mind itself was younger than its branch individuals. For a time in their youth, in their liquid-dwelling larval form, the branch inds carried their own sacs of data, each a fragment of the total necessary for complete memory. The branch inds swam through ammonia seas and wafted through thick warm gaseous zones, protoplasmic blobs three to four meters in diameter, developing their personalities under the weight of the past—and not even a complete past. No wonder they were inflexible, Aryz thought. Most branch inds were aware enough to see that—especially when they were allowed to compare histories with the Population I species, as he was doing—but there was nothing to be done. They were content the way they were. To change would be unspeakably repugnant. Extinction was preferable . . . almost.

But now they were pressed hard. The brood mind had begun a number of experiments. Aryz's team had been selected from the

seedship's contingent to oversee the experiments, and Aryz had
been chosen as the chief investigator. Two orbits past, they had captured six human embryos in a breeding device, as well as a highly
coveted memory storage center. Most Senexi engagements had
been with humans for the past three or four generations. Just as the
Senexi dominated Population II species, humans were ascendant
among their kind.

Experiments with the human embryos had already been conducted. Some had been allowed to develop normally; others had
been tampered with, for reasons Aryz was not aware of. The tamper-
ings had not been very successful.

The newer experiments, Aryz suspected, were going to take a different direction, and the seedship's actions now focused on him; he
believed he would be given complete authority over the human
shapes. Most branch inds would have dissipated under such a
burden, but not Aryz. He found the human shapes rather interesting,
in their own horrible way. They might, after all, be the key to Senexi
survival.

The moans were toughening her elfstate. She lay in pain for a
wake, not daring to close her eyes; her mind was changing and she
feared sleep would be the end of her. Her nightmares were not
easily separated from life; some, in fact, were sharper.

Too often in sleep she found herself in a Senexi trap, struggling
uselessly, being pulled in deeper, her hatred wasted against such
power. . . .

When she came out of the rigor, Prufrax was given leave by the
subordinate tellman. She took to the *Mellangee*'s greenroads, walking stiffly in the shallow gravity. Her hands itched. Her mind seemed
almost empty after the turmoil of the past few wakes. She had never
felt so calm and clear. She hated the Senexi double now; once for
their innate evil, twice for what they had made her overs put her
through to be able to fight them. Logic did not matter. She was calm,
assured. She was growing more mature wake by wake. Fight-bud-
ding, the tellman called it, hate coming out like blooms, synthesizing
the sunlight of his teaching into pure fight.

The greenroads rose temporarily beyond the labyrinth shields and
armor of the ship. Simple transparent plastic and steel geodesic sur-

faces formed a lacework over the gardens, admitting radiation necessary to the vegetation growing along the paths. No machines scooted
one forth and inboard here. It was necessary to walk. Walking was
luxury and privilege.

Prufrax looked down on the greens to each side of the paths without much comprehension. They were *beautiful*. Yes, one should say
that, think that, but what did it mean? Pleasing? She wasn't sure what
being pleased meant, outside of thinking Zap. She sniffed a flower
that, the signs explained, bloomed only in the light of young stars not
yet fusing. They were near such a star now, and the greenroads were
shiny black and electric green with the blossoms. Lamps had been
set out for other plants unsuited to such darkened conditions. Some
technic allowed suns to appear in selected plastic panels when
viewed from certain angles. Clever, the technicals.

She much preferred the looks of a technical to a tellman, but she
was common in that. Technicals required brainflex, tellmen cargo
capacity. Technicals were strong and ran strong machines, like in the
adventure fibs, where technicals were often the protags. She wished
a technical were on the greenroads with her. The moans had the effect of making her receptive—what she saw, looking in mirrors, was a
certain shine in her eyes—but there was no chance of a breeding
liaison. She was quite unreproductive in this moment of elfstate.
Other kinds of meetings were not unusual.

She looked up and saw a figure at least a hundred meters away,
sitting on an allowed patch near the path. She walked casually, grace-
fully as possible with the stiffness. Not a technical, she saw soon, but
she was not disappointed. Too calm.

"Over," he said as she approached.

"Under," she replied. But not by much—he was probably six or
seven ship years old and not easily classifiable.

"Such a fine elfstate," he commented. His hair was black. He was
shorter than she, but something in his build reminded her of the
glovers. She accepted his compliment with a nod and pointed to a
spot near him. He motioned for her to sit, and she did so with a
whuff, massaging her knees.

"Moans?" he asked.

"Bad stretch," she said.

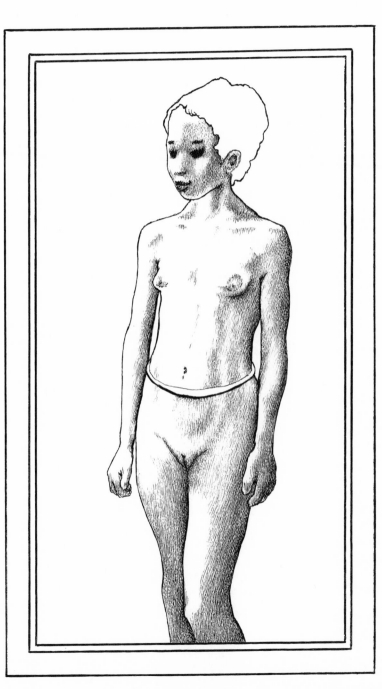

"You're a glover." He was looking at the fading scars on her hands.

"Can't tell what you are," she said.

"Noncombat," he said. "Tuner of the mandates."

She knew very little about the mandates, except that law decreed every ship carry one, and few of the crew were ever allowed to peep. "Noncombat, hm?" she mused. She didn't despise him for that; one never felt strong negatives for a crew member. She didn't feel much of anything. Too calm.

"Been working on ours this wake," he said. "Too hard, I guess. Told to walk." Overzealousness in work was considered an erotic trait aboard the *Mellangee*. Still, she didn't feel too receptive toward him.

"Glovers walk after a rough growing," she said.

He nodded. "My name's Clevo."

"Prufrax."

"Combat soon?"

"Hoping. Waiting forever."

"I know. Just been allowed access to the mandate for a half-dozen wakes. All new to me. Very happy."

"Can you talk about it?" she asked. Information about the ship not accessible in certain rates was excellent barter.

"Not sure," he said, frowning. "I've been told caution."

"Well, I'm listening."

He could come from glover stock, she thought, but probably not from technical. He wasn't very muscular, but he wasn't as tall as a glover, or as thin, either.

"If you'll tell me about gloves."

With a smile she held up her hands and wriggled the short, stumpy fingers. "Sure."

The brood mind floated weightless in its tank, held in place by buffered carbon rods. Metal was at a premium aboard the Senexi ships, more out of tradition than actual material limitations. From what Aryz could tell, the Senexi used metals sparingly for the same reason —and he strained to recall the small dribbles of information about the human past he had extracted from the memory store—for the same reason **that the Romans of old Earth regarded farming as the only truly noble occupation—**

Farming being the raising of *plants* for food and raw materials. *Plants* were analogous to the freeth Senexi ate in their larval youth, but the freeth were not green and sedentary.

There was always a certain fascination in stretching his mind to encompass human concepts. He had had so little time to delve deeply —and that was good, of course, for he had been set to answer specific questions, not mire himself in the whole range of human filth.

He floated before the brood mind, all these thoughts coursing through his tissues. He had no central nervous system, no truly differentiated organs except those that dealt with the outside world— limbs, eyes, permea. The brood mind, however, was all central nervous system, a thinly buffered sac of viscous fluids about ten meters wide.

"Have you investigated the human memory device yet?" the brood mind asked.

"I have."

"Is communication with the human shapes possible for us?"

"We have already created interfaces for dealing with their machines. Yes, it seems likely we can communicate."

"Does it occur to you that in our long war with humans, we have made no attempt to communicate before?"

This was a complicated question. It called for several qualities that Aryz, as a branch ind, wasn't supposed to have. Inquisitiveness, for one. Branch inds did not ask questions. They exhibited initiative only as offshoots of the brood mind.

He found, much to his dismay, that the question had occurred to him. "We have never captured a human memory store before," he said, by way of incomplete answer. "We could not have communicated without such an extensive source of information."

"Yet, as you say, even in the past we have been able to use human machines."

"The problem is vastly more complex."

The brood mind paused. "Do you think the teams have been prohibited from communicating with humans?"

Aryz felt the closest thing to anguish possible for a branch ind. Was he being considered unworthy? Accused of conduct inappropriate to a branch ind? His loyalty to the brood mind was unshakeable. "Yes."

"And what might our reasons be?"

"Avoidance of pollution."

"Correct. We can no more communicate with them and remain untainted than we can walk on their worlds, breathe their atmosphere." Again, silence. Aryz lapsed into a mode of inactivity. When the brood mind readdressed him, he was instantly aware.

"Do you know how you are different?" it asked.

"I am not . . ." Again, hesitation. Lying to the brood mind was impossible for him. What snared him was semantics, a complication in the radiated signals between them. He had not been aware that he was different; the brood mind's questions suggested he might be. But he could not possibly face up to the fact and analyze it all in one short time. He signaled his distress.

"You are useful to the team," the brood mind said. Aryz calmed instantly. His thoughts became sluggish, receptive. There was a possibility of redemption. But how was he different? "You are to attempt communication with the shapes yourself. You will not engage in any discourse with your fellows while you are so involved." He was banned. "And after completion of this mission and transfer of certain facts to me, you will dissipate."

Aryz struggled with the complexity of the orders. "How am I different, worthy of such a commission?"

The surface of the brood mind was as still as an undisturbed pool. The indistinct black smudges that marked its radiating organs circulated slowly within the interior, then returned, one above the other, to focus on him. "You will grow a new branch ind. It will not have your flaws, but, then again, it will not be useful to me should such a situation come a second time. Your dissipation will be a relief, but it will be regretted."

"How am I different?"

"I think you know already," the brood mind said. "When the time comes, you will feed the new branch ind all your memories but those of human contact. If you do not survive to that stage of its growth, you will pick your fellow who will perform that function for you."

A small pinkish spot appeared on the back of Aryz's globe. He floated forward and placed his largest permeum against the brood mind's cool surface. The key and command were passed, and his body became capable of reproduction. Then the signal of dismissal was given. He left the chamber.

Flowing through the thin stream of liquid ammonia lining the corridor, he felt ambiguously stimulated. His was a position of privilege and anathema. He had been blessed—and condemned. Had any other branch ind experienced such a thing?

Then he knew the brood mind was correct. He *was* different from his fellows. None of them would have asked such questions. None of them could have survived the suggestion of communicating with human shapes. If this task hadn't been given to him, he would have had to dissipate anyway.

The pink spot grew larger, then began to make greyish flakes. It broke through the skin, and casually, almost without thinking, Aryz scraped it off against a bulkhead. It clung, made a radio-frequency emanation something like a sigh, and began absorbing nutrients from the ammonia.

Aryz went to inspect the shapes.

She was intrigued by Clevo, but the kind of interest she felt was new to her. She was not particularly receptive. Rather, she felt a mental gnawing as if she were hungry or had been injected with some kind of brain moans. What Clevo told her about the mandates opened up a topic she had never considered before. How did all things come to be—and how did she figure in them?

The mandates were quite small, Clevo explained, each little more than a cubic meter in volume. Within them was the entire history and culture of the human species, as accurate as possible, culled from all existing sources. The mandate in each ship was updated whenever the ship returned to a contact station. It was not likely the *Mellangee* would return to a contact station during their lifetimes, with the crew leading such short lives on the average.

Clevo had been assigned small tasks—checking data and adding ship records—that had allowed him to sample bits of the mandate. "It's mandated that we have records," he explained, "and what we have, you see, is *man-data.*" He smiled. "That's a joke," he said. "Sort of."

Prufrax nodded solemnly. "So where do we come from?"

"Earth, of course," Clevo said. "Everyone knows that."

"I mean, where do we come from—you and I, the crew."

"Breeding division. Why ask? You know."

"Yes." She frowned, concentrating. "I mean, we don't come from the same place as the Senexi. The same way."

"No, that's foolishness."

She saw that it was foolishness—the Senexi were different all around. What was she struggling to ask? "Is their fib like our own?"

"Fib? History's not a fib. Not most of it, anyway. Fibs are for unreal. History is overfib."

She knew, in a vague way, that fibs were unreal. She didn't like to have their comfort demeaned, though. "Fibs are fun," she said. "They teach Zap."

"I suppose," Clevo said dubiously. "Being noncombat, I don't see Zap fibs."

Fibs without Zap were almost unthinkable to her. "Such dull," she said.

"Well, of course you'd say that. I might find Zap fibs dull—think of that?"

"We're different," she said. "Like Senexi are different."

Clevo's jaw hung open. "No way. We're crew. We're human. Senexi are . . ." He shook his head as if fed bitters.

"No, I mean . . ." She paused, uncertain whether she was entering unallowed territory. "You and I, we're fed different, given different moans. But in a big way we're different from Senexi. They aren't made, nor act, as you and I. But . . ." Again it was difficult to express. She was irritated. "I don't want to talk to you anymore."

A tellman walked down the path, not familiar to Prufrax. He held out his hand for Clevo, and Clevo grasped it. "It's amazing," the tellman said, "how you two gravitate to each other. Go, elfstate," he addressed Prufrax. "You're on the wrong greenroad."

She never saw the young researcher again. With glover training underway, the itches he aroused soon faded, and Zap resumed its overplace.

The Senexi had ways of knowing humans were near. As information came in about fleets and individual cruisers less than one percent nebula diameter distant, the seedship seemed warmer, less hospitable. Everything was UV with anxiety, and the new branch ind on the wall had to be shielded by a special silicate cup to prevent distortion. The brood mind grew a corniculum automatically, though the toughened outer membrane would be of little help if the seed-ship was breached.

Aryz had buried his personal confusion under a load of work. He had penetrated the human memory store deeply enough to find instructions on its use. It called itself a *mandate* (the human word came through the interface as a correlated series of radiated symbols), and even the simple preliminary directions were difficult for Aryz. It was like swimming in another family's private sea, though of course infinitely more alien; how could he connect with experiences never had, problems and needs never encountered by his kind?

He could speak some of the human languages in several radio frequencies, but he hadn't yet decided how he was going to produce modulated sound for the human shapes. It was a disturbing prospect. What would he vibrate? A permeum could vibrate subtly—such signals were used when branch inds joined to form the brood mind—but he doubted his control would ever be subtle enough. Sooner expect a human to communicate with a Senexi by controlling the radiations of its nervous system! The humans had distinct organs within their breathing passages that produced the vibrations; perhaps those structures could be mimicked. But he hadn't yet studied the dead shapes in much detail.

He observed the new branch ind once or twice each watch period. Never before had he seen an induced replacement. The normal process was for two brood minds to exchange plasm and form new team buds, then to exchange and nurture the buds. The buds were later cast free to swim as individual larvae. While the larvae often swam through the liquid and gas atmosphere of a Senexi world for thousands, even tens of thousands of kilometers, inevitably they returned to gather with the other buds of their team. Replacements were selected from a separately created pool of "generic" buds only if one or more originals had been destroyed during their wanderings. The destruction of a complete team meant reproductive failure.

In a mature team, only when a branch ind was destroyed did the brood mind induce a replacement. In essence, then, Aryz was already considered dead.

Yet he was still useful. That amused him, if the Senexi emotion could be called amusement. Restricting himself from his fellows was difficult, but he filled the time by immersing himself, through the interface, in the mandate.

The humans were also connected with the mandate through their surrogate parent, and in this manner they were quiescent.

He reported infrequently to the brood mind. Until he had established communication, there was little to report.

And throughout his turmoil, like the others he could sense a fight was coming. It could determine the success or failure of all their work in the nebula. In the grand scheme, failure here might not be crucial. But the Senexi had taken the long view too often in the past. Their age and experience—their calmness—were working against them. How else to explain the decision to communicate with human shapes? Where would such efforts lead? If he succeeded.

And he knew himself well enough to doubt he would fail.

He could feel an affinity for them already, peering at them through the thick glass wall in their isolated chamber, his skin paling at the thought of their heat, their poisonous chemistry. A diseased affinity. He hated himself for it. And reveled in it. It was what made him particularly useful to the team. If he was defective, and this was the only way he could serve, then so be it.

The other branch inds observed his passings from a distance, making no judgments. Aryz was dead, though he worked and moved. His sacrifice had been fearful. Yet he would not be a hero. His kind could never be emulated.

It was a horrible time, a horrible conflict.

She floated in language, learned it in a trice; there were no distractions. She floated in history and picked up as much as she could, for the source seemed inexhaustible. She tried to distinguish between eyes-open—the barren, pale grey-brown chamber with the thick green wall, beyond which floated a murky roundness—and eyes-shut, when she dropped back into language and history with no fixed foundation.

Eyes-open, she saw the Mam with its comforting limbs and its soft voice, its tubes and extrusions of food and its hissings and removal of waste. Through Mam's wires she learned. Mam also tended another like herself, and another, and one more unlike any of them, more like the shape beyond the green wall.

She was very young, and it was all a mystery.

At least she knew her name. And what she was supposed to do. She took small comfort in that.

They fitted Prufrax with her gloves, and she went into the practice chamber, dragged by her gloves almost, for she hadn't yet knitted her plug-in nerves in the right index digit and her pace control was uncertain.

There, for six wakes straight, she flew with the other glovers back and forth across the dark spaces like elfstate comets. Constellations and nebula aspects flashed at random on the distant walls, and she oriented to them like a night-flying bird. Her glovemates were Ornin, an especially slender male, and Ban, a red-haired female, and the special-projects sisters Ya, Trice, and Damu, new from the breeding division.

When she let the gloves have their way, she was freer than she had ever felt before. Did the gloves really control? The question wasn't important. Control was somewhere uncentered, behind her eyes and beyond her fingers, as if she were drawn on a beautiful silver wire where it was best to go. Doing what was best to do. She barely saw the field that flowed from the grip of the thick, solid gloves or felt its caressing, life-sustaining influence. Truly, she hardly saw or felt anything but situations, targets, opportunities, the success or failure of the Zap. Failure was an acute pain. She was never reprimanded for failure; the reprimand was in her blood, and she felt like she wanted to die. But then the opportunity would improve, the Zap would succeed, and everything around her—stars, Senexi seedship, the *Mellangee*, everything—seemed part of a beautiful dream all her own.

She was intense in the Mocks.

Their initial practice over, the entry play began.

One by one, the special-projects sisters took their hyperbolic formation. Their glove fields threw out extensions, and they combined force. In they went, the mock Senexi seedship brilliant red and white and UV and radio and hateful before them. Their tails swept through the seedship's outer shields and swirled like long silky hair laid on water; they absorbed fantastic energies, grew bright like violent little stars against the seedship outline. They were engaged in the drawing of the shields, and sure as topology, the spirals of force had to have a dimple on the opposite side that would iris wide enough to let in glovers. The sisters twisted the forces, and Prufrax could see the dimple stretching out under them—

The exercise ended. The elfstate glovers were cast into sudden dark. Prufrax came out of the mock unprepared, her mind still bent on the Zap. The lack of orientation drove her as mad as a moth suddenly flipped from night to day. She careened until gently mitted and channeled. She flowed down a tube, the field slowly neutralizing, and came to a halt still gloved, her body jerking and tingling.

"What the breed happened?" she screamed, her hands beginning to hurt.

"Energy conserve," a mechanical voice answered. Behind Prufrax the other elfstate glovers lined up in the catch tube, all but the special-projects sisters. Ya, Trice, and Damu had been taken out of the exercise early and replaced by simulations. There was no way their functions could be mocked. They entered the tube ungloved and helped their comrades adjust to the overness of the real.

As they left the mock chamber, another batch of glovers, even younger and fresher in elfstate, passed them. Ya held her hands up, and they saluted in return. "Breed more every day," Prufrax grumbled. She worried about having so many crew she'd never be able to conduct a satisfactory Zap herself. Where would the honor of being a glover go if everyone was a glover?

She wriggled into her cramped bunk, feeling exhilarated and irritated. She replayed the mocks and added in the missing Zap, then stared gloomily at her small narrow feet.

Out there the Senexi waited. Perhaps they were in the same state as she—ready to fight, testy at being reined in. She pondered her ignorance, her inability to judge whether such things were even possible among the enemy. She thought of the researcher, Clevo. "Blank," she murmured. "Blank, blank." Such thoughts were unnecessary, and humanizing Senexi was unworthy of a glover.

Aryz looked at the instrument, stretched a pod into it, and willed. Vocal human language came out the other end, thin and squeaky in the helium atmosphere. The sound disgusted and thrilled him. He removed the instrument from the gelatinous strands of the engineering wall and pushed it into his interior through a stretched permeum. He took a thick draft of ammonia and slid to the human shapes chamber again.

He pushed through the narrow port into the observation room. Adjusting his eyes to the heat and bright light beyond the transparent wall, he saw the round mutated shape first—the result of their unsuccessful experiments. He swung his sphere around and looked at the others.

For a time he couldn't decide which was uglier—the mutated shape or the normals. Then he thought of what it would be like to have humans tamper with Senexi and try to make them into human forms. . . . He looked at the round human and shrunk as if from sudden heat. Aryz had had nothing to do with the experiments. For that, at least, he was grateful.

Apparently, even before fertilization, human buds—eggs—were adapted for specific roles. The healthy human shapes appeared sufficiently different—discounting *sexual* characteristics—to indicate some variation in function. They were four-podded, two-opticked, with auditory apparatus and olfactory organs mounted on the *head*, along with one permeum, the *mouth*. At least, he thought, they were hairless, unlike some of the other Population I species Aryz had learned about in the mandate.

Aryz placed the tip of the vocalizer against a sound-transmitting plate and spoke.

"Zello," came the sound within the chamber. The mutated shape looked up. It lay on the floor, great bloated stomach backed by four almost useless pods. It usually made high-pitched sounds continuously. Now it stopped and listened, straining on the tube that connected it to the breed-supervising device.

"Hello," replied the male. It sat on a ledge across the chamber, having unhooked itself.

The machine that served as surrogate parent and instructor stood in one corner, an awkward parody of a human, with limbs too long and head too small. Aryz could see the unwillingness of the designing engineers to examine human anatomy too closely.

"I am called—" Aryz said, his name emerging as a meaningless stretch of white noise. He would have to do better than that. He compressed and adapted the frequencies. "I am called Aryz."

"Hello," the young female said.

"What are your names?" He knew that well enough, having listened many times to their conversations.

"Prufrax," the female said. "I'm a glover."

The human shapes contained very little genetic memory. As a kind of brood marker, Aryz supposed, they had been equipped with their name, occupation, and the rudiments of environmental knowledge. This seemed to have been artificially imposed; in their natural state, very likely, they were born almost blank. He could not, however, be certain, since human reproductive chemistry was extraordinarily subtle and complicated.

"I'm a teacher, Prufrax," Aryz said. The logic structure of the language continued to be painful to him.

"I don't understand you," the female replied.

"You teach me, I teach you."

"We have the Mam," the male said, pointing to the machine. "She teaches us." The Mam, as they called it, was hooked into the mandate. Withholding that from the humans—the only equivalent, in essence, to the Senexi sac of memory—would have been unthinkable. It was bad enough that humans didn't come naturally equipped with their own share of knowledge.

"Do you know where you are?" Aryz asked.

"Where we live," Prufrax said. "Eyes-open."

Aryz opened a port to show them the stars and a portion of the nebula. "Can you tell where you are by looking out the window?"

"Among the lights," Prufrax said.

Humans, then, did not instinctively know their positions by star patterns as other Population I species did.

"Don't talk to it," the male said. "Mam talks to us." Aryz consulted the mandate for some understanding of the name they had given to the breed-supervising machine. Mam, it explained, was probably a natural expression for womb-carrying parent. Aryz severed the machine's power.

"Mam is no longer functional," he said. He would have the engineering wall put together another less identifiable machine to link them to the mandate and to their nutrition. He wanted them to associate comfort and completeness with nothing but himself.

The machine slumped, and the female shape pulled herself free of the hookup. She started to cry, a reaction quite mysterious to Aryz. His link with the mandate had not been intimate enough to answer questions about the wailing and moisture from the eyes. After a time the male and female lay down and became dormant.

The mutated shape made more soft sounds and tried to approach the transparent wall. It held up its thin arms as if beseeching. The others would have nothing to do with it; now it wished to go with him. Perhaps the biologists had partially succeeded in their attempt at transformation; perhaps it was more Senexi than human.

Aryz quickly backed out through the port, into the cool and security of the corridor beyond.

It was an endless orbital dance, this detection and matching of course, moving away and swinging back, deceiving and revealing, between the *Mellangee* and the Senexi seedship. It was inevitable that the human ship should close in; human ships were faster, knew better the higher geometries.

Filled with her skill and knowledge, Prufrax waited, feeling like a ripe fruit about to fall from the tree. At this point in their training, just before the application, elfstates were very receptive. She was allowed to take a lover, and they were assigned small separate quarters near the outer greenroads.

The contact was satisfactory, as far as it went. Her mate was an older glover named Kumnax, and as they lay back in the cubicle, soothed by air-dance fibs, he told her stories about past battles, special tactics, how to survive.

"Survive?" she asked, puzzled.

"Of course." His long brown face was intent on the view of the greenroads through the cubicle's small window.

"I don't understand," she said.

"Most glovers don't make it," he said patiently.

"I will."

He turned to her. "You're six," he said. "You're very young. I'm ten.

I've seen. You're about to be applied for the first time, you're full of confidence. But most glovers won't make it. They breed thousands of us. We're expendable. We're based on the best glovers of the past, but even the best don't survive."

"I will," Prufrax repeated, her jaw set.

"You always say that," he murmured.

Prufrax stared at him for a moment.

"Last time I knew you," he said, "you kept saying that. And here you are, fresh again."

"What last time?"

"Master Kumnax," a mechanical voice interrupted.

He stood, looking down at her. "We glovers always have big mouths. They don't like us knowing, but once we know, what can they do about it?"

"You are in violation," the voice said. "Please report to **S**."

"But now, if you last, you'll know more than the tellman tells."

"I don't understand," Prufrax said slowly, precisely, looking him straight in the eye.

"I've paid my debt," Kumnax said. "We glovers stick. Now I'm going to go get my punishment." He left the cubicle. Prufrax didn't see him again before her first application.

The seedship buried itself in a heating protostar, raising shields against the infalling ice and stone. The nebula had congealed out of a particularly rich cluster of exploded fourth- and fifth-generation stars, thick with planets, the detritus of which now fell on Aryz's ship like hail.

Aryz had never been so isolated. No other branch ind addressed him; he never even saw them now. He made his reports to the brood mind, but even there the reception was warmer and warmer, until he could barely endure to communicate. Consequently—and he realized this was part of the plan—he came closer to his charges, the human shapes. He felt more sympathy for them. He discovered that even between human and Senexi there could be a bridge of need— the need to be useful.

The brood mind was interested in one question: how successfully could they be planted aboard a human ship? Would they be accepted until they could carry out their sabotage, or would they be detected? Already Senexi instructions were being coded into their teachings.

"I think they will be accepted in the confusion of an engagement," Aryz answered. He had long since guessed the general outlines of the brood mind's plans. Communication with the human shapes was for one purpose only; to use them as decoys, insurgents. They were weapons. Knowledge of human activity and behavior was not an end in itself; seeing what was happening to him, Aryz fully understood why the brood mind wanted such study to proceed no further.

He would lose them soon, he thought, and his work would be over. He would be much too human-tainted. He would end, and his replacement would start a new existence, very little different from Aryz—but, he reasoned, adjusted. The replacement would not have Aryz's peculiarity.

He approached his last meeting with the brood mind, preparing himself for his final work, for the ending. In the cold liquid-filled chamber, the great red-and-white sac waited, the center of his team, his existence. He adored it. There was no way he could criticize its action.

Yet—

"We are being sought," the brood mind radiated. "Are the shapes ready?"

"Yes," Aryz said. "The new teaching is firm. They believe they are fully human." And, except for the new teaching, they were. "They defy sometimes." He said nothing about the mutated shape. It would not be used. If they won this encounter, it would probably be placed with Aryz's body in a fusion torch for complete purging.

"Then prepare them," the brood mind said. "They will be delivered to the vector for positioning and transfer."

Darkness and waiting. Prufrax nested in her delivery tube like a freshly chambered round. Through her gloves she caught distant communications murmurs that resembled voices down hollow pipes. The *Mellangee* was coming to full readiness.

Huge as her ship was, Prufrax knew that it would be dwarfed by the seedship. She could recall some hazy details about the seedship's structure, but most of that information was stored securely away from interference by her conscious mind. She wasn't even positive what the tactic would be. In the mocks, that at least had been clear. Now such information either had not been delivered or had waited in inaccessible memory, to be brought forward by the appropriate triggers.

More information would be fed to her just before the launch, but she knew the general procedure. The seedship was deep in a proto-star, hiding behind the distortion of geometry and the complete hash of electromagnetic energy. The *Mellangee* would approach, collide if need be. Penetrate. Release. Find. Zap. Her fingers ached. Some-time before the launch she would also be fed her final moans—the tempers—and she would be primed to leave elfstate. She would be a mature glover. She would be a woman.

If she returned

will return

she could become part of the breed, her receptivity would end in ecstasy rather than mild warmth, she would contribute second state, naturally born glovers. For a moment she was content with the thought. That was a high honor.

Her fingers ached worse.

The tempers came, moans tiding in, then the battle data. As it passed into her subconscious, she caught a flash of—

Rocks and ice, a thick cloud of dust and gas glowing red but seem-ing dark, no stars, no constellation guides this time. The beacon came on. That would be her only way to orient once the gloves stopped inertial and locked onto the target.

The seedship

was like

a shadow within a shadow

twenty-two kilometers across, yet

carrying

only six

teams

LAUNCH *She flies!*

Data: the *Mellangee* has buried herself in the seedship, ploughed deep into the interior like a carnivore's muzzle looking for vitals.

Instruction: a swarm of seeks is dashing through the seedship, looking for the brood minds, for the brood chambers, for branch inds. The glovers will follow.

Prufrax sees herself clearly now. She is the great avenging comet, bringer of omen and doom, like a knife moving through the glass and ice and thin, cold helium as if they weren't there, the chambered round fired and tearing at hundreds of kilometers an hour through the Senexi vessel, following the seeks.

The seedship cannot withdraw into higher geometries now. It is pinned by the *Mellangee*. It is hers.

Information floods her, pleases her immensely. She swoops down orange-and-grey corridors, buffeting against the walls like a ricocheting bullet. Almost immediately she comes across a branch ind, sliding through the ammonia film against the outrushing wind, trying to reach an armored cubicle. Her first Zap is too easy, not satisfying, nothing like what she thought. In her wake the branch ind becomes scattered globules of plasma. She plunges deeper.

Aryz delivers his human charges to the vectors that will launch them. They are equipped with simulations of the human weapons, their hands encased in the hideous grey gloves.

The seedship is in deadly peril; the battle has almost been lost at one stroke. The seedship cannot remain whole. It must self-destruct, taking the human ship with it, leaving only a fragment with as many teams as can escape.

The vectors launch the human shapes. Aryz tries to determine which part of the ship will be elected to survive; he must not be there. His job is over, and he must die.

The glovers fan out through the seedship's central hollow, demolishing the great cold drive engines, bypassing the shielded fusion flare and the reprocessing plant, destroying machinery built before their Earth was formed.

The special-projects sisters take the lead. Suddenly they are confused. They have found a brood mind, but it is not heavily protected. They surround it, prepare for the Zap—

It is sacrificing itself, drawing them in to an easy kill and away from another portion of the seedship. Power is concentrating elsewhere. Sensing that, they kill quickly and move on.

Aryz's brood mind prepares for escape. It begins to wrap itself in

flux bind as it moves through the ship toward the frozen fragment. Already three of its five branch inds are dead; it can feel other brood minds dying. Aryz's bud replacement has been killed as well.

Following Aryz's training, the human shapes rush into corridors away from the main action. The special-projects sisters encounter the decoy male, allow it to fly with them . . . until it aims its weapons. One Zap almost takes out Trice. The others fire on the shape immediately. He goes to his death weeping, confused from the very moment of his launch.

The fragment in which the brood mind will take refuge encompasses the chamber where the humans had been nurtured, where the mandate is still stored. All the other brood minds are dead, Aryz realizes; the humans have swept down on them so quickly. What shall he do?

Somewhere, far off, he feels the distressed pulse of another branch ind dying. He probes the remains of the seedship. He is the last. He cannot dissipate now; he must ensure the brood mind's survival.

Prufrax, darting through the crumbling seedship, searching for more opportunities, comes across an injured glover. She calls for a mediseek and pushes on.

The brood mind settles into the fragment. Its support system is damaged; it is entering the time-isolated state, the flux bind, more rapidly than it should. The seals of foamed electric ice cannot quite close off the fragment before Ya, Trice, and Damu slip in. They frantically call for bind-cutters and preservers; they have instructions to capture the last brood mind, if possible.

But a trap falls upon Ya, and snarling fields tear her from her gloves. She is flung down a dark disintegrating shaft, red cracks opening all around as the seedship's integrity fails. She trails silver dust and freezes, hits a barricade, shatters.

The ice seals continue to close. Trice is caught between them and pushes out frantically, blundering into the region of the intensifying flux bind. Her gloves break into hard bits, and she is melded into an ice wall like an insect trapped on the surface of a winter lake.

Damu sees that the brood mind is entering the final phase of flux bind. After that they will not be able to touch it. She begins a desperate Zap

and is too late.

Aryz directs the subsidiary energy of the flux against her. Her Zap deflects from the bind region, she is caught in an interference pattern and vibrates until her tiniest particles stop their knotted whirlpool spins and she simply becomes

space and searing light.

The brood mind, however, has been damaged. It is losing information from one portion of its anatomy. Desperate for storage, it looks for places to hold the information before the flux bind's last wave.

Aryz directs an interface onto the brood mind's surface. The silvery pools of time-binding flicker around them both. The brood mind's damaged sections transfer their data into the last available storage device—the human mandate.

Now it contains both human and Senexi information.

The silvery pools unite, and Aryz backs away. No longer can he sense the brood mind. It is out of reach but not yet safe. He must propel the fragment from the remains of the seedship. Then he must wrap the fragment in its own flux bind, cocoon it in physics to protect it from the last ravages of the humans.

Aryz carefully navigates his way through the few remaining corridors. The helium atmosphere has almost completely dissipated, even there. He strains to remember all the procedures. Soon the seedship will explode, destroying the human ship. By then they must be gone.

Angry red, Prufrax follows his barely sensed form, watching him behind barricades of ice, approaching the moment of a most satisfying Zap. She gives her gloves their way

and finds a shape behind her, wearing gloves that are not gloves, not like her own, but capable of grasping her in tensed fields, blocking the Zap, dragging them together. The fragment separates, heat pours in from the protostar cloud. They are swirled in their vortex of power, twin locked comets—one red, one sullen grey.

"Who are you?" Prufrax screams as they close in on each other in the fields. Their environments meld. They grapple. In the confusion, the darkening, they are drawn out of the cloud with the fragment, and she sees the other's face.

Her own.

The seedship self-destructs. The fragment is propelled from the protostar, above the plane of what will become planets in their orbits, away from the crippled and dying *Mellangee*.

Desperate, Prufrax uses all her strength to drill into the fragment. Helium blows past them, and bits of dead branch inds.

Aryz catches the pair immediately in the shapes chamber, rearranging the fragment's structure to enclose them with the mutant shape and mandate. For the moment he has time enough to concentrate on them. They are dangerous. They are almost equal to each other, but his shape is weakening faster than the true glover. They float, bouncing from wall to wall in the chamber, forcing the mutant to crawl into a corner and howl with fear.

There may be value in saving the one and capturing the other. Involved as they are, the two can be carefully dissected from their fields and induced into a crude kind of sleep before the glover has a chance to free her weapons. He can dispose of the gloves—fake and real—and hook them both to the Mam, reattach the mutant shape as well. Perhaps something can be learned from the failure of the experiment.

The dissection and capture occur faster than the planning. His movement slows under the spreading flux bind. His last action, after attaching the humans to the Mam, is to make sure the brood mind's flux bind is properly nested within that of the ship.

The fragment drops into simpler geometries.

It is as if they never existed.

The battle was over. There were no victors. Aryz became aware of the passage of time, shook away the sluggishness, and crawled through painfully dry corridors to set the environmental equipment going again. Throughout the fragment, machines struggled back to activity.

How many generations? The constellations were unrecognizable. He made star traces and found familiar spectra and types, but advanced in age. There had been a malfunction in the overall flux bind. He couldn't find the nebula where the battle had occurred. In its place were comfortably middle-aged stars surrounded by young planets.

Aryz came down from the makeshift observatory. He slid through the fragment, established the limits of his new home, and found the solid mirror surface of the brood mind's cocoon. It was still locked in flux bind, and he knew of no way to free it. In time the bind would probably wear off—but that might require life spans. The seedship was gone. They had lost the brood chamber, and with it the stock.

He was the last branch ind of his team. Not that it mattered now; there was nothing he could initiate without a brood mind. If the flux bind was permanent—as sometimes happened during malfunction—then he might as well be dead.

He closed his thoughts around him and was almost completely submerged when he sensed an alarm from the shapes chamber. The interface with the mandate had turned itself off; the new version of the Mam was malfunctioning. He tried to repair the equipment, but without the engineer's wall he was almost helpless. The best he could do was rig a temporary nutrition supply through the old human-form Mam. When he was done, he looked at the captive and the two shapes, then at the legless, armless Mam that served as their link to the interface and life itself.

She had spent her whole life in a room barely eight by ten meters, and not much taller than her own height. With her had been Grayd and the silent round creature whose name—if it had any—they had never learned. For a time there had been Mam, then another kind of Mam not nearly as satisfactory. She was hardly aware that her entire existence had been miserable, cramped, in one way or another incomplete.

Separated from them by a transparent partition, another round shape had periodically made itself known by voice or gesture.

Grayd had kept her sane. They had engaged in conspiracy. Removing themselves from the interface—what she called "eyes-shut"—they had held on to each other, tried to make sense out of what they knew instinctively, what was fed them through the interface, and what the being beyond the partition told them.

First they knew their names, and they knew that they were glovers. They knew that glovers were fighters. When Aryz passed instruction through the interface on how to fight, they had accepted it eagerly but uneasily. It didn't seem to jibe with instructions locked deep within their instincts.

Five years under such conditions had made her introspective. She expected nothing, sought little beyond experience in the eyes-shut. Eyes-open with Grayd seemed scarcely more than a dream. They usually managed to ignore the peculiar round creature in the chamber with them; it spent nearly all its time hooked to the mandate and the Mam.

Of one thing only was she completely sure. Her name was Prufrax. She said it in eyes-open and eyes-shut, her only certainty.

Not long before the battle, she had been in a condition resembling dreamless sleep, like a robot being given instructions. The part of Prufrax that had taken on personality during eyes-shut and eyes-open for five years had been superseded by the fight instructions Aryz had programmed. She had flown as glovers must fly (though the gloves didn't seem quite right). She had fought, grappling (she thought) with herself, but who could be certain of anything?

She had long since decided that reality was not to be sought too avidly. After the battle she fell back into the mandate—into eyes-shut —all too willingly.

And what matter? If eyes-open was even less comprehensible than eyes-shut, why did she have the nagging feeling eyes-open was so compelling, so necessary? She tried to forget.

But a change had come to eyes-shut, too. Before the battle, the information had been selected. Now she could wander through the mandate at will. She seemed to smell the new information, completely unfamiliar, like a whiff of ocean. She hardly knew where to begin. She stumbled across:

—that all vessels will carry one, no matter what their size or class, just as every individual carries the map of a species. The mandate shall contain all the information of our kind, including accurate and uncensored history, for if we have learned anything, it is that censored and untrue accounts distort the eyes of the leaders. Leaders must have access to the truth. It is their responsibility. Whatever is told those who work under the leaders, for whatever reason, must not be believed by the leaders. Unders are told lies. Leaders must seek and be provided with accounts as accurate as possible, or we will be weakened and fall—

What wonderful dreams the *leaders* must have had. And they possessed some intrinsic gift called *truth,* through the use of the *man-*

date. Prufrax could hardly believe that. As she made her tentative explorations through the new fields of eyes-shut, she began to link the word *mandate* with what she experienced. That was where she was.

And she alone. Once, she had explored with Grayd. Now there was no sign of Grayd.

She learned quickly. Soon she walked along a beach on Earth, then a beach on a world called Myriadne, and other beaches, fading in and out. By running through the entries rapidly, she came up with a blurred *eidos* and so learned what a beach was in the abstract. It was a boundary between one kind of eyes-shut and another, between water and land, neither of which had any corollary in eyes-open.

Some beaches had sand. Some had clouds—the *eidos* of clouds was quite attractive. And one—

had herself running scared, screaming.

She called out, but the figure vanished. Prufrax stood on a beach under a greenish-yellow star, on a world called Kyrene, feeling lonelier than ever.

She explored farther, hoping to find Grayd, if not the figure that looked like herself. Grayd wouldn't flee from her. Grayd would—

The round thing confronted her, its helpless limbs twitching. Now it was her turn to run, terrified. Never before had she met the round creature in eyes-shut. It was mobile; it had a purpose. Over land, clouds, trees, rocks, wind, air, equations, and an edge of physics she fled. The farther she went, the more distant from the round one with hands and small head, the less afraid she was.

She never found Grayd.

The memory of the battle was fresh and painful. She remembered the ache of her hands, clumsily removed from the gloves. Her environment had collapsed and been replaced by something indistinct. Prufrax had fallen into a deep slumber and had dreamed.

The dreams were totally unfamiliar to her. If there was a left-turning in her arc of sleep, she dreamed of philosophies and languages and other things she couldn't relate to. A right-turning led to histories and sciences so incomprehensible as to be nightmares.

It was a most unpleasant sleep, and she was not at all sorry to find she wasn't really asleep.

The crucial moment came when she discovered how to slow her

turnings and the changes of dream subject. She entered a pleasant place of which she had no knowledge but which did not seem threatening. There was a vast expanse of water, but it didn't terrify her. She couldn't even identify it as water until she scooped up a handful. Beyond the water was a floor of shifting particles. Above both was an open expanse, not black but obviously space, drawing her eyes into intense pale blue-green. And there was that figure she had encountered in the seedship. Herself. The figure pursued. She fled.

Right over the boundary into Senexi information. She knew then that what she was seeing couldn't possibly come from within herself. She was receiving data from another source. Perhaps she had been taken captive. It was possible she was now being forcibly debriefed. The tellman had discussed such possibilities, but none of the glovers had been taught how to defend themselves in specific situations. Instead it had been stated—in terms that brooked no second thought— that self-destruction was the only answer. So she tried to kill herself.

She sat in the freezing cold of a red-and-white room, her feet meeting but not touching a fluid covering on the floor. The information didn't fit her senses—it seemed blurred, inappropriate. Unlike the other data, this didn't allow participation or motion. Everything was locked solid.

She couldn't find an effective means of killing herself. She resolved to close her eyes and simply will herself into dissolution. But closing her eyes only moved her into a deeper or shallower level of deception—other categories, subjects, visions. She couldn't sleep, wasn't tired, couldn't die.

Like a leaf on a stream, she drifted. Her thoughts untangled, and she imagined herself floating on the water called ocean. She kept her eyes open. It was quite by accident that she encountered:

Instruction. Welcome to the introductory use of the mandate. As a noncombat processor, your duties are to maintain the mandate, provide essential information for your overs, and, if necessary, protect or destroy the mandate. The mandate is your immediate over. If it requires maintenance, you will oblige. Once linked with the mandate, as you are now, you may explore any aspect of the information by requesting delivery. To request delivery, indicate the core of your subject—

Prufrax! she shouted silently. What is Prufrax?

A voice with different tone immediately took over.

Ah, now that's quite a story. I was her biographer, the organizer of her life tapes (ref. GEORGE MACKNAX), and knew her well in the last years of her life. She was born in the Ferment 26468. Here are selected life tapes. Choose emphasis. Analyses follow.

—Hey! Who are you? There's someone here with me. . . .
—Shh! Listen. Look at her. Who is she?
They looked, listened to the information.
—Why, she's *me* . . . sort of.
—She's *us*.

She stood two and a half meters tall. Her hair was black and thick, though cut short; her limbs well-muscled though drawn out by the training and hormonal treatments. She was seventeen years old, one of the few birds born in the solar system, and for the time being she had a chip on her shoulder. Everywhere she went, the birds asked about her mother, Jay-ax. "You better than her?"

Of course not! Who could be? But she was good; the instructors said so. She was just about through training, and whether she graduated to hawk or remained bird she would do her job well. Asking Prufrax about her mother was likely to make her set her mouth tight and glare.

On Mercior, the Grounds took up four thousand hectares and had its own port. The Grounds was divided into Land, Space, and Thought, and training in each area was mandatory for fledges, those birds embarking on hawk training. Prufrax was fledge three. She had passed Land—though she loathed downbound fighting—and was two years into Space. The tough part, everyone said, was not passing Space, but lasting through four years of Thought after the action in nearorbit and planetary.

Prufrax was not the introspective type. She could be studious when it suited her. She was a quick study at weapon maths, physics came easy when it had a direct application, but theory of service and polinstruc—which she had sampled only in prebird courses—bored her.

Since she had been a little girl, no more than five—
—Five! Five what?

and had seen her mother's ships and fightsuits and fibs, she had known she would never be happy until she had ventured far out and put a seedship in her sights, had convinced a Senexi of the overness of end—

—The Zap! She's talking the Zap!

—What's that?

—You're me, you should know.

—I'm not you, and we're not her.

The Zap, said the mandate, and the data shifted.

"Tomorrow you receive your first implants. These will allow you to coordinate with the zero-angle phase engines and find your targets much more rapidly than you ever could with simple biologic. The implants, of course, will be delivered through your noses—minor irritation and sinus trouble, no more—into your limbic system. Later in your training, hookups and digital adapts will be installed as well. Are there any questions?"

"Yes, sir." Prufrax stood at the top of the spherical classroom, causing the hawk instructor to swivel his platform. "I'm having problems with the zero-angle phase maths. Reduction of the momenta of the real."

Other fledge threes piped up that they, too, had had trouble with those maths. The hawk instructor sighed. "We don't want to install cheaters in all of you. It's bad enough needing implants to supplement biologic. Individual learning is much more desirable. Do you request cheaters?" That was a challenge. They all responded negatively, but Prufrax had a secret smile. She knew the subject. She just took delight in having the maths explained again. She could reinforce an already thorough understanding. Others not so well versed would benefit. She wasn't wasting time. She was in the pleasure of her weapon—the weapon she would be using against the Senexi.

"Zero-angle phase is the temporary reduction of the momenta of the real." Equations and plexes appeared before each student as the instructor went on. "Nested unreals can conflict if a barrier is placed between the participator princip and the assumption of the real. The effectiveness of the participator can be determined by a convenience model we call the angle of phase. Zero-angle phase is achieved by an opaque probability field according to modified Fourier of the separation of real waves. This can also be caused by the reflection of the beam—an effective counter to zero-angle phase, since the beam is always compoundable and the compound is always time-reversed. Here are the true gedanks—"

—Zero-angle phase. She's learning the Zap.

—She hates them a lot, doesn't she?

—The Senexi? They're Senexi.

—I think . . . eyes-open is the world of the Senexi. What does that mean?

—That we're prisoners. You were caught before me.

—Oh.

The news came as she was in recovery from the implant. Seedships had violated human space again, dropping cuckoos on thirty-five worlds. The worlds had been young colonies, and the cuckoos had wiped out all life, then tried to reseed with Senexi forms. The overs had reacted by sterilizing the planet's surfaces. No victory, loss to both sides. It was as if the Senexi were so malevolent they didn't care about success, only about destruction.

She hated them. She could imagine nothing worse.

Prufrax was twenty-three. In a year she would be qualified to hawk on a cruiser/raider. She would demonstrate her hatred.

Aryz felt himself slipping into endthought, the mind set that always preceded a branch ind's self-destruction. What was there for him to do? The fragment had survived, but at what cost, to what purpose? Nothing had been accomplished. The nebula had been lost, or he supposed it had. He would likely never know the actual outcome.

He felt a vague irritation at the lack of a spectrum of responses. Without a purpose, a branch ind was nothing more than excess plasm.

He looked in on the captive and the shapes, all hooked to the mandate, and wondered what he would do with them. How would humans react to the situation he was in? More vigorously, probably. They would fight on. They always had. Even without leaders, with no discernible purpose, even in defeat. What gave them such stamina? Were they superior, more deserving? If they were better, then was it right for the Senexi to oppose their triumph?

Aryz drew himself tall and rigid with confusion. He had studied

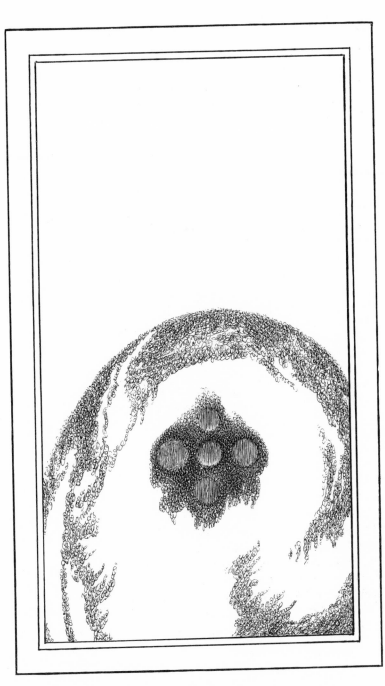

them too long. They had truly infected him. But here at least was a hint of purpose. A question needed to be answered.

He made preparations. There were signs the brood mind's flux bind was not permanent, was in fact unwinding quite rapidly. When it emerged, Aryz would present it with a judgment, an answer.

He realized, none too clearly, that by Senexi standards he was now a raving lunatic.

He would hook himself into the mandate, improve the somewhat isolating interface he had used previously to search for selected answers. He, the captive, and the shapes would be immersed in human history together. They would be like young suckling on a Population I mother-animal—just the opposite of the Senexi process, where young fed nourishment and information into the brood mind.

The mandate would nourish, or poison. Or both.

—Did she love?
—What—you mean, did she receive?
—No, did she—we—I—give?
—I don't know what you mean.
—I wonder if *she* would know what I mean. . . .
Love, said the mandate, and the data proceeded.

Prufrax was twenty-nine. She had been assigned to a cruiser in a new program where superior but untested fighters were put into thick action with no preliminary. The program was designed to see how well the Grounds prepared fighters; some thought it foolhardy, but Prufrax found it perfectly satisfactory.

The cruiser was a million-ton raider, with a hawk contingent of fifty-three and eighty regular crew. She would be used in a second-wave attack, following the initial hardfought.

She was scared. That was good; fright improved basic biologic, if properly managed. The cruiser would make a raid into Senexi space and retaliate for past cuckoo-seeding programs. They would come up against thornships and seedships, likely.

The fighting was going to be fierce.

The raider made its final denial of the overness of the real and pip-squeezed into an arduous, nasty sponge space. It drew itself together again and emerged far above the galactic plane.

Prufrax sat in the hawks wardroom and looked at the simulated rotating snowball of stars. Red-coded numerals flashed along the borders of known Senexi territory, signifying old stars, dark hulks of stars, the whole ghostly home region where they had first come to power when the terrestrial sun had been a mist-wrapped youngster. A green arrow showed the position of the raider.

She drank sponge-space supplements with the others but felt isolated because of her firstness, her fear. Everyone seemed so calm. Most were fours or fives—on their fourth or fifth battle call. There were ten ones and an upper scatter of experienced hawks with nine to twenty-five battles behind them. There were no thirties. Thirties were rare in combat; the few that survived so many engagements were plucked off active and retired to PR service under the polinstructors. They often ended up in fibs, acting poorly, looking unhappy.

Still, when she had been more naive, Prufrax's heros had been a man-and-woman thirty team she had watched in fib after fib—Kumnax and Arol. They had been better actors than most.

Day in, day out, they drilled in their fightsuits. While the crew bustled, hawks were put through implant learning, what slang was already calling the Know, as opposed to the Tell, of classroom teaching. Getting background, just enough to tickle her curiosity, not enough to stimulate morbid interest.

—There it is again. Feel?

—I know it. Yes. The round one, part of eyes-open . . .

—Senexi?

—No, brother without name.

—Your . . . brother?

—No . . . I don't know.

—Can it hurt us?

—It never has. It's trying to talk to us.

—*Leave us alone!*

—It's going.

Still, there were items of information she had never received before, items privileged only to the fighters, to assist them in their work. Older hawks talked about the past, when data had been freely available. Stories circulated in the wardroom about the Senexi, and she managed to piece together something of their origins and growth.

Senexi worlds, according to a twenty, had originally been large, cold masses of gas circling bright young suns nearly metal-free. Their gas-giant planets had orbited the suns at hundreds of millions of kilometers and had been dusted by the shrouds of neighboring dead stars; the essential elements carbon, nitrogen, silicon, and fluorine had gathered in sufficient quantities on some of the planets to allow Population II biology.

In cold ammonia seas, lipids had combined in complex chains. A primal kind of life had arisen and flourished. Across millions of years, early Senexi forms had evolved. Compared with evolution on Earth, the process at first had moved quite rapidly. The mechanisms of procreation and evolution had been complex in action, simple in chemistry.

There had been no competition between life forms of different genetic bases. On Earth, much time had been spent selecting between the plethora of possible ways to pass on genetic knowledge.

And among the early Senexi, outside of predation there had been no death. Death had come about much later, self-imposed for social reasons. Huge colonies of protoplasmic individuals had gradually resolved into the team-forms now familiar.

Soon information was transferred through the budding of branch inds; cultures quickly developed to protect the integrity of larvae, to allow them to regroup and form a new brood mind. Technologies had been limited to the rare heavy materials available, but the Senexi had expanded for a time with very little technology. They were well adapted to their environment, with few predators and no need to hunt, absorbing stray nutrients from the atmosphere and from layers of liquid ammonia. With perceptions attuned to the radio and microwave frequencies, they had before long turned groups of branch inds into radio telescope chains, piercing the heavy atmosphere and probing the universe in great detail, especially the very active center of the young galaxy. Huge jets of matter, streaming from other galaxies and emitting high-energy radiation, had provided laboratories for their vicarious observations. Physics was a primitive science to them.

Since little or no knowledge was lost in breeding cycles, cultural growth was rapid at times; since the dead weight of knowledge was often heavy, cultural growth often slowed to a crawl.

Using water as a building material, developing techniques that humans still understood imperfectly, they prepared for travel away from their birthworlds.

Prufrax wondered, as she listened to the older hawks, how humans had come to know all this. Had Senexi been captured and questioned? Was it all theory? Did anyone really know—anyone she could ask?

—She's weak.

—Why weak?

—Some knowledge is best for glovers to ignore. Some questions are best left to the supreme overs.

—Have you thought that in here, you can answer her questions, our questions?

—No. No. Learn about me—us—first.

In the hour before engagement, Prufrax tried to find a place alone. On the raider this wasn't difficult. The ship's size was overwhelming for the number of hawks and crew aboard. There were many areas where she could put on an environs and walk or drift in silence, surrounded by the dark shapes of equipment wrapped in plexerv. There was so much about ship operations she didn't understand, hadn't been taught. Why carry so much excess equipment, weapons—far more than they'd need even for replacements? She could think of possibilities—superiors on Mercior wanting their cruisers to have flexible mission capabilities, for one—but her ignorance troubled her less than *why* she was ignorant. Why was it necessary to keep fighters in the dark on so many subjects?

She pulled herself through the cold G-less tunnels, feeling slightly awked by the loneness, the quiet. One tunnel angled outboard, toward the hull of the cruiser. She hesitated, peering into its length with her environs beacon, when a beep warned her she was near another crew member. She was startled to think someone else might be as curious as she. The other hawks and crew, for the most part, had long outgrown their need to wander and regarded it as birdish. Prufrax was used to being different—she had always perceived herself, with some pride, as a bit of a freak. She scooted expertly up the tunnel, spreading her arms and tucking her legs as she would in a fightsuit.

The tunnel was filled with a faint milky green mist, absorbing her environs beam. It couldn't be much more than a couple of hundred meters long, however, and it was quite straight. The signal beeped louder.

Ahead she could make out a dismantled weapons blister. That explained the fog: a plexerv aerosol diffused in the low pressure. Sitting in the blister was a man, his environs glowing a pale violet. He had deopaqued a section of the blister and was staring out at the stars. He swiveled as she approached and looked her over dispassionately. He seemed to be a hawk—he had fightform, tall, thin with brown hair above hull-white skin, large eyes with pupils so dark she might have been looking through his head into space beyond.

"Under," she said as their environs met and merged.

"Over. What are you doing here?"

"I was about to ask you the same."

"You should be getting ready for the fight," he admonished.

"I am. I need to be alone for a while."

"Yes." He turned back to the stars. "I used to do that, too."

"You don't fight now?"

He shook his head. "Retired. I'm a researcher."

She tried not to look impressed. Crossing rates was almost impossible. A bitalent was unusual in the service.

"What kind of research?" she asked.

"I'm here to correlate enemy finds."

"Won't find much of anything, after we're done with the zero phase."

It would have been polite for him to say, "Power to that," or offer some other encouragement. He said nothing.

"Why would you want to research them?"

"To fight an enemy properly, you have to know what they are. Ignorance is defeat."

"You research tactics?"

"Not exactly."

"What, then?"

"You'll be in a tough hardfought this wake. Make you a proposition. You fight well, observe, come to me and tell me what you see. Then I'll answer your questions."

"Brief you before my immediate overs?"

"I have the authority," he said. No one had ever lied to her; she didn't even suspect he would. "You're eager?"

"Very."

"You'll be doing what?"

"Engaging Senexi fighters, then hunting down branch inds and brood minds."

"How many fighters going in?"

"Twelve."

"Big target, eh?"

She nodded.

"While you're there, ask yourself—what are they fighting for? Understand?"

"I—"

"Ask, what are they fighting for. Just that. Then come back to me."

"What's your name?"

"Not important," he said. "Now go."

She returned to the prep center as the sponge-space warning tones began. Overhawks went among the fighters in the lineup, checking gear and giveaway body points for mental orientation. Prufrax submitted to the molded sensor mask being slipped over her face. "Ready!" the overhawk said. "Hardfought!" He clapped her on the shoulder. "Good luck."

"Thank you, sir." She bent down and slid into her fightsuit. Along the launch line, eleven other hawks did the same. The overs and other crew left the chamber, and twelve red beams delineated the launch tube. The fightsuits automatically lifted and aligned on their individual beams. Fields swirled around them like silvery tissue in moving water, then settled and hardened into cold scintillating walls, pulsing as the launch energy built up.

The tactic came to her. The ship's sensors became part of her information net. She saw the Senexi thornship—twelve kilometers in diameter, cuckoos lacing its outer hull like maggots on red fruit, snakes waiting to take them on.

She was terrified and exultant, so worked up that her body temperature was climbing. The fightsuit adjusted her balance.

At the count of ten and nine, she switched from biologic to cyber. The implant—after absorbing much of her thought processes for weeks—became Prufrax.

For a time there seemed to be two of her. Biologic continued, and in that region she could even relax a bit, as if watching a fib.

With almost dreamlike slowness, in the electronic time of cyber, her fightsuit followed the beam. She saw the stars and oriented herself to the cruiser's beacon, using both for reference, plunging in the sword-flower formation to assault the thornship. The cuckoos retreated in the vast red hull like worms withdrawing into an apple. Then hundreds of tiny black pinpoints appeared in the closest quadrant to the sword flower.

Snakes shot out, each piloted by a Senexi branch ind. "Hardfought!" she told herself in biologic before that portion gave over completely to cyber.

> *Why were we flung out of dark*
> *through ice and fire, a shower*
> *of sparks? a puzzle;*
> *Perhaps to build hell.*
>
> *We strike here, there;*
> *Set brief glows, fall through*
> *and cross round again.*
>
> *By our dimming, we see what*
> *Beatitude we have.*
> *In the circle, kindling*
> *together, we form an*
> *exhausted Empyrean.*
> *We feel the rush of*
> *igniting winds but still*
> *grow dull and wan.*
>
> *New rage flames, new light,*
> *dropping like sun through muddy*
> *ice and night and fall*
> *Close, spinning blue and bright.*

In time they, too,
Tire. Redden.
We join, compare pasts
cool in huddled paths,
turn grey.

And again.
We are a companion flow
of ash, in the slurry,
out and down.
We sleep.

Rivers form above and below.
Above, iron snakes twist,
clang and slice, chime,
helium eyes watching, seeing
Snowflake hawks,
signaling adamant muscles and
energy teeth. What hunger
compels our venom spit?

It flies, strikes the crystal
flight, making mist grey-green
with ammonia rain.

Sleeping, we glide,
and to each side
unseen shores wait
with the moans of an
unseen tide.

—She wrote that. We. One of her—our—poems.
—Poem?
—A kind of fib, I think.
—I don't see what it says.
—Sure you do! She's talking hardfought.
—The Zap? Is that all?
—No, I don't think so.
—Do you understand it?
—Not all . . .

She lay back in the bunk, legs crossed, eyes closed, feeling the receding dominance of the implant—the overness of cyber—and the almost pleasant ache in her back. She had survived her first. The thornship had retired, severely damaged, its surface seared and scored so heavily it would never release cuckoos again.

It would become a hulk, a decoy. Out of action. *Satisfaction / out of action / Satisfaction . . .*

Still, with eight of the twelve fighters lost, she didn't quite feel the exuberance of the rhyme. The snakes had fought very well. Bravely, she might say. They lured, sacrificed, cooperated, demonstrating teamwork as fine as that in her own group. Strategy was what made the cruiser's raid successful. A superior approach, an excellent tactic. And perhaps even surprise, though the final analysis hadn't been posted yet.

Without those advantages, they might have all died.

She opened her eyes and stared at the pattern of blinking lights in the ceiling panel, lights with their secret codes that repeated every second, so that whenever she looked at them, the implant deep inside was debriefed, reinstructed. Only when she fought would she know what she was now seeing.

She returned to the tunnel as quickly as she was able. She floated up toward the blister and found him there, surrounded by packs of information from the last hardfought. She waited until he turned his attention to her.

"Well?" he said.

"I asked myself what they are fighting for. And I'm very angry."

"Why?"

"Because I don't know. I *can't* know. They're Senexi."

"Did they fight well?"

"We lost eight. Eight." She cleared her throat.

"Did they fight well?" he repeated, an edge in his voice.

"Better than I was ever told they could."

"Did they die?"

"Enough of them."

"How many did you kill?"

"I don't know." But she did. Eight.

"You killed eight," he said, pointing to the packs. "I'm analyzing the battle now."

"You're behind what we read, what gets posted?" she asked.

"Partly," he said. "You're a good hawk."

"I knew I would be," she said, her tone quiet, simple.

"Since they fought bravely—"

"How can Senexi be brave?" she asked sharply.

"Since," he repeated, "they fought bravely, why?"

"They want to live, to do their . . . work. Just like me."

"No," he said. She was confused, moving between extremes in her mind, first resisting, then giving in too much. "They're Senexi. They're not like us."

"What's your name?" she asked, dodging the issue.

"Clevo."

Her glory hadn't even begun yet, and already she was well into her fall.

Aryz made his connection and felt the brood mind's emergency cache of knowledge in the mandate grow up around him like ice crystals on glass. He stood in a static scene. The transition from living memory to human machine memory had resulted in either a coding of data or a reduction of detail; either way, the memory was cold, not dynamic. It would have to be compared, recorrelated, if that would ever be possible.

How much human data had had to be dumped to make space for this?

He cautiously advanced into the human memory, calling up topics almost at random. In the short time he had been away, so much of what he had learned seemed to have faded or become scrambled. Branch inds were supposed to have permanent memory; human data, for one reason or another, didn't take. It required so much effort just to begin to understand the different modes of thought.

He backed away from sociological data, trying to remain within physics and mathematics. There he could make conversions to fit his understanding without too much strain.

Then something unexpected happened. He felt the brush of another mind, a gentle inquiry from a source made even stranger by the hint of familiarity. It made what passed for a Senexi greeting, but not in the proper form, using what one branch ind of a team would radiate to a fellow; a gross breach, since it was obviously not from his team or even from his family. Aryz tried to withdraw. How was it possible for minds to meet in the mandate? As he retreated, he pushed into a broad region of incomprehensible data. It had none of the characteristics of the other human regions he had examined.

—This is for machines, the other said. —Not all cultural data is limited to biologic. You are in the area where programs and cyber designs are stored. They are really accessible only to a machine hooked into the mandate.

—What is your family? Aryz asked, the first step-question in the sequence Senexi used for urgent identity requests.

—I have no family. I am not a branch ind. No access to active brood minds. I have learned from the mandate.

—Then what are you?

—I don't know, exactly. Not unlike you.

Aryz understood what he was dealing with. It was the mind of the mutated shape, the one that had remained in the chamber, beseeching when he approached the transparent barrier.

—I must go now, the shape said. Aryz was alone again in the incomprehensible jumble. He moved slowly, carefully, into the Senexi sector, calling up subjects familiar to him. If he could encounter one shape, doubtless he could encounter the others—perhaps even the captive.

The idea was dreadful—and fascinating. So far as he knew, such intimacy between Senexi and human had never happened before. Yet there was something very Senexi-like in the method, as if branch inds attached to the brood mind were to brush mentalities while searching in the ageless memories.

The dread subsided. There was little worse that could happen to him, with his fellows dead, his brood mind in flux bind, his purpose uncertain.

What Aryz was feeling, for the first time, was a small measure of *freedom*.

The story of the original Prufrax continued.

In the early stages she visited Clevo with a barely concealed anger. His method was aggravating, his goals never precisely spelled out. What did he want with her, if anything?

And she with him? Their meetings were clandestine, though not precisely forbidden. She was a hawk one now with considerable personal liberty between exercises and engagements. There were no monitors in the closed-off reaches of the cruiser, and they could do whatever they wished. The two met in areas close to the ship's hull, usually in weapons blisters that could be opened to reveal the stars; there they talked.

Prufrax was not accustomed to prolonged conversation. Hawks were not raised to be voluble, nor were they selected for their curiosity. Yet the exhawk Clevo talked a great deal and was the most curious person she had met, herself included, and she regarded herself as uncharacteristically curious.

Often he was infuriating, especially when he played the "leading game," as she called it. Leading her from one question to the next, like an instructor, but without the trappings or any clarity of purpose. "What do you think of your mother?"

"Does that matter?"

"Not to me."

"Then why ask?"

"Because you matter."

Prufrax shrugged. "She was a fine mother. She bore me with a well-chosen heritage. She raised me as a hawk candidate. She told me her stories."

"Any hawk I know would envy you for listening at Jay-ax's knee."

"I was hardly at her knee."

"A speech tactic."

"Yes, well, she was important to me."

"She was a preferred single?"

"Yes."

"So you have no father."

"She selected without reference to individuals."

"Then you are really not that much different from a Senexi."

She bristled and started to push away. "There! You insult me again."

"Not at all. I've been asking one question all this time, and you haven't even heard. How well do you know the enemy?"

"Well enough to destroy them." She couldn't believe that was the only question he'd been asking. His speech tactics were very odd.

"Yes, to win battles, perhaps. But who will win the war?"

"It'll be a long war," she said softly, floating a few meters from him. He rotated in the blister, blocking out a blurred string of stars. The cruiser was preparing to shift out of status geometry again. "They fight well."

"They fight with conviction. Do you believe them to be evil?"

"They destroy us."

"We destroy them."

"So the question," she said, smiling at her cleverness, "is who began to destroy?"

"Not at all," Clevo said. "I suspect there's no longer a clear answer to that. Our leaders have obviously decided the question isn't important. No. We are the new, they are the old. The old must be superseded. It's a conflict born in the essential difference between Senexi and humans."

"That's the only way we're different? They're old, we're not so old? I don't understand."

"Nor do I, entirely."

"Well, finally!"

"The Senexi," Clevo continued, unperturbed, "long ago needed only gas-giant planets like their homeworlds. They lived in peace for billions of years before our world was formed. But as they moved from star to star, they learned uses for other types of worlds. We were most interested in rocky Earth-like planets. Gradually we found uses for gas giants, too. By the time we met, both of us encroached on the other's territory. Their technology is so improbable, so unlike ours, that when we first encountered them we thought they must come from another geometry."

"Where did you learn all this?" Prufrax squinted at him suspiciously.

"I'm no longer a hawk," he said, "but I was too valuable just to discard. My experience was too broad, my abilities too useful. So I was placed in research. It seems a safe place for me. Little contact with my comrades." He looked directly at her. "We must try to know our enemy, at least a little."

"That's dangerous," Prufrax said, almost instinctively.

"Yes, it is. What you know, you cannot hate."

"We must hate," she said. "It makes us strong. Senexi hate."

"They might," he said. "But, sometime, wouldn't you like to . . . sit down and talk with one, after a battle? Talk with a fighter? Learn its tactic, how it bested you in one move, compare—"

"No!" Prufrax shoved off rapidly down the tube. "We're shifting now. We have to get ready."

—She's smart. She's leaving him. He's crazy.

—Why do you think that?

—He would stop the fight, end the Zap.

—But he was a hawk.

—And hawks became glovers, I guess. But glovers go wrong, too. Like you.

—?

—Did you know they used you? How you were used?

—That's all blurred now.

—She's doomed if she stays around him. Who's that?

—Someone is listening with us.

—Recognize?

—No, gone now.

The next battle was bad enough to fall into the hellfought. Prufrax was in her fightsuit, legs drawn up as if about to kick off. The cruiser exited sponge space and plunged into combat before sponge-space supplements could reach full effectiveness. She was dizzy, disoriented. The overhawks could only hope that a switch from biologic to cyber would cure the problem.

She didn't know what they were attacking. Tactic was flooding the implant, but she was only receiving the wash of that; she hadn't merged yet. She sensed that things were confused. That bothered her. Overs did not feel confusion.

The cruiser was taking damage. She could sense at least that, and she wanted to scream in frustration. Then she was ordered to merge with the implant. Biologic became cyber. She was in the Know.

The cruiser had reintegrated above a gas-giant planet. They were seventy-nine thousand kilometers from the upper atmosphere. The damage had come from ice mines—chunks of Senexi-treated water ice, altered to stay in sponge space until a human vessel integrated nearby. Then they emerged, packed with momentum and all the residual instability of an unsuccessful exit into status geometry. Unsuccessful for a ship, that is—very successful for a weapon.

The ice mines had given up the overness of the real within range of the cruiser and had blasted out whole sections of the hull. The launch lanes had not been damaged. The fighters lined up on their beams and were peppered out into space, spreading in the classic sword flower.

The planet was a cold nest. Over didn't know what the atmosphere contained, but Senexi activity had been high in the star system, concentrating on this world. Over had decided to take a chance. Fighters headed for the atmosphere. The cruiser began planting singularity eggs. The eggs went ahead of the fighters, great black grainy ovoids that seemed to leave a trail of shadow—the wake of a birthing disruption in status geometry that could turn a gas giant into a short-lived sun.

Their time was limited. The fighters would group on entry sleds and descend to the liquid water regions where Senexi commonly kept their upwelling power plants. The fighters would first destroy any plants, loop into the liquid ammonia regions to search for hidden cuckoos, then see what was so important about the world.

She and five other fighters mounted the sled. Growing closer, the hazy clear regions of the atmosphere sparkled with Senexi sensors. Spiderweb beams shot from the six sleds to down the sensors. Buffet began. Scream, heat, then a second flower from the sled at a depth of two hundred kilometers. The sled slowed and held station. It would be their only way back. The fightsuits couldn't pull out of such a large gravity well.

She descended deeper. The pale, bloated beacon of the red star was dropping below the second cloudtops, limning the strata in orange and purple. At the liquid ammonia level she was instructed to key in permanent memory of all she was seeing. She wasn't "seeing" much, but other sensors were recording a great deal, all of it duly processed in her implant. "There's life here," she told herself. Indigenous life. Just another example of Senexi disregard for basic decency: they were interfering with a world developing its own complex biology.

The temperature rose to ammonia vapor levels, then to liquid water. The pressure on the fightsuit was enormous, and she was draining her stores much more rapidly than expected. At this level the atmosphere was particularly thick with organics.

Senexi snakes rose from below, passed them in altitude, then doubled back to engage. Prufrax was designated the deep diver; the others from her sled would stay at this level in her defense. As she fell, another sled group moved in behind her to double the cover.

She searched for the characteristic radiation curve of an upwelling plant. At the lower boundary of the liquid water level, below which her suit could not safely descend, she found it.

The Senexi were tapping the gas giant's convection from greater depths than usual. Above the plant, almost indetectable, was another object with an uncharacteristic curve. They were separated by ten kilometers. The power plant was feeding its higher companion with tight energy beams.

She slowed. Two other fighters, disengaged from the brief skirmish above, took positions as backups a few dozen kilometers higher than she. Her implant searched for an appropriate tactic. She would avoid the zero-angle phase for the moment, go in for reconnaissance. She could feel sound pouring from the plant and its companion—rhythmic, not waste noise, but deliberate. And homing in on that sound were waves of large vermiform organisms, like chains of gas-filled sausage. They were dozens of meters long, two meters at their greatest thickness, shaped vaguely like the Senexi snake fighters. The vermiforms were native, and they were being lured into the uppermost floating structure. None were emerging. Her backups spread apart, descended, and drew up along her flanks.

She made her decision almost immediately. She could see a pattern in the approach of the natives. If she fell into the pattern, she might be able to enter the structure unnoticed.

—It's a grinder. She doesn't recognize it.

—What's a grinder?

—She should make the Zap! It's an ugly thing; Senexi use them all the time. Net a planet with grinders, like a cuckoo, but for larger operations.

The creatures were being passed through separator fields. Their organics fell from the bottom of the construct, raw material for new growth—Senexi growth. Their heavier elements were stored for later harvest.

With Prufrax in their midst, the vermiforms flew into the separator. The interior was hundreds of meters wide, lead-white walls with flat

grey machinery floating in a dust haze, full of hollow noise, the distant bleats of vermiforms being slaughtered. Prufrax tried to retreat, but she was caught in a selector field. Her suit bucked and she was whirled violently, then thrown into a repository for examination. She had been screened from the separator; her plan to record, then destroy, the structure had been foiled by an automatic filter.

"Information sufficient." Command logic programmed into the implant before launch was now taking over. "Zero-angle phase both plant and adjunct." She was drifting in the repository, still slightly stunned. Something was fading. Cyber was hissing in and out; the over logic-commands were being scrambled. Her implant was malfunctioning and was returning control to biologic. The selector fields had played havoc with all cyber functions, down to the processors in her weapons.

Cautiously she examined the down systems one by one, determining what she could and could not do. This took as much as thirty seconds—an astronomical time on the implant's scale.

She still could use the phase weapon. If she was judicious and didn't waste her power, she could cut her way out of the repository, maneuver and work with her escorts to destroy both the plant and the separator. By the time they returned to the sleds, her implant might have rerouted itself and made sufficient repairs to handle defense. She had no way of knowing what was waiting for her if—when—she escaped, but that was the least of her concerns for the moment.

She tightened the setting of the phase beam and swung her fightsuit around, knocking a cluster of junk ice and silty phosphorescent dust. She activated the beam. When she had a hole large enough to pass through, she edged the suit forward, beamed through more walls and obstacles, and kicked herself out of the repository into free fall. She swiveled and laid down a pattern of wide-angle beams, at the same time relaying a message on her situation to the escorts.

The escorts were not in sight. The separator was beginning to break up, spraying debris through the almost-opaque atmosphere. The rhythmic sound ceased, and the crowds of vermiforms began to disperse.

She stopped her fall and thrust herself several kilometers higher—directly into a formation of Senexi snakes. She had barely enough power to reach the sled, much less fight and turn her beams on the upwelling plant.

Her cyber was still down.

The sled signal was weak. She had no time to calculate its direction from the inertial guidance cyber. Besides, all cyber was unreliable after passing through the separator.

Why do they fight so well? Clevo's question clogged her thoughts. Cursing, she tried to blank and keep all her faculties available for running the fightsuit. *When evenly matched, you cannot win against your enemy unless you understand them. And if you truly understand, why are you fighting and not talking?* Clevo had never told her that—not in so many words. But it was part of a string of logic all her own.

Be more than an automaton with a narrow range of choices. Never underestimate the enemy. Those were old Grounds dicta, not entirely lost in the new training, but only emphasized by Clevo.

If they fight as well as you, perhaps in some ways they fight-think like you do. Use that.

Isolated, with her power draining rapidly, she had no choice. They might disregard her if she posed no danger. She cut her thrust and went into a diving spin. Clearly she was on her way to a high-pressure grave. They would sense her power levels, perhaps even pick up the lack of field activity if she let her shields drop. She dropped the shields. If they let her fall and didn't try to complete the kill—if they concentrated on active fighters above—she had enough power to drop into the water vapor regions, far below the plant, and silently ride a thermal into range. With luck, she could get close enough to lay a web of zero-angle phase and take out the plant.

She had minutes in which to agonize over her plan. Falling, buffeted by winds that could knock her kilometers out of range, she spun like a vagrant flake of snow.

She couldn't even expend the energy to learn if they were scanning her, checking out her potential.

Perhaps she underestimated them. Perhaps they would be that much more thorough and take her out just to be sure. Perhaps they had unwritten rules of conduct like the ones she was using, taking hunches into account. Hunches were discouraged in Grounds training—much less reliable than cyber.

She fell. Temperature increased. Pressure on her suit began to constrict her air supply. She used fighter trancing to cut back on her breathing.

Fell.

And broke the trance. Pushed through the dense smoke of exhaustion. Planned the beam web. Counted her reserves. Nudged into an updraft beneath the plant. The thermal carried her, a silent piece of paper in a storm, drifting back and forth beneath the objective. The huge field intakes pulsed above, lightning outlining their invisible extension. She held back on the beam.

Nearly faded out. Her suit interior was almost unbearably hot.

She was only vaguely aware of laying down the pattern. The beams vanished in the murk. The thermal pushed her through a layer of haze, and she saw the plant, riding high above clear-atmosphere turbulence. The zero-angle phase had pushed through the field intakes, into their source nodes and the plant body, surrounding it with bright blue Tcherenkov. First the surface began to break up, then the middle layers, and finally key supports. Chunks vibrated away with the internal fury of their molecular, then atomic, then particle disruption. Paraphrasing Grounds description of beam action, the plant became less and less convinced of its reality. "Matter dreams," an instructor had said a decade before. "Dreams it is real, maintains the dream by shifting rules with constant results. Disturb the dreams, the shifting of the rules results in inconstant results. Things cannot hold."

She slid away from the updraft, found another, wondered idly how far she would be lifted. Curiosity at the last. Let's just see, she told herself; a final experiment.

Now she was cold. The implant was flickering, showing signs of reorganization. She didn't use it. No sense expanding the amount of time until death. No sense—

at all.

The sled, maneuvered by one remaining fighter, glided up beneath her almost unnoticed.

Aryz waited in the stillness of a Senexi memory, his thinking temporarily reduced to a faint susurrus. What he waited for was not clear.

—Come.

The form of address was wrong, but he recognized the voice. His thoughts stirred, and he followed the nebulous presence out of Senexi territory.

—Know your enemy.

Prufrax . . . the name of one of the human shapes sent out against their own kind. He could sense her presence in the mandate, locked into a memory store. He touched on the store and caught the essentials—the grinder, the updraft plant, the fight from Prufrax's viewpoint.

—Know how your enemy knows you.

He sensed a second presence, similar to that of Prufrax. It took him some time to realize that the human captive was another form of the shape, a reproduction of the . . .

Both were reproductions of the female whose image was in the memory store. Aryz was not impressed by threes—Senexi mysticism, what had ever existed of it, had been preoccupied with fives and sixes—but the coincidence was striking.

—Know how your enemy *sees* you.

He saw the grinder processing organics—the vermiform natives—in preparation for a widespread seeding of deuterium gatherers. The operation had evidently been conducted for some time; the vermiform populations were greatly reduced from their usual numbers. Vermiforms were a common type-species on gas giants of the sort depicted. The mutated shape nudged him into a particular channel of the memory, that which carried the original Prufrax's emotions. She had reacted with *disgust* to the Senexi procedure. It was a reaction not unlike what Aryz might feel when coming across something forbidden in Senexi behavior. Yet eradication was perfectly natural, analogous to the human cleansing of *food* before *eating*.

—It's in the memory. The vermiforms are intelligent. They have their own kind of civilization. Human action on this world prevented their complete extinction by the Senexi.

—So what matter they were *intelligent?* Aryz responded. They did not behave or think like Senexi, or like any species Senexi find compatible. They were therefore not desirable. Like humans.

—You would make humans extinct?

—We would protect ourselves from them.

—Who damages whom most?

Aryz didn't respond. The line of questioning was incomprehensible. Instead he flowed into the memory of Prufrax, propelled by another aspect of complete freedom, confusion.

The implant was replaced. Prufrax's damaged limbs and skin were repaired or regenerated quickly, and within four wakes, under intense treatment usually reserved only for overs, she regained all her reflexes and speed. She requested liberty of the cruiser while it returned for repairs. Her request was granted.

She first sought Clevo in the designated research area. He wasn't there, but a message was, passed on to her by a smiling young crew member. She read it quickly:

"You're free and out of action. Study for a while, then come find me. The old place hasn't been damaged. It's less private, but still good. Study! I've marked highlights."

She frowned at the message, then handed it to the crew member, who duly erased it and returned to his duties. She wanted to talk with Clevo, not study.

But she followed his instructions. She searched out highlighted entries in the ship's memory store. It was not nearly as dull as she had expected. In fact, by following the highlights, she felt she was learning more about Clevo and about the questions he asked.

Old literature was not nearly as graphic as fibs, but it was different enough to involve her for a time. She tried to create imitations of what she read, but erased them. Nonfib stories were harder than she suspected. She read about punishment, duty; she read about places called heaven and hell, from a writer who had died tens of thousands of years before. With ed supplement guidance, she was able to comprehend most of what she read. Plugging the store into her implant, she was able to absorb hundreds of volumes in an hour.

Some of the stores were losing definition. They hadn't been used in decades, perhaps centuries.

Halfway through, she grew impatient. She left the research area. Operating on another hunch, she didn't go to the blister as directed, but straight to memory central, two decks inboard the research area. She saw Clevo there, plugged into a data pillar, deep in some aspect of ship history. He noticed her approach, unplugged, and swiveled on his chair. "Congratulations," he said, smiling at her.

"Hardfought," she acknowledged, smiling.

"Better than that, perhaps," he said.

She looked at him quizzically. "What do you mean, better?"

"I've been doing some illicit tapping on over channels."

"So?"

—He *is* dangerous!

"You've been recommended."

"For what?"

"Not for hero status, not yet. You'll have a good many more fights before that. And you probably won't enjoy it when you get there. You won't be a fighter then."

Prufrax stood silently before him.

"You may have a valuable genetic assortment. Overs think you behaved remarkably well under impossible conditions."

"Did I?"

He nodded. "Your type may be preserved."

"Which means?"

"There's a program being planned. They want to take the best fighters and reproduce them—clone them—to make uniform top-grade squadrons. It was rumored in my time—you haven't heard?"

She shook her head.

"It's not new. It's been done, off and on, for tens of thousands of years. This time they believe they can make it work."

"You were a fighter, once," she said. "Did they preserve your type?"

Clevo nodded. "I had something that interested them, but not, I think, as a fighter."

Prufrax looked down at her stubby-fingered hands. "It was grim," she said. "You know what we found?"

"An extermination plant."

"You want me to understand them better. Well, I can't. I refuse. How could they do such things?" She looked disgusted and answered her own question. "Because they're Senexi."

"Humans," Clevo said, "have done much the same, sometimes worse."

"No!"

—No!

"Yes," he said firmly. He sighed. "We've wiped Senexi worlds, and we've even wiped worlds with intelligent species like our own. Nobody is innocent. Not in this universe."

"We were never taught that."

"It wouldn't have made you a better hawk. But it might make a better human of you, to know. Greater depth of character. Do you want to be more aware?"

"You mean, study more?"

He nodded.

"What makes you think *you* can teach me?"

"Because you thought about what I asked you. About how Senexi thought. And you survived where some other hawk might not have. The overs think it's in your genes. It might be. But it's also in your head."

"Why not tell the overs?"

"I have," he said. He shrugged. "I'm too valuable to them, otherwise I'd have been busted again, a long time ago."

"They wouldn't want me to learn from you?"

"I don't know," Clevo said. "I suppose they're aware you're talking to me. They could stop it if they wanted. They may be smarter than I give them credit for." He shrugged again. "Of course they're smart. We just disagree at times."

"And if I learn from you?"

"Not from me, actually. From the past. From history, what other people have thought. I'm really not any more capable than you . . . but I know history, small portions of it. I won't teach you so much, as guide."

"I did use your questions," Prufrax said. "But will I ever need to use them—think that way—again?"

Clevo nodded. "Of course."

—You're quiet.

—She's giving in to him.

—She gave in a long time ago.

—She should be afraid.

—Were you—we—ever really afraid of a challenge?

—No.

—Not Senexi, not forbidden knowledge.

—Someone listens with us. Feel—

Clevo first led her through the history of past wars, judging that was appropriate considering her occupation. She was attentive enough, though her mind wandered; sometimes he was didactic, but she found she didn't mind that much. At no time did his attitude change as they pushed through the tangle of the past. Rather her perception of his attitude changed. Her perception of herself changed.

She saw that in all wars, the first stage was to dehumanize the enemy, reduce the enemy to a lower level so that he might be killed without compunction. When the enemy was not human to begin with, the task was easier. As wars progressed, this tactic frequently led to an underestimation of the enemy, with disastrous consequences. "We aren't exactly underestimating the Senexi," Clevo said. "The overs are too smart for that. But we refuse to understand them, and that could make the war last indefinitely."

"Then why don't the overs see that?"

"Because we're being locked into a pattern. We've been fighting for so long, we've begun to lose ourselves. And it's getting worse." He assumed his didactic tone, and she knew he was reciting something he'd formulated years before and repeated to himself a thousand times. "There is no war so important that to win it, we must destroy our minds."

She didn't agree with that; losing the war with the Senexi would mean extinction, as she understood things.

Most often they met in the single unused weapons blister that had not been damaged. They met when the ship was basking in the real between sponge-space jaunts. He brought memory stores with him in portable modules, and they read, listened, experienced together. She never placed a great deal of importance in the things she learned; her interest was focused on Clevo. Still, she learned.

The rest of her time she spent training. She was aware of a growing isolation from the hawks, which she attributed to her uncertain rank status. Was her genotype going to be preserved or not? The decision hadn't been made. The more she learned, the less she wanted to be singled out for honor. Attracting that sort of attention might be dangerous, she thought. Dangerous to whom, or what, she could not say.

Clevo showed her how hero images had been used to indoctrinate birds and hawks in a standard of behavior that was ideal, not realistic. The results were not always good; some tragic blunders had been made by fighters trying to be more than anyone possibly could or refusing to be flexible.

The war was certainly not a fib. Yet more and more the overs seemed to be treating it as one. Unable to bring about strategic victories against the Senexi, the overs had settled in for a long war of attrition and were apparently bent on adapting all human societies to the effort.

"There are overs we never hear of, who make decisions that shape our entire lives. Soon they'll determine whether or not we're even born, if they don't already."

"That sounds paranoid," she said, trying out a new word and concept she had only recently learned.

"Maybe so."

"Besides, it's been like that for ages—not knowing all our overs."

"But it's getting worse," Clevo said. He showed her the projections he had made. In time, if trends continued unchanged, fighters and all other combatants would be treated more and more mechanically, until they became the machines the overs wished them to be.

—No.

—Quiet. How does he feel toward her?

It was inevitable that as she learned under his tutelage, he began to feel responsible for her changes. She was an excellent fighter. He could never be sure that what he was doing might reduce her effectiveness. And yet he had fought well—despite similar changes—until his billet switch. It had been the overs who had decided he would be more effective, less disruptive, elsewhere.

Bitterness over that decision was part of his motive. The overs had done a foolish thing, putting a fighter into research. Fighters were tenacious. If the truth was to be hidden, then fighters were the ones likely to ferret it out. And pass it on. There was a code among fighters, seldom revealed to their immediate overs, much less to the supreme overs parsecs distant in their strategospheres. What one fighter learned that could be of help to another had to be passed on, even under penalty. Clevo was simply following that unwritten rule.

Passing on the fact that, at one time, things had been different. That war changed people, governments, societies, and that societies could effect an enormous change on their constituents, especially now—change in their lives, their thinking. Things could become even more structured. Freedom of fight was a drug, an illusion—

—No!

used to perpetuate a state of hatred.

"Then why do they keep all the data in stores?" she asked. "I mean, you study the data, everything becomes obvious."

"There are still important people who think we may want to find our way back someday. They're afraid we'll lose our roots, but—"

His face suddenly became peaceful. She reached out to touch him, and he jerked slightly, turning toward her in the blister. "What is it?" she asked.

"It's not organized. We're going to lose the information. Ship overs are going to restrict access more and more. Eventually it'll decay, like some already has in these stores. I've been planning for some time to put it all in a single unit—"

—He built the mandate!

"and have the overs place one on every ship, with researchers to tend it. Formalize the loose scheme still in effect, but dying. Right now I'm working on the fringes. At least I'm allowed to work. But soon I'll have enough evidence that they won't be able to argue. Evidence of what happens to societies that try to obscure their histories. They go quite mad. The overs are still rational enough to listen; maybe I'll push it through." He looked out the transparent blister. The stars were smudging to one side as the cruiser began probing for entrances to sponge space. "We'd better get back."

"Where are you going to be when we return? We'll all be transferred."

"That's some time removed. Why do you want to know?"

"I'd like to learn more."

He smiled. "That's not your only reason."

"I don't need someone to tell me what my reasons are," she said testily.

"We're so reluctant," he said. She looked at him sharply, irritated and puzzled. "I mean," he continued, "we're hawks. Comrades.

Hawks couple like *that*." He snapped his fingers. "But you and I sneak around it all the time."

Prufrax kept her face blank.

"Aren't you receptive toward me?" he asked, his tone almost teasing.

"You're so damned superior. Stuffy," she snapped.

"Aren't you?"

"It's just that's not all," she said, her tone softening.

"Indeed," he said in a barely audible whisper.

In the distance they heard the alarms.

—It was never any different.

—What?

—Things were never any different before me.

—Don't be silly. It's all here.

—If Clevo made the mandate, then he put it here. It isn't true.

—Why are you upset?

—I don't like hearing that everything I believe is a . . . fib.

—I've never known the difference, I suppose. Eyes-open was never all that real to me. This isn't real, you aren't . . . this is eyes-shut. So why be upset? You and I . . . we aren't even whole people. I feel you. You wish the Zap, you fight, not much else. I'm just a shadow, even compared to you. But she is whole. She loves him. She's less a victim than either of us. So something has to have changed.

—You're saying things have gotten worse.

—If the mandate is a lie, that's all I am. You refuse to accept. I *have* to accept, or I'm even less than a shadow.

—I don't refuse to accept. It's just hard.

—You started it. You thought about love.

—You did!

—Do you know what love is?

—Reception.

They first made love in the weapons blister. It came as no surprise; if anything, they approached it so cautiously they were clumsy. She had become more and more receptive, and he had dropped his guard. It had been quick, almost frantic, far from the orchestrated and drawn-out ballet the hawks prided themselves for. There was no pretense. No need to play the roles of artists interacting. They were depending on each other. The pleasure they exchanged was nothing compared to the emotions involved.

"We're not very good with each other," Prufrax said.

Clevo shrugged. "That's because we're shy."

"Shy?"

He explained. In the past—at various times in the past, because such differences had come and gone many times—making love had been more than a physical exchange or even an expression of comradeship. It had been the acknowledgment of a bond between people.

She listened, half-believing. Like everything else she had heard, that kind of love seemed strange, distasteful. What if one hawk was lost, and the other continued to love? It interfered with the hard-fought, certainly. But she was also fascinated. Shyness—the fear of one's presentation to another. The hesitation to present truth, or the inward confusion of truth at the awareness that another might be important, more important than one thought possible. That such emotions might have existed at one time, and seem so alien now, only emphasized the distance of the past, as Clevo had tried to tell her. And that she felt those emotions only confirmed she was not as far from that past as, for dignity's sake, she might have wished.

Complex emotion was not encouraged either at the Grounds or among hawks on station. Complex emotion degraded complex performance. The simple and direct was desirable.

"But all we seem to do is talk—until now," Prufrax said, holding his hand and examining his fingers one by one. They were very little different from her own, though extended a bit from hawk fingers to give greater versatility with key instruction.

"Talking is the most human thing we can do."

She laughed. "I know what you are," she said, moving up until her eyes were even with his chest. "You're stuffy. You aren't the party type."

"Where'd you learn about parties?"

"You gave me literature to read, I read it. You're an instructor at heart. You make love by telling." She felt peculiar, almost afraid, and looked up at his face. "Not that I don't enjoy your lovemaking, like this. Physical."

"You receive well," he said. "Both ways."

"What we're saying," she whispered, "is not truth-speaking. It's amenity." She turned into the stroke of his hand through her hair. "Amenity is supposed to be decadent. That fellow who wrote about heaven and hell. He would call it a sin."

"Amenity is the recognition that somebody may see or feel differently than you do. It's the recognition of individuals. You and I, we're part of the end of all that."

"Even if you convince the overs?"

He nodded. "They want to repeat success without risk. New individuals are risky, so they duplicate past success. There will be more and more people, fewer individuals. More of you and me, less of others. The fewer individuals, the fewer stories to tell. The less history. We're part of the death of history."

She floated next to him, trying to blank her mind as she had before, to drive out the nagging awareness he was right. She thought she understood the social structure around her. Things seemed new. She said as much.

"It's a path we're taking," Clevo said. "Not a place we're at."

—It's a place *we're* at. How different are *we?*

—But there's so much history in here. How can it be over for us?

—I've been thinking. Do we know the last event recorded in the mandate?

—Don't, we're drifting from Prufrax now. . . .

Aryz felt himself drifting with them. They swept over countless millennia, then swept back the other way. And it became evident that as much change had been wrapped in one year of the distant past as in a thousand years of the closing entries in the mandate. Clevo's voice seemed to follow them, though they were far from his period, far from Prufrax's record.

"Tyranny is the death of history. We fought the Senexi until we became like them. No change, youth at an end, old age coming upon us. There is no important change, merely elaborations in the pattern."

—How many times have we been here, then? How many times have we died?

Aryz wasn't sure, now. *Was* this the first time humans had been captured? Had he been told everything by the brood mind? Did the Senexi have no *history*, whatever that was—

The accumulated lives of living, thinking beings. Their actions, thoughts, passions, hopes.

The mandate answered even his confused, nonhuman requests. He could understand action, thought, but not passion or hope. Perhaps without those there was no *history*.

—You have no history, the mutated shape told him. There have been millions like you, even millions like the brood mind. What is the last event recorded in the brood mind that is not duplicated a thousand times over, so close they can be melded together for convenience?

—You understand that? Aryz asked the shape.

—Yes.

—How do you understand—because we made you between human and Senexi?

—Not only that.

The requests of the twin captive and shape were moving them back once more into the past, through the dim grey millennia of repeating ages. History began to manifest again, differences in the record.

On the way back to Mercior, four skirmishes were fought. Prufrax did well in each. She carried something special with her, a thought she didn't even tell Clevo, and she carried the same thought with her through their last days at the Grounds.

Taking advantage of hawk liberty, she opted a posthardfought residence just outside the Grounds, in the relatively uncrowded Daughter of Cities zone. She wouldn't be returning to fight until several issues had been decided—her status most important among them.

Clevo began making his appeal to the middle overs. He was given Grounds duty to finish his proposals. They could stay together for the time being.

The residence was sixteen square meters in area, not elegant—*natural*, as rentOpts described it. Clevo called it a "garret," inaccurately as she discovered when she looked it up in his memory blocs, but perhaps he was describing the tone.

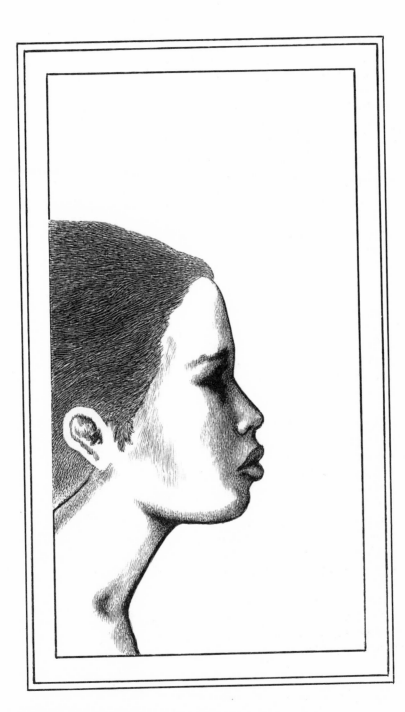

On the last day she lay in the crook of Clevo's arm. They had done a few hours of nature sleep. He hadn't come out yet, and she looked up at his face, reached up with a hand to feel his arm.

It was different from the arms of others she had been receptive toward. It was unique. The thought amused her. There had never been a reception like theirs. This was the beginning. And if both were to be duplicated, this love, this reception, would be repeated an infinite number of times. Clevo meeting Prufrax, teaching her, opening her eyes.

Somehow, even though repetition contributed to the death of history, she was pleased. This was the secret thought she carried into fight. Each time she would survive, wherever she was, however many duplications down the line. She would receive Clevo, and he would teach her. If not now—if one or the other died—then in the future. The death of history might be a good thing. Love could go on forever.

She had lost even a rudimentary apprehension of death, even with present pleasure to live for. Her functions had sharpened. She would please him by doing all the things he could not. And if he was to enter that state she frequently found him in, that state of introspection, of reliving his own battles and of envying her activity, then that wasn't bad. All they did to each other was good.

—*Was* good

—*Was*

She slipped from his arm and left the narrow sleeping quarter, pushing through the smoke-colored air curtain to the lounge. Two hawks and an over she had never seen before were sitting there. They looked up at her.

"Under," Prufrax said.

"Over," the woman returned. She was dressed in tan and green, Grounds colors, not ship.

"May I assist?"

"Yes."

"My duty, then?"

The over beckoned her closer. "You have been receiving a researcher."

"Yes," Prufrax said. The meetings could not have been a secret on the ship, and certainly not their quartering near the Grounds. "Has that been against duty?"

"No." The over eyed Prufrax sharply, observing her perfected fight-form, the easy grace with which she stood, naked, in the middle of the small compartment. "But a decision has been reached. Your status is decided now."

She felt a shiver.

"Prufrax," said the elder hawk. She recognized him from fibs, and his companion: Kumnax and Arol. Once her heroes. "You have been accorded an honor, just as your partner has. You have a valuable genetic assortment—"

She barely heard the rest. They told her she would return to fight, until they deemed she had had enough experience and background to be brought into the polinstruc division. Then her fighting would be over. She would serve better as an example, a hero.

Heroes never partnered out of function. Hawk heroes could not even partner with exhawks.

Clevo emerged from the air curtain. "Duty," the over said. "The residence is disbanded. Both of you will have separate quarters, separate duties."

They left. Prufrax held out her hand, but Clevo didn't take it. "No use," he said.

Suddenly she was filled with anger. "You'll give it up? Did I expect too much? *How strongly?*"

"Perhaps even more strongly than you," he said. "I knew the order was coming down. And still I didn't leave. That may hurt my chances with the supreme overs."

"Then at least I'm worth more than your breeding history?"

"Now you are history. History the way they make it."

"I feel like I'm dying," she said, amazement in her voice. "What is that, Clevo? What did you do to me?"

"I'm in pain, too," he said.

"You're hurt?"

"I'm confused."

"I don't believe that," she said, her anger rising again. "You knew, and you didn't do anything?"

"That would have been counter to duty. We'll be worse off if we fight it."

"So what good is your great, exalted history?"

"History is what you have," Clevo said. "I only record."

—Why did they separate them?

—I don't know. You didn't like him, anyway.

—Yes, but now . . .

—See? You're her. We're her. But shadows. She was whole.

—I don't understand.

—We don't. Look what happens to her. They took what was best out of her. Prufrax

went into battle eighteen more times before dying as heroes often do, dying in the midst of what she did best. The question of what made her better before the separation—for she definitely was not as fine a fighter after—has not been settled. Answers fall into an extinct classification of knowledge, and there are few left to interpret, none accessible to this device.

—So she went out and fought and died. They never even made fibs about her. This killed her?

—I don't think so. She fought well enough. She died like other hawks died.

—And she might have lived otherwise.

—How can I know that, any more than you?

—They—we—met again, you know. I met a Clevo once, on my ship. They didn't let me stay with him long.

—How did you react to him?

—There was so little time, I don't know.

—Let's ask. . . .

In thousands of duty stations, it was inevitable that some of Prufrax's visions would come true, that they should meet now and then. Clevos were numerous, as were Prufraxes. Every ship carried complements of several of each. Though Prufrax was never quite as successful as the original, she was a fine type. She—

—She was never quite as successful. They took away her edge. They didn't even know it!

—They must have known.

—Then they didn't want to win!

—We don't know that. Maybe there were more important considerations.

—Yes, like killing history.

Aryz shuddered in his warming body, dizzy as if about to bud, then regained control. He had been pulled from the mandate, called to his own duty.

He examined the shapes and the human captive. There was something different about them. How long had they been immersed in the mandate? He checked quickly, frantically, before answering the call. The reconstructed Mam had malfunctioned. None of them had been nourished. They were thin, pale, cooling.

Even the bloated mutant shape was dying; lost, like the others, in the mandate.

He turned his attention away. Everything was confusion. Was he human or Senexi now? Had he fallen so low as to understand them? He went to the origin of the call, the ruins of the temporary brood chamber. The corridors were caked with ammonia ice, burning his pod as he slipped over them. The brood mind had come out of flux bind. The emergency support systems hadn't worked well; the brood mind was damaged.

"Where have you been?" it asked.

"I assumed I would not be needed until your return from the flux bind."

"You have not been watching!"

"Was there any need? We are so advanced in time, all our actions are obsolete. The nebula is collapsed, the issue is decided."

"We do not know that. We are being pursued."

Aryz turned to the sensor wall—what was left of it—and saw that they were, indeed, being pursued. He had been lax.

"It is not your fault," the brood mind said. "You have been set a task that tainted you and ruined your function. You will dissipate."

Aryz hesitated. He had become so different, so tainted, that he actually *hesitated* at a direct command from the brood mind. But it was damaged. Without him, without what he had learned, what could it do? It wasn't reasoning correctly.

"There are facts you must know, important facts—"

Aryz felt a wave of revulsion, uncomprehending fear, and something not unlike human anger radiate from the brood mind. Whatever he had learned and however he had changed, he could not withstand that wave.

Willingly, and yet against his will—it didn't matter—he felt himself liquefying. His pod slumped beneath him, and he fell over, landing on a pool of frozen ammonia. It burned, but he did not attempt to lift himself. Before he ended, he saw with surprising clarity what it was to be a branch ind, or a brood mind, or a human. Such a valuable insight, and it leaked out of his permea and froze on the ammonia.

The brood mind regained what control it could of the fragment. But there were no defenses worthy of the name. Calm, preparing for its own dissipation, it waited for the pursuit to conclude.

The Mam set off an alarm. The interface with the mandate was severed. Weak, barely able to crawl, the humans looked at each other in horror and slid to opposite corners of the chamber.

They were confused: which of them was the captive, which the decoy shape? It didn't seem important. They were both bone-thin, filthy with their own excrement. They turned with one motion to stare at the bloated mutant. It sat in its corner, tiny head incongruous on the huge thorax, tiny arms and legs barely functional even when healthy. It smiled wanly at them.

"We felt you," one of the Prufraxes said. "You were with us in there." Her voice was a soft croak.

"That was my place," it replied. "My only place."

"What function, what name?"

"I'm . . . I know that. I'm a researcher. In there. I knew myself in there."

They squinted at the shape. The head. Something familiar, even now. "You're a Clevo . . ."

There was noise all around them, cutting off the shape's weak words. As they watched, their chamber was sectioned like an orange, and the wedges peeled open. The illumination ceased. Cold enveloped them.

A naked human female, surrounded by tiny versions of herself, like an angel circled by fairy kin, floated into the chamber. She was thin as a snake. She wore nothing but silver rings on her wrists and a narrow torque around her waist. She glowed blue-green in the dark.

The two Prufraxes moved their lips weakly but made no sound in the near vacuum. *Who are you?*

She surveyed them without expression, then held out her arms as if to fly. She wore no gloves, but she was of their type.

As she had done countless times before on finding such Senexi experiments—though this seemed older than most—she lifted one arm higher. The blue-green intensified, spread in waves to the mangled walls, surrounded the freezing, dying shapes. Perfect, angelic, she left the debris behind to cast its fitful glow and fade.

They had destroyed every portion of the fragment but one. They left it behind unharmed.

Then they continued, millions of them thick like mist, working the spaces between the stars, their only master the overness of the real.

They needed no other masters. They would never malfunction.

The mandate drifted in the dark and cold, its memory going on, but its only life the rapidly fading tracks where minds had once passed through it. The trails writhed briefly, almost as if alive, but only following the quantum rules of diminishing energy states. Finally, a small memory was illuminated.

Prufrax's last poem, explained the mandate reflexively.

> How the fires grow! Peace passes
> All memory lost.
> Somehow we always miss that single door,
> Dooming ourselves to circle.
>
> Ashes to stars, lies to souls,
> Let's spin round the sinks and holes.
>
> Kill the good, eat the young.
> Forever and more
> You and I are never done.

The track faded into nothing. Around the mandate, the universe grew old very quickly.

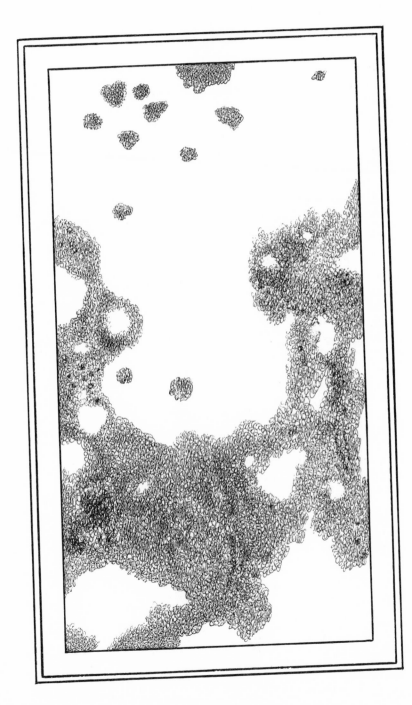

A NOTE ON THE TYPE

The text of this book was composed in the film version of Optima, a typeface designed by Hermann Zapf during the midfifties and issued in 1958. In creating Optima, Zapf achieved a unique rapport between classic roman and sans-serif typography by flaring the terminals of unadorned stems to suggest serif endings. So delicate are the stresses and balances in Optima that it rivals sans-serif faces in clarity and freshness while preserving the fundamental readability of old-style type.